Foote

TOM BREDEHOFT

FOOTE

A MYSTERY NOVEL

WEST VIRGINIA UNIVERSITY PRESS
MORGANTOWN

Copyright © 2022 by Tom Bredehoft
All rights reserved
First edition published 2022 by West Virginia University Press
Printed in the United States of America

ISBN 978-1-952271-60-1 (paperback) / 978-1-952271-61-8 (ebook)

Library of Congress Cataloging-in-Publication Data is available from
the Library of Congress

Cover design by Rachel Willey
Book design by Than Saffel / WVU Press

CHAPTER 1

FRIDAY

———

It was a drizzly morning in April, and all I knew was that someone was standing outside the door. That was all right. Sometimes folks need a few minutes to get their courage up, to really convince themselves that they need my kind of help. My office, to tell the truth, isn't exactly inviting from the outside: it's just a plain metal door, bracketed by a couple of windows with the blinds closed. And the door itself stands in a little blackened brick building crouched beneath the PRT tracks, not too far from the downtown stop. That also makes it not too far from the county courthouse, as a matter of fact.

The sign on the door says "Big Jim Foote: Private Investigator," and I know well enough that that doesn't always encourage the curious to come in, either. Even the mailman rarely says hello. If someone really needs me, they open the door. They come in.

And, eventually, this one did.

It's a little-known fact that a small, but significant, community of bigfoot live, more or less in the open, in and around Morgantown, West Virginia. They are, some might say, passing for humans, though the truth is that most of them don't mix very much with the humans around them. It's a small enough step from hiding in the woods and wild to hiding in plain sight. So if you're in Morgantown, and you see a lumbering great figure pushing a buggy through the grocery store, with a heavy coat and unruly hair, and with two or more bags of cheese puffs but no beer, there's a good chance it's a bigfoot. There's a good chance it's me.

Most of the Morgantown bigfoot live a little way out of town: they do their share of hunting and fishing (not all of it in season, naturally), and they know all the best places to find ramps and morels and pawpaws and serviceberries. Their ability to track something—human or otherwise—through the woods is second to none. But a few of us bigfoot live right in town, playing a part in the human community, and yet we are always at least a little apart from it, living in secret. I suppose that's why being a private investigator always seemed like a natural-enough career choice for me. It's all about secrets.

"It's just a nickname," I said about the name on the door, when the prospective client finally came in and sat down across from me. They don't always ask first off, but unless they know me already, they do always ask. She was a human female, and she looked like she might be a college student, or maybe a year or two older than that. Pale hair; not very tall, even for a human; blue-gray eyes: probably the average human male would find her attractive, but I wasn't much of a judge. She said her name was Emily Smart.

"It seemed like you couldn't make up your mind about coming in here," I said to her. "What made you decide?"

"I don't really know," she answered uncertainly. "Hobo Joe said you were a good guy."

I had to laugh. I hardly ever said more than two words to Hobo

Joe, but we've both been around a long time, and Morgantown isn't that big a place once you get away from the university. I'll never forget seeing him at the post office one time; he was telling some other customer about being a hobo (not a homeless man, no), and about his various travels. "I'm writin' a book," he had said to this guy. "Yeah, I know him," I said now to Emily Smart. "Old school hat, great big backpack."

"Yeah, that's him."

I knew I just needed to wait: at this point, she'd either tell me what she needed to tell me, or she'd duck back out the door. It didn't look much like she'd be able to pay the fee, so I didn't see why I needed to do much to encourage her. She wasn't exactly squirming as she sat in the hard wooden chair across my desk, but she was close.

"It's my mom. I haven't heard from her in over a month."

"Police?"

"I talked to them, but they haven't found her. They haven't found anything, and they don't act like they're going to."

Well, it wasn't unusual for the police to fail to find a missing person. Already this sounded a lot more interesting than anything else on my plate. As a rule, I tried to take on as little work as possible, but a missing mother? I wasn't coldhearted enough to refuse.

"Husband, boyfriend?" I asked, though surely the cops had already asked.

"My dad lives in Texas," she said. "I don't think there's anyone else. But maybe."

"Any brothers or sisters?"

"No, just me."

"What's she do for a living?"

"She's a surveyor," came the answer, and I immediately had a

3

kind of foreboding. Surveying probably sounds innocent enough to most people, but measuring the land has gotten folks into trouble before.

"The fee is fifty bucks an hour, plus incidentals." It wasn't really enough to pay the bills, but I wasn't exactly working for the money anyhow.

"I've got two hundred dollars," she said, though she made no move at all to open up her little purse. "I'm sure my mom will cover the rest, once you find her."

I managed to avoid laughing outright, but I'm afraid I couldn't hold back a bit of a bigfoot snort. "I'll tell you what," I said, "I can't do anything at all until next week: I've got to work the ramps festival this weekend. But I'll take a hundred up front, and if you answer all my questions right now, I can at least take a look around, ask around, and maybe even turn over some rocks. Maybe we can figure something out, and if we're both lucky, your mom will pay your bills for you one more time." She had the grace to look embarrassed, and I hoped that embarrassment was the worst thing she had coming from her troubles.

"Thanks, Mr. Foote," she said when I was finally done asking her questions. "I hope you find her."

"I hope I do too, kid," I said.

Diane Smart, Emily had told me, had been working for PaVaMa Power, a big conglomerate with holdings in coal and gas and electric generation and transmission. Pennsylvania, Virginia, Maryland. West Virginia, too, but as usual, the West Virginia component of the company didn't mean much to the rest of the world. A PaVaMa surveyor might do any number of things: Emily said she thought her mother had been working on laying out a proposed route for a pipeline, or maybe an electrical transmission line. She didn't really know, but I knew that either of those might have led her into some tricky places. Diane Smart had been working with a partner, Harlan Stephens, and I took down what information about him that Emily had. I'd probably need to talk to him, and to Diane's boss, too, if I could manage it.

I took Emily's phone number, gave her mine, and said I'd be in touch. A hundred dollars cash was always welcome. Just minutes after she'd left, I slipped the Closed sign into the window behind the blinds and headed out. It wasn't more than a few blocks, and only slightly uphill, to the Cottonwood Café, a local coffee shop where the coffee was okay, the internet service was generally reliable, the floor was always grimy, and the kitchen probably was too. It was my kind of place.

"Hey, Big!" one or two of the regulars said when I came in. I nodded and grunted and ordered a bagel and some chicken salad. I wasn't especially big for a bigfoot, but I stood over two meters tall, and the nickname suited me out here in the human world. I took my coffee—black—over to an empty table and plugged the laptop in. A reputation for occasional surliness usually kept most of the regulars away.

As anybody who's ever searched for "bigfoot" on the internet knows, not everything you find there is necessarily true, or reliable, and it's certainly not the sum of human—or other—knowledge. Still, the internet can be a useful starting point in an investigation, and I'd been working with it long enough to know a few tricks and to have at least enough sense to be able to tell information from misinformation, which is a surprisingly useful skill. To hear PaVaMa tell it, the new pipeline they were planning was going to be the best thing for their customers since the discovery of natural gas, and if they were going to make any profit from it, well, that was hardly their concern. To those opposed to the line, it was terrible for the environment, it was a political boondoggle, it would only benefit out-of-staters, it was bad for Coal, and some of the older posts still suggested that it was probably a secret plot of Barack Obama and his Muslim friends.

I quickly found that two potential routes had been in the final proposal, and one of them passed not twenty miles from Morgantown. I expanded the Google Maps view and took a second look: it passed even more closely by the Homeland, where most of the bigfoot in the area still lived. That might be trouble.

Google, and Google Street View in particular, might give you the impression that all the world has been thoroughly mapped and even photographed. But a satellite view of miles upon miles of forest tells you very little about who or what might live there, and no Google Street View car had ever come close to the Homeland. In fact, the Homeland has literally been kept off the map from the time Mason and Dixon passed by in my grandfather's youth to the digital present. No roads led to it, no search of the county courthouse records would turn up an owner, no taxes had ever been paid on it. No surveyor had ever set foot on it.

Well, maybe that had changed recently.

Seeing where those routes lay, I was glad Emily Smart had tracked me down: I wouldn't want anyone else traipsing up through the woods out there, maybe stumbling into the Homeland. My only regret was that I would have to wait until Monday to follow up on this, and it was hardly any consolation to know that Diane Smart had been gone long enough that she either didn't really want to be found, or else the extra couple days wouldn't matter to her. I'd told Emily I couldn't do anything until Monday, and she'd seemed to understand.

I finished my little lunch and went back to the office. I had a studio apartment in the back: I never called it home, but the truth was that I lived there. It was still raining a bit; it might get worse later in the day. I'd already packed my bag for the festival, but I had a decent hike in front of me. I made a quick change: boots, tracksuit, extra jacket in case the rain got really heavy. The backpack held my hammock and another change of clothes. I wasn't going to impress anyone with my fashion sense, but I needed to look the part.

The beauty of the big, bulky tracksuit was its roomy and unconstraining fit. The basketball coach at the university always seemed to be wearing something similar, and although my ponytail meant that I'd never been mistaken for him, no one ever looked twice at me when I was wearing it, especially if I was out on the rail-trail. And that's where I started out; I then headed up to the Mason-Dixon line for the ramps festival. By the time I left, it was around one; I made my way out to the park by four.

"I can't believe you hike out here every year, Big," said Mike Merrill, the festival organizer, once I managed to track him down.

"I never did learn to drive," I said. "You know the exercise doesn't hurt me any, either." I'd only ever driven a human vehicle once or twice, and I had never even tried to get a license, though I probably could have managed it if I had to. I interacted with the state government as little as I could. "Is it pretty much the usual crowd out this year?" I asked.

"Pretty much everyone is back from last year," he said. "One or two new faces. Why don't you go get your gear unpacked, and then I'll introduce you around?"

I took my backpack and hammock out past the little area where the Airstream trailers were all parked, and I strung it up between two trees just a little way back into the woods. If it kept raining all night, I'd get a pretty good soaking, but a little rain had never hurt me—I'm not made of sugar, I've always said. It wasn't going to get all that cold, either, if I could trust what I heard on the

7

radio. The trees had finally started to leaf out in the last week or two, so I'd be at least a little protected from the rain. I expected it to clear up by morning, regardless.

It didn't take me more than ten minutes to get my little camp set up, and I found Mike Merrill over by the Lovingood clan's long tables, half of which were under little pop-up awnings better suited to keeping off the sun than the rain. Every year they put together what they called a "ramp banquet" where festival attendees could get a plateful of various ramp dishes masquerading as traditional fare: ramp salad, with ramp vinaigrette dressing; ramp pickled eggs and deviled eggs; ramp butter on a slice of home-baked rampy salt-risin' bread. The whole thing was topped off with a ramp cookie, believe it or not. They charged six bucks a plate, and they made out like bandits, or so they always said.

Mike Merrill was talking with old Sut Lovingood himself, the old man of the Morgantown side of the family. He was at least the fourth of the name, to my knowledge. This branch of the Lovingoods had come up here from Tennessee sometime before 1850, and by this point Lovingoods were all over Appalachia. Sut and I had a history; I'd known him for over thirty years, and I still owed him and a couple of other folks favors for when they'd all helped me out one time. "You got any of that ginseng tea?" I asked him when I came up. "You just can't get that stuff anywhere else anymore." Part of why you couldn't get it was that there was a restricted harvesting season for ginseng, and it was in the fall. I was sure that if I asked, Sut Lovingood would tell me he'd harvested this months ago, and kept it hanging in a root cellar somewhere. I didn't ask.

"Sure, Jim, sure," he said, glancing over at his daughter-in-law. "Mary'll get that for you. No charge for Jim," he told her, as if she might have asked me to pay.

"Thanks, Mary," I said when she brought it over in a plastic cup.

"Sure, Jim, no problem. How's business?"

Although most humans called me Big, the Lovingoods always called me by name. Mary had married into the family some fifteen or twenty years earlier, though what she saw in Bill Lovingood, I never did understand. She always called me by name, too. The family homestead was not far from the Homeland, and the Lovingoods knew almost everything there was to know about their bigfoot neighbors, but as far as I knew, there'd never been any trouble. They were always good neighbors to us. "Business as usual, Mary," I answered. "Seems like I'm always short on cash flow."

"Us too," she said, laughing. "We're hoping for a big turnout this year."

"Every year."

"Well, yeah."

"You know," I said then, "I might be out your way, early next week."

"Visiting?" she asked.

'Yeah, maybe," I answered. "And a case. A missing woman."

"Oh, I hope you find her, Jim," Mary told me, and I could only nod. Hope is a strange, strange thing, but it seemed to be something bigfoot and humans shared.

But before I could answer her, Mike Merrill turned toward us. "Well, I'm going to introduce Big here to the new vendors."

"Sure enough," said Sut Lovingood. "See you at the party, Jim."

Besides being the organizer of the ramps festival, Mike Merrill was an Airstream aficionado from way back. Since it was his festival, there was always an Airstream meet-up at the same time. Most of the Airstreamers probably didn't care one way or the other about ramps, and very few of the local festival vendors would have ever spent their spare money on an antique camper-trailer, but the festival had been going on long enough that the two groups knew each other by now. Everybody pulled into the little state park where the festival was held for setup some time on Friday, before the official ten o'clock start on Saturday morning, and a big music jam and party was always held in the picnic shelter on Friday night. Of course I'd be there.

For now, Mike Merrill was walking me around, and we nodded at the old hands. Here was Hank Marshall using an old pair of tinsnips on a Mountain Dew can. He made whirligigs and wind chimes from old cans, and he always seemed to do a good business. Across the way were the O'Reillys with a booth full of brightly printed T-shirts, stuffed dinosaurs, and classic rock and country music mirrors. Next to them was a portable wood-working setup, though I hadn't seen the outhouse-shaped toilet paper holders before. The ones with the crescent moons on the doors were traditional enough, but I thought the ones with the crosses looked a little jarring. At the end of one row, I could see they already had the logs set up for chainsaw carving and amateur hatchet-throwing.

"Big, this is Seth Jones," said Mike as we headed down the second row. "This is his first time here as a vendor. I've got him signed up to set up for the reenactment down at Prickett's Fort next week, too," he added, and then turned to Jones. "This is Big Jim Foote; he provides security for the festival."

"Glad to meet you, Mr. Foote."

"Same here," I answered, shaking his hand. I supposed he was what might be called a hipster these days: somewhere between twenty and thirty years old, with glasses and a flannel shirt. His age was hard to figure, because he was wearing the sort of facial hair that had last been fashionable in the human world during my grandfather's day. His tables were under an awning, too, and I could see from a chalkboard list of prices that he'd be selling food. "Ramp quiche?" I said. "Sounds good!"

"I'll be bringing some to the party. If you like it, tell everybody tomorrow," he said, grinning.

"I'll look forward to it," I said.

"I'll pass," said Mike Merrill. "Believe it or not, I'm allergic to the damn things."

"No kidding," said Seth Jones. "How'd you end up organizing the festival?"

"It's a long story, but the short version of it is I hoped to be able to make a little money."

Seth Jones laughed.

"He's down from Pittsburgh," Mike Merrill said, as we walked on. "He says he thinks we might get a couple folks in from Philadelphia, or even from New York City. Ramps are big in the foodie world these days, he says."

"That's what I hear."

"He's really the only new vendor, I think," he went on. "We've got one or two new Airstream folks, but I'm not sure where they're parked. I'm sure you'll meet them at the party, though."

"I look forward to it," I said again, and I meant it.

If you've never eaten ramps, I hardly know how to describe them. They're sometimes described as wild leeks, but they have a flavor closer to fresh garlic, but spicier, somehow. They have a little white bulb at the base, a purplish stem, and a broad green leaf, and if you eat them today, you'll reek of them tomorrow. They're one of the earliest greens of spring that you can eat, and they've been a seasonal staple of the northern Appalachian woodland cuisine since before the Mayflower. Bigfoot have eaten them forever, of course.

I wouldn't touch Sut Lovingood's ramp banquet if you paid me, but Seth Jones's ramp quiche sounded pretty good. I was glad to see a kind of foodie presence this year, even though I doubted anything would be as good as the beer-battered ramps that the volunteer firemen always served. They were what made the festival worthwhile, as far as I was concerned. The firemen were all locals, so they usually didn't camp at the festival like most of the vendors, but they always came out and fired up the fryer on Friday evening. My mouth was already watering.

I took a trip around the perimeter of the big field where the festival was held. The only road in was a twisty, uneven one that went down to a single lane in places, and I knew that those were always potential trouble spots. But the truth was that working security here was an easy gig. Trouble was rare, and hardly anyone came from farther away than Morgantown, except for a few curious folks from Pittsburgh, like Seth Jones. Everything seemed in perfectly good order, and I made it back to the big picnic shelter just as the sun was going down.

I walked around, saying hello to various familiar faces, and when the line had shrunken down to only one or two people, I got in it and waited for a paper plate full of the beer-battered ramps. Tomorrow, the firemen would be charging five bucks a plate for about half the amount, but tonight everybody who wanted them could get their fill. When I reached the end of the line, I saw Seth Jones sitting at a picnic table with a couple of his quiches. "I'll take a slice," I told him.

He cut me a largish piece and squeezed it onto my paper plate, already soaking through with the frying grease. "I hope you like it, Mr. Foote," he said.

"I will, I'm sure." I picked up a little plastic fork and took my plate over to an empty picnic table at one side of the shelter.

Although we were technically on the grounds of a state park, the rules against alcohol consumption were somehow never enforced on the Friday before the festival. I didn't drink, of course: for me, like all the bigfoot I've ever known, the effects of alcohol always seemed to proceed straight to headache and hangover, with no pleasurable interval of euphoria, overconfidence, or freedom preceding. But just about all of the humans who were over twenty-one seemed to be drinking their share, and a few of the younger folks seemed to have had a sip or two as well. A couple of folks had fiddles out (it was no more correct to call them violins than to say that Hobo Joe was homeless), and a couple guitars were playing, too.

Mostly, they played either bluegrass classics or radio hits from the 1970s. It was almost mandatory around these parts that an evening like this would end with a sing-along to John Denver's "Country Roads," although I personally could live without it. And the version of "Jesus Is Just All Right" that I heard took on a whole different feeling from the Doobie Brothers hit, and I didn't think it was improved by the change. I didn't sing along to any of the songs; I just don't have the voice for it.

Instead, I watched. I suppose that was my job in some ways. Security, Mike Merrill called it, but really it amounted to night watchman and, very occasionally, bouncer. But at the Friday party, I probably wouldn't need to do either, unless a fight broke out. I knew from experience that it was a possibility, if a slim one.

People moved around from table to table, carrying their cans or bottles of beer, and sometimes a little plastic cup of something stronger. The Lovingoods camped out at a pair of tables and didn't move, but most everyone knew one or another member of the clan, and people came to them.

At one point, Seth Jones stopped by my table with a couple

unmarked brown bottles. "This is just a little homebrew cider I've been making on the side. I can't sell it tomorrow, of course, but I thought maybe you'd like a taste."

"Thanks, man," I said, "but I'm technically working, you know."

"Keep this one for later, then," he said. He took a small drink from his own bottle. "You always do security here?"

"Yeah, it's a regular gig for me, once a year. And I like the people. And the batter-dipped ramps."

"I can't compete with them, I'm afraid, but I hope it'll be worth my while to be here."

"I'm sure it will. Most of the food here isn't all that good, if you ask me. It's technically a food festival, but people don't seem to come here for the food. It's the idea of the thing, a chance to get out in the springtime weather. An excuse to risk getting rained on."

He nodded, not entirely sure what I meant, probably. Of course, I might be completely wrong about why humans come to the festival: I've lived among them for a long time, but I can't say that I always understand what a human is thinking. We sat in semi-companionable silence for a while until we were joined by one of the Airstream crowd, Darla Something-or-other.

"Hey, Big," she said, sitting down on the bench on my side of the picnic table. She had a bottle a lot like Seth's and her own paper plate full of the beer-battered ramps.

"It's Darla, right?" I asked.

"That's right, honey," she answered. "I just had to get away from that Bill Lovingood." She said. "He's got none of your charm at all, Big."

"Mom!" said Seth Jones, much to my surprise.

"This is your mother?"

"None other," she said, looking at me over the bottle as she took a drink.

Something seemed to pass without words, then, between mother and son, and I had no real idea of what it might be. But Seth Jones picked up his bottle and the one he'd put down next to me and slumped off with what I thought might be an unhappy look on his face without another word to her or me.

"Ungrateful child," she said, with what seemed to me to be a perfectly cheerful expression.

I didn't really know how to respond to that, so I tried another tack. "Bill Lovingood being his usual self?" I'd always thought of him as kind of a blowhard and a jerk. Some of the Lovingoods grew up respecting their bigfoot neighbors, some of them didn't, and Bill had always seemed like one of the latter.

"He made me an offer that I could refuse," she said, cryptically. "And I refused it. He didn't seem to be expecting that."

I had lived among humans long enough—and watched enough TV and movies—to have at least some idea of how uncomfortable human sexual negotiations could be, and I figured that was what she was talking about. I didn't feel like it was a conversational area I needed to move into, at the moment. "Your boy seems like a good kid," I tried.

"He wouldn't even be here if I hadn't told him about the festival. He runs a food truck up in Pittsburgh," she added, as if this explained everything.

"He make a good living that way?" I asked, with no idea what she really was doing here. Being social, I guessed.

"I can hardly hear you over the music," she said, sliding down the bench. "My, you really are big aren't you?" she said then.

I wasn't sure I was happy with the direction this was taking. She was, as far as I could tell, what many human males would find sexually attractive: she wasn't as thin as the models I saw on TV, or as young, but she was here, and the shorts and the V-necked T-shirt she was wearing seemed to catch a lot of the men's eyes. No doubt they had caught Bill Lovingood's eye. "I'm about two meters tall," I said noncommittally. I wondered who might be looking her way right now and what they'd see.

"Mmm," she hummed. "There's probably barely room for you in my Airstream. But I'm sure I could fit you in."

I may not always be able to tell what the humans are thinking, but I was pretty sure I knew a double entendre when I heard one. The hand she had placed on my thigh was also a clue.

Though my experience with humans in this mood is, frankly, limited, I know enough to know that there are some lines of attack that you just have to head off. This was one of them. "I'm afraid you're barking up the wrong tree, ma'am," I said.

"Ma'am?" she said indignantly. "You're older than I am, I'll bet!" She was laughing a little, I thought, and she had the grace, at this point, to pull her hand away.

"That I am," I said, though she probably had no idea how much older. Bigfoot are a long-lived bunch. "But it never hurts to be polite, I've found, when I've had to turn someone down."

"Hmmm," she said, looking halfway askance at me. "Happens all the time, I suppose."

I could only laugh. "Almost never, since you ask. It's not that I don't appreciate the offer," I said, "but the truth is you've got nothing for me."

"Well, I never," she said, but if I was any judge, she seemed genuinely amused, rather than irritated. Undoubtedly, she thought I preferred men, and it was a misunderstanding I was happy enough to let go unchallenged. "But I think I'll sit here and drink with you a while, even so," she added. "I don't think I could stand to have to talk to that Bill Lovingood anymore."

"Sitting and talking and laughing? That'd I'd enjoy greatly," I said to her.

"Let me get another couple of my son's bottles," she said, and she was up and gone before I could tell her I didn't need one.

"You sure you don't want some company up in that hammock?" she asked around midnight, when the party was winding down.

"Darla, I've had a fine evening," I said. "And I like you a lot. But when I say you're not my type, you've got to believe me."

"Oh, I do, Big. Just checking, really." She smiled her little half-smile.

"You'll be all right, I think," I said to her as we parted.

I didn't know then how wrong I was.

CHAPTER 2

SATURDAY

———

I woke to my hammock rocking wildly. "Big!" said a voice. "Get your ass up; there's been a murder!"

It was Mike Merrill, standing there in my little campsite. I struggled against the ropes of the hammock for a moment before managing to get a leg over the edge. I rubbed my face a moment. "Who killed who?" I said, regardless of the grammar.

"You don't know?" Even as he said it, it seemed a strange thing to say to me.

"No idea!" I said, irritated. "How could I know?"

"It was Darla Jones," he answered. "Far as anyone knows, you were the last one to talk to her."

"Huh. That's terrible." Had she been looking for protection, last evening? Had there been some danger I hadn't even known about? Whether there had been or not, I felt like I'd failed her. "How do you know it's murder?" I asked.

"It was done with a hatchet," Mike answered. "Couldn't be an accident. You'd better come see."

So I walked along with him over to where the Airstreamers

were camping. It was still the dark side of daybreak, and no one much seemed to be stirring. There was no outcry yet, no crowd of onlookers. Well, that wouldn't last, I thought grimly.

"I was just going around," he said. "I'm always up early out here, worried about the festival, I guess, and I always walk around to make sure everyone's all right. Nothing like this has ever happened here before!"

"You got anything we can fence this area off with?" I asked. "The police won't want everybody pawing all over it." The body was spilled on the ground not far from the camper's little door, which stood open. Sure enough, a hatchet lay nearby, and there was an open wound high up on her back, the T-shirt sliced open and soaked with blood. Her spine had probably been severed, I guessed, though it would take a doctor to be certain. But anyone could see she was dead.

"I suppose I could get some barriers or something. And I've got some rope we could use."

"And a tarp," I added. "Something to cover the body. No one needs to see this."

He bustled away to look for those things, and I knelt down to take a closer look at the body in the dim morning light. The hatchet was the normal kind, like anybody might use to split kindling or break up branches for a fire. Even so, I'd have to check in on the hatchet throwers, to see if it was one of theirs. I doubted it, though. Someone must have been incredibly angry with her to hit her from behind after she'd turned her back. But I know that human emotions can be powerful, dangerous things.

I stood up, looked around, and tried to think who could possibly have wanted her dead. She must have had a whole life away from the ramps festival, but it seemed likely that it was someone here who'd done it: we were out in the middle of nowhere and I couldn't really picture anyone making their way out here in the dark of the night just to kill Darla Jones with a hatchet. It seemed much more likely to be a spur-of-the-moment act.

They always say to look at the family first, but Seth Jones didn't seem the type from anything I had seen. He might have looked unhappy when he'd stalked off last night, but he was hardly surprised. His mother had probably been embarrassing him for years. Seth must have had a father somewhere in the picture, but who that might have been, and if he was even still alive was nothing I knew anything about. I remembered that Darla had complained last evening about Bill Lovingood, who'd apparently been pursuing her, right under the nose of his own wife Mary. Darla had turned him down, but he might have tried again, later. Or maybe Mary had done it, angry at her husband and taking it out on Darla Jones. The kinds of emotions that might have been working among those three were nothing I really knew how to understand.

"You get any kind of phone signal out here?" I asked Mike when he came back with his rope and one of those crinkly blue tarps.

"I wish!" he said. "Can you give me a hand with this?"

"Sure," I said, and we started to gently stake down the tarp over the body. Mike had brought only three stakes, so at one corner, I just weighed the tarp down with a brick that Darla had been using to chock one of the camper's wheels. "Somebody's going to have to go into town, maybe, or at least to somewhere there's a signal, and get the sheriff out here."

Mike grunted, either from the effort of getting back up from the ground or as all the answer I was going to get. He looked at me, but before he could suggest it was my job, I pointed out what he must have already known. "I don't drive," I said. "Someone with a car will get them out here much faster."

I could see him thinking—probably trying to decide if he was going to have to shut down the festival or whether to let it go on. I didn't know how much money he took in, but the parking alone had to be in the hundreds or thousands, which could be a significant amount in these parts, as I well knew. "I'll go," he said finally. "Billy can handle the parking when the gates open at ten o'clock if I'm not back before then. We're going to have hundreds of people out here whether the festival's open or not, so we might as well go on with it. I don't know what else we can do."

Obviously posting a cancellation notice out by the park entrance was something we could do, but I'm really no judge of what humans find appropriate or inappropriate at such times, so I just nodded.

"Have you told her boy?" I asked.

"Her boy?" he said.

"Seth Jones, the young guy with the ramp quiche," I answered. "He's her son."

"I had no idea!" he said, plainly surprised.

"Well," I said, "you fetch the sheriff; I'll tell him about his mama."

Before I went to talk to Seth, I took one last look around, and in the growing light, I saw something I hadn't noticed before. Over near the rounded rear corner of the little camper, I found a pile of vomit sitting on the grass—the kind of thing you find on a Morgantown sidewalk just about any morning during the school year before the owners of the various storefronts hose down the walks. In Morgantown, it is drunken college students purging poisons from their bodies. Darla had drunk a fair amount last evening, but I wouldn't have said she'd poisoned herself with the stuff, at least not when I'd last seen her. What happened afterward was another question. One thing that had happened to her was fatally certain.

Maybe she'd come out of the camper to throw up. Or maybe she'd seen something she shouldn't have. It couldn't have been an accident. I'd seen dead bodies before, human and bigfoot both, but all of a sudden, I almost felt like throwing up myself. Last evening, she'd made me laugh, more than once, and now here she lay, inert.

The smell of bile was in the air, the smell of vomit. There was alcohol in it, too. But something seemed odd, and I took a closer look, and a sniff. The bigfoot sense of smell might be better than the equivalent human sense, and it might not be; who can tell, for sure, what another person senses? But I knew one thing right away: I knew who had killed Darla Jones.

I poked my head into the little camper and looked around. There was a little drying rack alongside a tiny sink, and a little plastic container and lid sitting there in it, along with some stainless flatware. I picked the container up, took it outside, scooped about half the pile of vomit up, and closed the lid on it. Even I can't believe the kind of things I find myself doing on this job sometimes.

I continued to putter around Darla's campsite a bit longer. I wished that I had given Mike a good sniff when he had come back with the tarp: I would have known for sure if he had eaten any of the ramps last evening. The puke wasn't Darla's, I knew: I'd seen her eating the beer-battered ramps right at my own picnic table. Mike was probably the only human in the whole place who hadn't eaten any ramps last evening. If he hadn't killed her himself, I was betting he still knew something about it. I probably would have noticed if he had had the ramps, I told myself. It just would have been nice if I had been able to confirm it before he'd left.

But I could hear his car, even then; he was driving off to Morgantown to look for the sheriff. If he didn't just call it in, he'd probably go all the way to the sheriff's offices and then ride along with the deputies back here, leaving his car in order to fill their ears with his story of me being the last person to see Darla alive. On second thought, if I was right, and he'd done it, he probably wouldn't just call it in, for that very reason.

This was going to be more interesting than I'd really like. I wasn't at all sure I'd be able to convince even the sharpest deputy that a pile of stale puke was a vital piece of evidence in a murder investigation. That, and my ability to smell the ramps on the bodies and breath of anyone who'd eaten them. After all, I could hardly say that some special bigfoot sense of smell was the key to solving the case, although I had heard that humans also could smell the ramps the next day wafting off people who had eaten them. One thing that absolutely couldn't happen was for me to be taken in, fingerprinted, and investigated. I needed to tie this up with a bow before the sheriff's deputies got here. Somehow, I had to find a way to get them to take the barf evidence seriously.

Finally, I poked my head back into Darla's camper. In a minute or two, I found what I was looking for, a little pad of notepaper. I grabbed a pen, too, and then made my way to Seth Jones's camper.

"Mr. Jones?" I said, knocking gently. "Seth?"

"Who is it?" I heard, a sleepy, grumpy voice.

"It's me, Jim Foote," I answered. "I'm afraid I have some terrible news about your mother." Maybe that wasn't the best way to phrase it, but I wanted him up and awake.

He came to the door of the camper in his boxers. "What is it?"

"She's dead," I said. "I'm sorry, but there's no way to break it any gentler."

"What? What happened?"

"The police are on the way, so it's probably best for them to investigate. But I can walk you over there, and you can see what they are going to see. I'd better warn you: it wasn't an accident—she was killed with a hatchet."

"Just a minute," he said, closing the door. I heard some more thumping around from inside the vehicle, and then he came out the door, dressed. "Where is she?"

"Right by her own camper." We were already walking that way. I didn't know what to say. A human, in this situation, might have some clue, some idea, about what was going through his mind, or his heart, but I felt lost. Probably he did, too, I decided. It wasn't hard to guess that he'd be hurting, one way or another.

"We put this tarp over her," I said when we got there. It was much lighter out now, and he pulled up the brick at the one corner and peeked under it, shaking his head and giving an involuntary shiver at what he saw. He pointed at the hatchet lying nearby. "Somebody hit her with this?" he asked.

"Looks like. I'm sure there'll be a police investigation, maybe an autopsy."

"Ugh. You never really think that stuff will happen to you. Or to your mom." Before I knew it, he had plopped down on the ground right beside her. I didn't see tears or hear sobbing, but they couldn't be far off, I guessed. But I couldn't let him just sit there; we had things to do.

"You don't have any ideas who did this?" I asked.

"How could I?" he asked, angry.

I had a plan for trying to get the police to take the barf evidence seriously, but the longer we waited, the trickier it would get. I knew I hadn't done it, and I didn't think he had, either. For one thing, I'd seen him eating the beer-battered ramps. "There's one piece of evidence I think the cops will need to see," I said, gesturing toward the diminished pile of puke.

"She threw up?" he asked, obviously confused.

24

"I don't think so: there's no ramps in that vomit."

He peered at the little pile of evidence. "It would smell different if there were," I added.

"I don't think I want to know how you found that out," he said. "But everyone at the festival must have had at least some ramps at the party last night."

"Almost everyone, I'm sure. But you can't say anything about this to anyone," I said. "Whoever did this could cover their tracks, just by eating some ramps this morning, if they know what we know."

"You think the killer threw up here?"

"Yeah, I do. And if not, at the least, it was someone who was here, on the spot, sometime last night." I tore the little notepad I'd picked up in Darla Jones's camper in two, and Seth Jones's eyes grew wide to see me do it. But I acted like it was nothing, and I gave him half. "I know this is a terrible time," I told him. "But I need your help. I want to go talk to everyone this morning and tell them we think there's been an outbreak of food poisoning, and it'll close down the whole festival if we can't pin it down. Make everyone write down everything they ate and drank last night. We'll see if there's anyone who didn't have any ramps."

"Mike Merrill," he said. "He said he was allergic."

I hadn't been sure if I had remembered correctly that Seth had also heard Mike say this, and I hadn't known if he'd remember it even if he had, but now it seemed he did remember. "Yeah, maybe," I answered. "That's why we've got to find out if there's anyone else who's allergic to 'em and without giving anything away. I don't think anyone knows your mom is dead yet, and I'd like to keep it under wraps until the cops get here. Is that all right?"

He looked down at the tarp where we had staked it down again over his mother's body. Something seemed to pass through his mind, but I had no idea what. "You had some ramps, I know it," he said finally. "You want me to help prove who did it. Yeah, I'll do it. I'll help you ask everyone what they had."

"Food poisoning," I said. "Remember to tell 'em you're asking because of a case of food poisoning."

I hated to send him off on his own the way he must have been feeling, but I didn't see what else there was to do. We split up; Seth went out canvassing among the Airstreamers while I knocked on camper doors among the vendors. "If we can pin down what's making people sick," I kept telling them, "we can let the festival open. Otherwise, we'll probably have to shut it down." I didn't really like lying to folks, but I'd learned over the years that humans usually couldn't tell when I was lying or when I was telling the truth; it worked both ways, of course. Surprisingly, this hadn't been a problem in my work as an investigator: I just didn't believe anything anyone told me until I'd checked it out.

I didn't know how long we'd have until the sheriff or his people would come in and take over, but I didn't think it would be very long, so I moved as quickly as I could. People were cooperative once I'd explained what I wanted, though I woke more than one person up, and many had hangovers. Pretty soon, I had a handful of little written notes. Everyone I spoke to had had the ramps, in one form or another, as far as I could see. I was lucky: I got all of the way around my half of the crowd before I saw the sheriff's deputies coming in, two cars with lights flashing but no sirens. Everyone's attention was on them immediately.

They parked at the very front of what would later become the public parking area, and I made my way toward them. Mike got out of the passenger seat of one car as two deputies stepped out from the drivers' seats. I realized I knew them both, Deputies Bowling and Evans, but not very well. I might be a private investigator, but even so, I usually try to steer clear of law enforcement. Bowling was tall for a human, he had brown hair going gray, and it always seemed like he looked at me suspiciously—as if he didn't trust anyone bigger than he was. Evans was no bigger than Mike or Seth and was a bit on the portly side, with hair a few shades darker than his skin. I wasn't always certain about human racial categories, but I'd heard him describe himself as Black once. "I haven't made any kind of announcement," I said by way of greeting. "I thought I'd leave that to you gentlemen."

Bowling's look seemed even more irritated than usual. It had been his car that Mike had been riding in. "Big Jim Foote," he said without offering a hand to shake, probably just making sure I knew he remembered me. "Let's take a look at the scene," he said.

I let Mike lead them to Darla's camper. "We covered over the body with this tarp," Mike was saying, "but we didn't touch it. Or the hatchet." He and Deputy Evans lifted the tarp up off the body.

The deputies looked, snapping a few digital pictures with their phones. "Is this one of the hatchets from those axe-throwing guys?" asked Evans.

Mike didn't seem like he was going to answer, so I did. "I don't think so: I think it's just a kindling splitter. Probably belonged to her." I nodded at Darla's body as I said it.

"You knew the victim?" asked Bowling, turning.

"Sure, enough to say hi to. She'd been coming here for a few years, and I've been working security here since the festival started."

"We have a witness who says she was cuddled up pretty close to you last evening."

I looked at Mike, then at Bowling again. I wondered who he thought he was fooling with the circumlocution.

"Sure," I said, "Mike here and probably half the people at the party saw her chatting with me last night. But I slept in my hammock. Alone."

"Noted," said Bowling briefly, as if already disbelieving.

I opened the little door and reached into the camper, where I'd stored the little Tupperware container of puke. "I scooped this up from the pile over there," I said pointing. "I think it might be the killer's."

"Jesus, Foote!" said Bowling then. "Tampering with evidence and making sure that we can see you've put your fingerprints all over the scene of the crime. A PI ought to know better."

"Yeah, well, I got nothing to hide."

"And you thought we'd need the help?"

I knew better than to agree, even if that's exactly what I had thought. Mike and Deputy Evans were watching this exchange with their eyes wide, though I suspected Mike might have had a hint of satisfaction about him.

"And you think there's evidence in this vomit?" Bowling continued. "You're crazier than I thought."

"It could be anybody's, here behind the trailer," Mike said. "There was a lot of drinking last night. Could have been anybody walking by." I thought he was a fool for speaking out, but I could see Bowling nod, and Evans seemed to be going along with it.

I added my own two cents, anyway. "Yeah, I thought there was some alcohol in it when I scooped it up and that it might evaporate if I didn't seal some of it up." At this point, Seth came up and gave me a look that I couldn't figure.

"Gentlemen," I said to the two deputies, "this is Seth Jones, Darla Jones's son."

Evans held out his hand, and Seth Jones shook it. "I'm sorry this happened to your mother," he said. "We'll get the guy, count on it."

"We will," echoed Bowling.

"I'd love to see the guys in the lab," Evans said then, glancing with a half-smile on his face at the container that was still in my hand, "when we bring them a container of barf to evaluate!"

"It'll never happen," said Bowling. "Big Jim Foote here has had half the morning to tamper with the evidence, and anything about this that points away from him is useless, as far as I can see."

"Yeah," I said, finally seeing my way. "Because you know I didn't drink last night. I never do: so the presence of alcohol in the puke means it wasn't mine."

"Exactly," said Bowling. "All you'd need to do would be to pour a bit in here and seal it up. As if that would be proof you were never here."

"You guys are missing the point," I said. "Nobody could ever prove they weren't here, unless they could prove they were somewhere else. I already told you I was alone. This isn't evidence I wasn't here: it's evidence that someone else was."

"It's probably Darla's anyway," said Mike. "She was drinking, sure enough."

"She never drank that much," said Seth Jones then. "I never saw her drunk."

"Still means nothing," Bowling said.

"But it does," I said finally. "There's one thing about this little pile of puke you guys are missing: there's no ramps in it."

There was a brief pause, and then: "Jesus, I hate those things," Bowling said.

"Seth," I said, "what'd you see me eating last night?"

"You had the beer-battered ramps, and I gave you a slice of the ramp quiche. Same as my mom."

I have to admit, I smiled a bit, turning to Bowling. "And you drove all the way out here with Mike," I said, "who's allergic. Did you smell any ramps on him, cooped up with him in that car?"

It wasn't real evidence, of course, but even Bowling was smart enough to realize that he'd been fed a line of suspicion all through that car ride, one pointing not so subtly or indirectly at me. Seth and I produced our notes on what everyone else had eaten, and sure enough, everyone else at the festival had had ramps, in one form or another, right down to half a dozen children and Bill Lovingood's dog, who'd pulled a plate of ramp cookies right from the table. It was enough to make the deputies suspicious. Once Evans pointed out that there must be DNA evidence in the barf and then asked Mike for a sample, Mike told them he wanted to speak to his lawyer. Even that statement wasn't any kind of evidence they could actually use, but it was like blood in the water to a couple of sharks. From there on, it was just a matter of moving to the endgame.

"You really think he did it?" Seth asked me, late in the day.

"I do think so."

"But why?"

What could I say? Human motivations are always a mystery to me. "He must have been angry with her," I finally said.

"But why?"

"I don't know. Maybe even he doesn't know or doesn't really remember."

"On TV, they always talk about means, motive, and opportunity," he said.

"I know it. But truth is different from fiction. I won't say it's stranger, but it's different, sure enough. In this case, it was all about the ramps."

The rest of the festival, I guess I can say, was uneventful by comparison. Billy Mayhew, who'd always been Mike Merrill's helper, had managed everything on his own—running the gate, getting the cars parked, and collecting everybody's fees before closing up the place on Sunday. Where the money that Billy took in was going to end up was unclear. Probably, it would go to pay for Mike's lawyer, though something seemed very wrong about that idea. Most of the visitors to the festival would probably never know there'd been a murder until they read the paper on Monday morning or saw the brief story on the Clarksburg TV station. It wouldn't even make the Pittsburgh news.

I spent a good part of Sunday talking to Seth Jones, who cycled from anger to hurt and back again. I think he stuck close by me precisely because he figured I was nobody's shoulder to cry on, but I hoped he had someone who could be. He had gone ahead and baked up the rest of the ramp quiches he'd prepared, not wanting to let the food go to waste, and I carried them over to the Lovingoods, who were willing to sell them alongside their own food. Old Sut even promised me that he'd give all the money from the quiches to Seth without even taking a cut. As the festival was winding down, I told Seth he could call me if there was ever anything he needed done down in Morgantown, and we traded business cards. He was taking the loss pretty hard, understandably, and I was reminded very much of Emily Smart, who was worried herself that her own mother might be gone.

And then the festival was over. Everyone packed up and went their own way. I put my hammock back into my pack and made my way back to Morgantown. The afternoon sun was hot, and I decided that I preferred the cool and the rain we'd had on Friday.

I tried, as I walked, to wrestle my thoughts back to Emily Smart and her missing mother, but somehow it was Darla and Seth that I spent most of my time thinking about.

CHAPTER 3

MONODAY

———

The next morning, I spent a few minutes on the internet again, checking my email and the social site I lurked on. I also looked over some of the pages I'd bookmarked last week after my long interview with Emily Smart.

Nothing had changed, naturally. Her mother was still missing, and the fact that her mother worked as a surveyor still seemed like it might give me a place to start, although I had no way of knowing if starting from this angle would turn anything up. I still thought there was a chance she might have ended up close to the Homeland, given her most recent assignment, and I needed to get up there and at least try to find her before anyone started to comb those woods as part of a search. I told myself that I could also use a day in the Homeland, a day when I didn't need to pretend to be a human.

I sent Emily Smart a brief email just to let her know I was working, and then I put my tracksuit back on. The ramps festival had been west of town; this time I headed east, down to Decker's Creek Trail, which I followed right up into the hills. Along the way, I stopped at one of the grocery stores and picked up a few things. Once I had these provisions packed, I started out in a comfortable jog, knowing that I had some distance to cover. Mike Merrill had commented that he couldn't believe how I always hiked out to the state park where he held the festival, and I knew that most humans nowadays would probably never think of making a fifteen- or twenty-mile trip on foot, unless they were in an actual race or training for one. They might run five miles on a treadmill, but most of them wouldn't walk even a mile to get to the gym. They'd rather drive a car to get to somewhere where they could run in place. What that meant for me was that once I was only a mile or two out of town, I had the trail pretty much to myself.

There is nothing special about Decker's Creek. It isn't all that scenic or picturesque, especially in the lower part, and it's not important to the local economy, but a rail line had been laid down along it in the nineteenth century, and not long after the last mine on the line closed in 2000, it had been rehabilitated into a gravel or cinder trail for bikers, hikers, and runners. No steeper than a steam train could manage, it was a far easier trail than I needed.

I finally settled in to a steady walking pace and tried to think. Diane Smart could have gotten into fifteen different kinds of trouble out in this direction. Worst case, from my point of view, was the possibility that she might have stumbled across the Homeland. I'd like to say bigfoot never use lethal force when they have any option, but not everyone I know finds humans as tolerable as I do. Diane could also have stumbled across some entrepreneur's patch of marijuana, or if this had been years ago, when I was younger, I'd have guessed that she might have run across a still. She might have also come across someone who was real upset about the possibility that PaVaMa might put a pipeline too close to their place. Or a tree or a rock might have fallen on her—although that was, admittedly, unlikely. I didn't really have any reason to be certain that she'd ever come out this way at all, but I've ignored my gut before, and I've almost always regretted it. Well, I'd just see what I could see.

Eventually I reached the turn off: it was just a spot in the trail where you could scramble up the hillside to another trail, a deer track, really. Another hour or so up this way, and I'd be at the edge of the Homeland.

"Yo, Jim," I heard when I was close to the border line. A shadowy figure stepped out from beside a tree.

"Ezra," I said. Someone is always stationed out here near the trail to greet folks who know where they are going—some of them even humans—and to discourage everyone else. Ezra is one of the regular rotation—a good bit bigger than me, his hair and beard are dark to the point of being almost black. He was dressed in a truly awful tracksuit with extensions sewn onto the legs. Barefoot, of course. I don't know what these guys are thinking, sometimes. I can leave all the footprints I want, anywhere I go, and all that any human who sees them will do is marvel at the size of my shoes. I suppose Ezra probably looked at me and my shoes and figured I was losing my touch. "Any news?" I asked.

"Not a thing," he said. "You're the first person I've seen out here all day."

"Just the way you like it, I bet."

"Yep." He paused. "What brings you back home?"

"I'm working," I answered. "Just looking for some information."

"What kind of case?"

"Missing person. Human."

"It wasn't me; I swear!"

"Very funny, Ezra. Just keep your eyes open. I don't know that anything about this case points up this way, but it might, so you could find yourself a bit busier than usual up here. I don't know for sure, but it's a possibility."

"Huh. Well, thanks for the heads up."

I headed on in. I was looking for my cousin Martha, and I found her not half an hour later, just as twilight was really starting to grip the mountainside. She had a little nook up between two rocks—a boulder split in two, really—and she was tidying things up when I found her. Out beyond the rocks, she had a rope hammock strung up between two trees. A bigfoot doesn't need much in the way of comforts to make a home, but it was Martha's policy in the Homeland to make sure that every bigfoot lair or nest had something human about it: a hammock, a rumpled old blanket, a handful of old beer cans or plastic bottles. That way, if some human ever did manage to find their way up here and came across one of our places, it would look like some kind of human camp or dump. Even for a bigfoot, a hammock was a lot more comfortable than a bed on the ground. I held the little plastic grocery bag I'd been carrying out in my hand. "I brought a couple of sandwiches and some chips," I told her. "And I've got a couple of questions I need to ask."

Bigfoot are omnivores, like most humans are. What that means is that although we'll eat rabbit or squirrel or fish or deer or bear when we can get them, most of the time we forage for what the woods will provide. Martha was happy enough with the sandwiches—a change of pace is always nice—and I wouldn't have expected her to feed me on no notice at all. It may be true that a few handfuls of acorns are something just about anyone in the Homeland can always spare, but I was already asking her for more than one favor: the least I could do was bring her some food from town.

"Cuz," she said, looking up. "Nice outfit."

I couldn't help but laugh. She didn't have any kind of human clothes on at all. With a fine fur coat, cold temperatures and rain aren't a problem for bigfoot, and only those of us who live among the humans usually bother with clothes. Guys like Ezra, who may run into the odd hiker, can go either way. Fashion isn't something most bigfoot care about, maybe because the humans do. Anyway, Martha is old school, and she has always found human clothes amusing. "I can always count on you to keep me in my place," I said, still laughing.

"I should have known you'd be turning up," she said then.

"Has there been any trouble?"

"No," she answered easily. "Just a feeling."

"Yeah. Me too. And a case," I added.

It didn't take me long at all to tell her everything I knew about the case. It wasn't much. She listened. She hasn't spent nearly as much time among the humans as I have, but she has a lot of wisdom, I've always found. She also knows almost everything that has happened in the Homeland. She doesn't run the place, exactly: bigfoot are loners, as a rule, and the Homeland mostly runs on its own. But she is the person everyone knows they can go to when they need or want something.

"You'd better get a good night's sleep," was all she said, when I'd finished.

"You know something about this?" I asked, surprised.

"I'll show you in the morning," she said. And she refused to say any more. She took the hammock; I found a flat spot on the ground.

"I don't know for sure whether this will have anything to do with your case," she said as we hiked along the next morning. "But it might. I'll let you decide what to do about it, either way."

It didn't sound good, though she still refused to give any details. The route we were taking was pretty rough: nothing I couldn't handle, but not anywhere easy, either. We were heading up toward the ridge, and in some places, the rhododendrons were almost impassable. Finally, she pointed to an opening between two trees. "I haven't gotten too close," she said. "But it looks like a body to me."

My heart sank. It did look like a body, even from a distance: a pile of artificial colors that didn't belong in the forest any more than the primary colors of my tracksuit did. I crept a bit closer. "Yeah," I said, as I saw a hand, and then a face. Human, I thought. Probably a woman.

"How long's it been here?" I asked turning back to Martha.

"I don't know: I only came across it three or four days ago. I forgot all about it until I heard your story last night."

"Hmm," I said, thinking. I pulled my phone from my pocket. No signal, but you always have to check. "Where do you suppose the nearest real road is?" I asked.

She pointed downhill. "About half an hour or so, I think."

I thought the same: I know that I don't spend as much time up here in the mountains as I should, but you never really lose your sense of direction. "You'd probably better get out of here," I told her. "I'll have to call this one in when I can get somewhere where I can get a signal. We'll probably have the cops up here, maybe the coroner and an ambulance, too."

"Yeah, that's what I figured," she said. "You think it's her?"

"I don't know, but even if it's not, it's someone that somebody's probably looking for."

"Yeah. Okay. Well, you need anything, you come on back, right?"

"I will, cuz," I said. "Thanks."

"I'll let you know if I hear anything," she said, and then she melted back into the woods so smoothly that even I couldn't see her.

I don't know why I crept up to the body so carefully; it wasn't like I expected it to move. But it was the second dead human I'd seen in the past few days, and there's always something about a corpse, even a human one, that asks for calm and care. It was hard to tell without turning her, but it looked like she'd been shot. The place was a crime scene, and I really did know better than to touch anything. The puke evidence at the ramps festival had been an exception. But not touching anything doesn't mean that one can't look. I knew I was going to be a suspect again: any cops who hiked up here on this ridge would be asking themselves why in the world I had been here. Worse, I thought I was still in Mononga-lia County; it'd probably be Deputies Bowling and Evans who'd have to come out here, and they really weren't going to think my involvement was a coincidence. There wasn't much that I could do about that, but I was sure I wouldn't get a better chance to look over the scene.

There was nothing around besides the body and the clothes it was wearing: no purse, no hiker's pack, no surveyor's equipment. I couldn't be sure how long it had lain out here, but it must have been a couple of weeks or more. Fortunately, the April weather had mostly been on the chilly side. I thought there was a bullet hole at the front of the jacket, and traces of some blood, but I didn't think there was enough to match the wound, and there was no obvious exit wound. Maybe the body had been moved here, or maybe the blood had just soaked into the ground or had been washed away by rain. I didn't see any obvious trail or tracks, but all that meant was that whoever had done this had been care-ful. It would have been more of a surprise if they hadn't been. I couldn't be sure, but I thought this must be Diane Smart. Her daughter had shown me a picture, and there were some similarities, but human faces were similar enough to me that I wasn't very confident in the identification. I took out the phone and snapped a few pictures. I didn't think that Emily would want to see them, but they might be useful later.

I stood and looked all around again. I was at least a mile or two from the Homeland, but it was still too close for real comfort. Everything about this setup was bad, but I didn't see that there was anything more I could do. I set out on a kind of rambling route back down off the ridge, the kind of aimless path that I hoped I could sell as a bored and meaningless rambler's walk, if anyone bothered to track me. There's no point in not being ready for the question you know you'll be asked.

I made it down to the road sometime around mid-morning. I thought I had a good idea of which direction to go to get reception on my phone at which point I knew I'd need to call the police. Before I did that, though, I sat down at the base of a tree and thought. It was certain to come out that Emily Smart had hired me on Friday morning, and it would not look good at all if I called in a report of the body along with a claim that'd I'd just gone out on a long morning hike and had just happened to find it. If it was Diane Smart, the coincidence was far too great. I'd be better off, I figured, if I could plausibly suggest I'd been following a lead, or a tip, or something. Martha would never forgive me if I brought her into this, so telling the truth was not an option. I thought some more. This was going to take all day, I soon realized.

I decided my best bet was to say I'd come out here to check out the proposed route for the PaVaMa pipeline, which ought to pass within a few miles of here. Then, I figured, my story would have to be that I had gotten lost somehow: I knew that could happen to humans in the woods. It would have taken me about three hours to jog out here from Morgantown, so if I'd left first thing in the morning, I'd be getting here about now. All I could see to do was to put in another three or four hours of purposefully aimless hiking in the woods, until I could stumble my way onto the body again.

I began to wander. I had hoped this would have been a great chance to get some thinking done, but I discovered that I just didn't have enough data to work with. I thought plenty, but I got nowhere. And I was literally just walking in a giant circle through the trackless woods, killing time.

With every step, I saw even more clearly just how little information I had. For one, I wasn't even sure this was the woman I was looking for, though I admitted to myself that it probably was. Beyond that, I had no real idea who might have shot her and nowhere to start on finding that out, either. Eventually, I made my way back down to the road—by now it was getting on toward late afternoon—and I headed uphill again to try to get a phone signal. One thing I had been able to decide on was who to call, and when I finally got a signal, I dialed up Deb Armstrong, the only Morgantown policewoman I knew.

"Holy cow, Big," she said, when I told her what I'd found. "That sounds awful. But call the county sheriff! You know how touchy they are!"

"Well, I thought it might be someone you've got a missing persons report on, Diane Smart."

"Yeah, well, it's still the sheriff you've got to call."

"They don't treat me as good as you," I said, which might have been laying it on a bit too thick.

"Yeah, well, that's probably because you call me first," she said, which covered it well enough, actually. I told her I didn't have the number in my phone, and I didn't think it was a 911 emergency, so really I was just calling her for the number, and that seemed to ease her mind a bit. "Thanks," she even said, once she'd given me the number.

So I called the sheriff's office, and they told me to wait and meet them where I was so I could lead them up to the scene. As I had hoped, Deb drove up even before the sheriff's officers arrived, and we waited together. She didn't ask any questions, and I kept my mouth shut. The only thing she asked about was what had happened out at the ramps festival, and that story took some time.

Sure enough, it was Deputies Bowling and Evans who drove up a few minutes later; they parked the single car they'd brought behind Deb's cruiser. Behind them were a couple of paramedics in an ambulance, traveling without lights or siren. Bowling looked unhappy, I thought, but he shook my hand. "Another body?" was all he said.

"This one's been dead a couple weeks, I think. Nothing to do with the ramps festival," I said.

"What can you tell us?"

So I told him my tale of being hired by Emily Smart, that I had been looking into the PaVaMa line her mother might have been surveying, that I had gotten lost, and that I had then wandered about until I stumbled across the body. There was nothing in my story that they could check to see that it wasn't true, as far as I could figure it. "I don't know if it's my client's mother or not," I finished, "but I think it probably is."

"Well," he answered, "I guess you need to lead us to where you say you saw this body."

I didn't know what he was thinking, but I thought that he might at least give me credit for knowing when I'd seen a body. It wouldn't do me any good to give it back to him, so I just nodded and headed up the hill. Let 'em scramble to keep up, I thought.

"I didn't touch anything," I said, when we'd all gotten up there. "But I walked up pretty close. I took a few pictures on my phone, if you want them."

"Stay back now," Bowling said, still breathing hard from the climb. I hadn't actually made any move toward the body at all, but that's what he said. Deb gave me a look that told me not to press him. Then she stepped forward toward the scene, too.

There was nothing for me to do then but wait and watch. The two deputies snapped a few digital pictures of their own, and then before I knew it, they were rolling the body over, looking for some kind of ID, probably. The guys from the ambulance, who'd struggled up the hillside with a stretcher, watched along with me. Deb was taking her own set of photos, just in case.

"Looks like she's been shot," Evans said, and I resisted the temptation to say I'd said as much to their dispatcher. "Anyone you know?" he asked Deb.

"I'm not sure," I heard her say. "We do have a missing person's report on Diane Smart, and this is the picture we've got." She handed Evans a color photocopy, the same snapshot Emily had shown to me.

"Could be her," Evans said, passing the copy to Bowling. "Guess we'll have to wait for the coroner."

Bowling looked at the image for a moment and grunted. "Once we've got her on the stretcher," he said to Evans, "get a couple pictures of where she was lying and then I guess we should take a look around."

As quick as that, the squad guys came in, picked up the corpse, and strapped it to the stretcher. They took her right away, making their awkward way downhill as best they could.

"Two calls in one week," Bowling finally said to me, "both with a dead woman, and both times you're all alone at the scene, with all the time in the world to doctor up the evidence and invent a line of bullshit for us to follow. But maybe," he added, turning now to Evans, "maybe we got us a serial killer."

"I'm an investigator," I said. "I was hired to look for someone missing. Just doing my job."

"Just a coincidence, you're saying."

"They do happen."

He looked unhappy to hear me say it, as if even making the observation seemed suspicious to him. He looked like he was thinking hard, though perhaps I was misreading his expression. Eventually he spoke again.

"Mike Merrill says you threatened him, probably threatened Seth Jones, too."

This wasn't anything I'd expected, and it took me a second to work it through. Of course, Mike would have had to change his story if he really was guilty, unless he outright confessed. But if I'd threatened him, as he said, it had been spectacularly unsuccessful, since he'd ridden all the way back to the park feeding Bowling the tale of my guilt. The pile of puke put him at the scene, I was sure. He must now be saying that I'd said not to tell anyone he'd seen me there and that he hadn't dared tell them that first, because he'd taken my words as a threat. He must be owning up to the pile of puke but still insisting he'd only been a witness, not the killer.

I probably should have expected something like this, but I hadn't. Whatever it was that Mike was saying now could be putting me in a pretty bad light.

"We still think he did it," Evans chimed in, and for a second, I actually thought they were trying to good cop/bad cop me.

"Only folks who've got something to hide change their stories," I said.

"Yeah, that's usually right," Bowling answered. "But you're still a suspect, and coincidences don't sell very well to juries."

Was he threatening me, now? I thought that he was, but I really couldn't decide if he was for sure. Apparently, he was done giving information away and was now starting the interrogation phase. "Why don't you tell us how you found her again?"

So I told the tale once more, adding nothing, making extra sure that I did not change my story.

"So, you think the body is this Diane Smart?" Bowling said when I was done.

"It might be," I said. "But I couldn't say for sure."

"You own a gun?" he asked me then.

"No."

"You're a private investigator, and you don't own a gun?"

"Never saw the need," I said.

"Huh. Where's your car parked at?"

He wasn't going to believe this, but I couldn't lie to him on this one. "I jogged out here from Morgantown."

"You expect me to believe that?"

"Look at me," I said. "I can definitely stand to lose the extra weight."

"Yeah, whatever," he said, after looking me up and down. "We'll want to talk to you tomorrow, I think. Two o'clock, county sheriff's office."

It wasn't a request.

"I'll be there," I said.

About this time, it was starting to get dark, and there wasn't anything else we were going to be able to see, so we hiked back down to the road. Deb Armstrong asked me if I wanted a ride back into town. I guessed that she might want to talk in private, so I agreed, despite having misgivings. "You really did jog out here?" she asked, when we got in the car and started back to Morgantown.

"Sure! I don't drive, you know."

"Huh," she said. "Lost your license?"

"Never had one."

"Unbelievable," was all she said.

We drove along in silence for a while, and I didn't have any ideas about a way to break it. In her eyes maybe the only reason to give me a ride was that I was too much of a suspect to be let loose. Regardless, she didn't have much to say to me.

I have never enjoyed riding in cars: I've never been in one that is roomy enough, and there is something disorienting about the sheer speed at which they travel. My discomfort didn't put me in any mood for small talk.

"Could you drop me off at the grocery store?" I finally asked, as we were coming into Sabraton. "I need to pick up a few things."

"Sure," she said, putting on her signal. A moment later, she had pulled into a parking space. "Anything you want to tell me about all that?" she asked. I didn't know what, exactly, she thought was suspicious, but there must have been something.

"Nothing," I said, probably sending all the wrong signals. Sometimes it was a real disadvantage not to actually be human, not to feel any emotions in quite the same way they did.

"Yeah, well, thanks for the tip," she said then, looking out the front of the car. There was nothing I could do but get out.

"Thanks for the ride," I said.

She didn't answer.

I pushed the buggy around the grocery store, using up another chunk of Emily Smart's hundred dollars on stuff that would keep since I only had a tiny dorm-sized refrigerator. "Plastic," I said at the checkout when the cashier asked what kind of bags I wanted. When I was checked out, I gathered the bags up and then went behind the store to pick up the Decker's Creek Trail again to head downtown.

As I walked, I tried to figure out how much of the hundred dollars I'd actually earned. I wouldn't charge for my travel time, and Martha had walked me straight to the body. All my wandering around in the woods had been just to keep Martha out of it. In the end, it was really only the hour or so I'd spent on the internet that I could charge for. Emily Smart deserved at least another hour of my time.

I climbed back up the hill to my office and unpacked the grocery bags. I got the phone out of my tracksuit pocket and called Emily. I couldn't put it off any longer. Fortunately, it went straight to voicemail.

"Hi Emily," I said. "This is Jim Foote. I don't know if you heard from the sheriff's office today, but we found a body out in the woods a few miles out of town: it might be your mother. If they determine it is her, you should be getting an official call or visit from them, but I thought I should let you know it was a possibility. Call me, tonight or tomorrow, if you want to hear anything more about it."

CHAPTER 4

WEDNESDAY

———

The next morning, I had my coffee in the Cottonwood Café, still spending Emily Smart's cash. Not all the substances humans call drugs affect bigfoot the way they affect humans, but the caffeine in coffee is always welcome enough in my system in the morning. Do I get the same feeling as humans get from it? Who knows.

I was looking over the paper when another customer stopped at my table.

"Hey, Big, what's up?"

Kenny Hetrick, human. He was a professor from the university, though I thought maybe he was retired. I thought he'd taught literature, or history; I was never too clear on which but leaned toward literature. He is one of the few humans who's figured out I am a bigfoot without me needing to drop any hints, but he's never told a soul, as far as I know. I like a guy who can keep a secret.

"I'm just killing time, Kenny," I answered.

And it was true: I had nothing that I needed to be doing until I heard from Emily Smart, or until two o'clock rolled around, when I had to face another round of questions from Deputy Bowling, and maybe his boss, too.

"Have a seat," I suggested.

Kenny put his coat and laptop on a nearby table and chair, then sat down at my table. He liked to come down here and look busy; for all I knew, he really was working on some project or other, but he always seemed to spend a lot of time chatting with me, or with some of the other regulars. He is a useful acquaintance for me to have: he's lived in Morgantown a long time, though not as long as I have. Unlike me, he seems to know everyone, and everyone seems to know him.

"You need a refill on that coffee?" he asked, sitting.

"No, I'm fine."

"How's business?" he asked, as he usually did.

"Moving along, moving along," I answered—as I always did. It was a conversational opening, rather than a real inquiry, and we both knew it. "I've got a big afternoon ahead of me, though—being interrogated by the county."

"Really!" he said. "Not guilty, I presume?"

"Not so far as I know. There was a body found up in the woods south of the Cheat yesterday. No ID on it, so it's a little suspicious. Could be a missing person I was looking for, though."

"And so you're a suspect, since you found it."

"That's about the size of it," I said.

"It's an interesting problem, I suppose," he said, a sparkle in his eye, "how you identify a body."

"Especially one that looks like it's been in the woods for a couple of weeks," I said.

"You know, this reminds me of a story I heard once, about a chemistry professor here at the university, oh, a few years before I was hired. I got this story straight from one of his colleagues, who swore up and down that it really happened."

He paused, as if knowing that I might object at this point, but I said nothing. I knew from experience it was best to let him go.

"Anyway, this chem prof had somehow wrangled his way into teaching a course in ornithology: you know, back in those days, it was easier to teach outside your field, especially if you had a legitimate knowledge area that the university needed. Anyway, this guy was a world-class expert on birds, it seems, and he was teaching the class as a kind of course in physical ornithology, a serious analysis of the physical form and function of various species and types of bird."

I couldn't see quite yet where this story was going, but if it was a true story, I'd eat my hat, as humans say.

"Anyway, for the midterm exam, this professor brought in a tatty old stuffed bird, mounted and hidden under a sheet. He put it up on the front table of the lecture hall, and then shifted the sheet just a bit, so only the bird's feet and legs were visible. 'If you've learned what I've tried to teach you this term,' he said to the students, 'if you've understood the material, everything you need to know about this animal can be seen or deduced just from this part I've made visible. Open up your bluebooks and write everything you can tell me about this bird, its species, habitat, feeding habits, and so on. You have fifty minutes.'

"Well, there's no telling what the students thought of this, but there was an audible grumbling. Most of the students, though, seemed to take it seriously, scribbling away at their little exam booklets. Then, when time was winding down, they started trickling out, piling up the bluebooks on the front table. At last one surly student stood up and trudged to the front of the room. 'What a stupid test!' he said, obviously angry. 'It was a stupid test, and if there's one thing I've learned in this class, it's that you're a fool and an idiot yourself!'

"The professor was angry of course. 'Don't take that tone

with me, young man!' he said, blustering around the table. 'Tell me your name, so I can mark you down in my book!' The student took his test and slipped it into the middle of the pile on the table. 'You don't know my name?' he asked, laughing. 'Here's everything you need.' And he pulled up his pants legs a couple inches, so his feet and ankles were showing."

I laughed, of course, and I heard a chuckle or two from nearby tables; Kenny never felt a good story should be told quietly. But there was really nothing I could say after that performance. What was I supposed to do, say that I wished I'd taken a closer look at the poor dead woman's feet? Human humor sometimes fails to make much sense to me, but I knew that to Kenny, the dead woman wasn't anything he had any personal connection to.

"That's a good one," I finally managed. I opened up my laptop and plugged it in. "But I've got some work to do this morning, Ken."

"Ah, don't we all," he said, standing up and moving over to his own table. "Don't we all."

A little before two o'clock, I presented myself at the sheriff's office, where I was eventually shown into an interrogation room. Deputies Bowling and Evans were both there. They gave me the standard boilerplate, and I waived my right to an attorney, though I told them that, of course, if I suddenly felt I needed one, I might have to ask for one.

"Of course, of course," Bowling said. "Walk us through it once more, for the record, if you would, how you found the body."

I knew they'd be recording all of this, and so I told them the whole story yet again: my meeting with Emily Smart, my internet searches, my trip out on Tuesday morning to start looking, just where I'd left the road, and how long I'd wandered lost. Sure,

I was lying, but the tells a bigfoot might show mean nothing to them. Or so I always hoped.

"So you thought you'd walk the possible PaVaMa line, is that right?"

"Yeah."

"Any idea how far from it you were when you found her?" Evans asked. To their credit, they weren't giving me any kind of good cop/bad cop routine today as far as I could tell.

"No idea, really: I wasn't entirely lost, but it's hard to walk a straight line in the mountains."

"Okay, sure enough," he said. "But you did pretty well: she was right smack on the line, close as we can tell."

"Huh," I said. I still had no idea why they'd be volunteering any information to me. Maybe I wasn't really a suspect after all, or they wanted me to think I wasn't. I didn't say anything more. It was their turn; they were the ones asking the questions.

"You think there's a connection?" Evans asked.

"It's possible. I suppose it might be more likely if you've been able to confirm the identity of the body."

"Well, we can't say about that quite yet," Evans said.

"You really don't have a car?" asked Bowling.

I didn't see how knowing that would help their investigation, but I didn't see any harm in answering it. "No car, and I don't drive either. I've got a bicycle, but I don't really need to use it very often."

"No car and no gun. You sure you're a PI?"

I just looked at Bowling. Apparently, he still had no compunctions about antagonizing me. It wasn't a question that needed an answer, and we both knew it.

"Well, then," I finally said. "This really doesn't seem to be going anywhere." I didn't know why they had even made me come in. I supposed they would try to trace my movements, but no one they'd be able to find had seen me yesterday, as I well knew, so they wouldn't have any luck with that. They probably figured I was hiding something and, of course, I was. But I wasn't about to change my story, either, and what I was hiding wasn't relevant to their job. I stood up. "You can reach me, I think, if you have any other questions. Good luck with your investigation."

Bowling looked like he wanted to be able to make me stay, but there wasn't more they could really ask: I'd done my duty, called in the body, told my story about how I'd found it and what I'd been looking for up there. The rest was up to them.

"We'll be in touch," said Evans.

I headed back to the office, letting myself in with the key. The trash and recycling bills were in the mail, but nothing much else. I moved into the tiny living area in the back, ducking my head at the doorway: it was crammed with a fridge, microwave, sink, washing machine, clothesline, dresser, and hammock. A shower stall, another sink, and a toilet were behind a curtain. It was a kind of all-in-one room, and I tried not to spend much time in there. I grabbed a can of pop from the fridge and sat behind my desk in the main office. I left the blinds closed, as I usually did.

My work for Emily Smart was done, unless the body turned out to be someone else's. Hmm. That, at least, was something I could check up on. I got my phone out and pulled up Deb Armstrong's number. "Just wondering if you'd heard anything," I said when her voicemail picked up. "I don't know what to tell my client, whether it's her mother or not. Let me know, either way, if you can." I thought that would probably do the trick: since she was in charge of the missing person sheet, she'd definitely hear as soon as anyone, and she'd probably be willing to tell me, off the record. It'd be in the newspaper in a day or two, anyway.

Part of me hoped that it wouldn't be Emily's mom. Whenever I agreed to look for someone, there was always a chance that I'd need to ask someone to pay me for bringing them bad news. I'd be a monster if I didn't find it uncomfortable, or worse, and it was just a couple days ago that I'd had to tell Seth Jones about his own mother. Two dead single mothers, just about the same age: I could see why the deputies had to consider me as a suspect. There were enough coincidences to make anyone wonder if they made a pattern. If there was a pattern, it was one I played no role in, as far as I knew, but I might still have work to do to make the deputies see it that way.

Of course, it was only a pattern if the body in the woods really was Diane Smart, and if it didn't turn out to be her, I'd need to keep looking. I probably should start by finding Diane's partner, Harlan Stephens. He wasn't in the phone book; I'd checked that on Friday. But now I decided to look online. Yep—he was still posting on social media, or at least someone with that name was, from a profile that said he lived up in Point Marion, a little Pennsylvania river town just north of the state line. It had to be the same guy, although I didn't see much on the site. Either the account was almost inactive or he valued his privacy.

Maybe I could bike up there tomorrow on the rail-trail path and see if I could find him. There really wasn't much else I could see to do at this point. I'd have to check out the bike before I left, though. It hadn't been an especially cold winter, but I hadn't ridden in months, and for all I knew, the tires were flat, or worse.

I keep the bike in what I always describe as the storage shed. It's in the same building as my office, but it has an external entrance. Really, it's just a room behind a little garage door that is almost too small to let a car in. The space is crammed with all sorts of oddball stuff, all covered in a nasty layer of dust. This is one of the reasons, if I am honest, why I am not sure I'd ever really be able to move back out to the Homeland: I have too much stuff, and up there, there's almost nothing to own and nowhere to keep it. It's the purer way of life, but I've lived among the humans too long to be pure.

The tires were flat, as it turned out, so I got out the little foot pump and tried to fill them up. I hated the thing—it kept coming apart—but I kept at it until I thought the bike would roll. I locked the shed, did the same to the front door, and pushed the bike up the hill. At one end of High Street is an outdoor sports shop, the kind of place where you can get everything from bike gloves to a fiberglass kayak. Every spring, I take the bike in there for a kind of tune-up. I wheeled it in the front door, and after they took the bike to the back, they told me I could pick it up in the morning.

I was just opening the door to leave when Hobo Joe stepped in. "Big," he said to me nodding, clearly intending to pass me by.

"Joe," I said, equally curt. Then I stopped, and turned to him. "Hey, Joe," I said. "I wanted to thank you for doing me a good turn."

"When was that?" he asked, pivoting to half face me.

"Emily Smart said you said I was a good guy."

He looked like he was racking his brain, not too successfully. "Ah, Emily. Yeah, she pours the coffee most mornings up at the Jackalope." That is the other coffee shop/bar Morgantown has going for it. We may be the only town in the state where there are two coffee joints where the humans can also buy beer at ten o'clock in the morning.

"Anyway, thanks for the good word," I said, turning back to the door.

He still didn't seem to remember giving it.

It was sprinkling as I made my way back to the office: forty-five degrees and raining. Standing by my door was Emily Smart.

"I was hoping you'd be back soon," she said. "I'm ready to get out of this weather."

"Come on in," I said. I had expected her to call me back, maybe send me a text, but I couldn't turn her away from my door. "Sit down," I said as I pulled my phone from my jacket pocket and turned it off.

She did sit down, then, shaking out her hair a bit. She wasn't carrying an umbrella. "Thanks for calling me," she said.

"Have you heard from the police?" I asked. I figured it was the reason she was here.

"Yeah, they called about half an hour ago. They said they were pretty sure it was my mom."

And there it was. At least I hadn't had to be the bearer of the bad news, even if I was sort of responsible for it. She didn't cry, though if I had to guess, it was probably a close thing. "I was so afraid it would turn out like this," she said eventually. "I'm glad you were able to find her so quickly."

"It was pure dumb luck," I said. "Who knows what she was doing out in the woods."

"They said she'd been shot."

"Yeah," I answered. "That's what it looked like to me, too."

"What could she possibly have been doing that would make someone shoot her?" she asked me, and even I could see her real anguish. That emotion I knew all too well. All bigfoot did.

"Well," I answered slowly. "I hope the police will be able to tell you. At the least, they'll be looking for who did it."

She looked at me, and she seemed confused. "The case is over for me," I told her.

"What?"

"You mother has been found, and it looks like she's been the victim of a crime. It's a police matter, and they really don't like it when people don't trust them do their work."

"What if they don't find who did it?"

"Well, if they don't find who did it, I probably can't either. They are professionals, you know. They will want to solve this."

"Yeah, I'm sure you're right," she said, sighing.

"I will give you some free advice, though," I said. I wished I could figure out a way to make what I had to say next reassuring, but if there was a way, I couldn't see it.

"Yeah?" she said, as if advice was the last thing she wanted.

"Yeah. Get ready to learn some things about your mother, things that maybe you'd rather not know."

"What do you mean?"

"What I mean is, when someone gets shot, and nobody knows who the shooter is, there are secrets in it somewhere: secrets the shooter wants to stay secret, and probably secrets that involve the victim somehow."

"What kind of secrets?"

"Important ones, I suppose. Desperate ones. But nobody knows them."

"Or they wouldn't be secrets," she said.

"That's right." I really didn't know what more to say, but Emily didn't seem quite ready to stand up and walk away. I couldn't just shoo her out the door. She didn't know it yet, I supposed, but she was also about to be caught up in the grinding wheels of the justice system. She probably wouldn't be taken any more seriously as a suspect than I had been, but if they didn't find somebody soon, they'd turn their eyes her way, I didn't doubt it. If there's one thing that every cop knows, it's that every family has its secrets. It was probably best if I tried to give her some warning about what she'd be facing.

Finally I spoke up. "I'd offer you a drink," I said, pulling open the big bottom drawer of the desk, "but I don't keep any of the stuff around. All I can offer you is some of these cheese curls." I had a clothes pin at the folded-over opening.

She looked like she was about to laugh. Then she reached forward and slipped the pin off, taking a handful. "These things are terrible for you, you know."

"Well, I come from a long-lived family," I said.

"What happened to your hands?"

I tried my best to keep them out of sight, but sooner or later, everyone noticed them. I could shave my face, shape my hair, wear clothes that covered most of my body, but there was nothing I could do about the hands. Or the feet. "I was born this way," I said, knowing from experience that it was an answer that seemed to explain, without actually explaining everything. And it happened to be true.

"Oh."

"At this point in my life, they're part of who I am," I said, telling a bit more of the truth. "Most people never even notice." Not so much of the truth, but close enough. I held one hand up so she could look. My thumbs were built differently from a human's: not completely different, like the pictures I've seen of some primates' hands, but different enough. Some people asked about them when they saw them, some didn't. There is a human phrase these days, "differently abled," that I might have used, but it didn't quite seem to fit.

"Secrets," she said then, surprising me.

"Sort of," I answered, "but right out in the open."

Before she left, I offered to give back fifty dollars of the advance she'd given me, and it was this, of all the things I said, that caused her to finally burst into tears. I had tissues, and she took one when I offered it, but there was nothing that I knew how to say. "You can keep the money," she said eventually. "You've done more than I could have expected, and I've taken up more than an hour of your time just today."

Which was true enough. "Thank you," I told her, but I knew I still hadn't told her everything she needed to hear, and as gently as I could, I tried again to warn her that the sheriff's office would probably consider her a suspect. She'd be asked in to answer more questions, I said, and she might want to have a lawyer present, if she was at all anxious about it. "But I didn't do anything!" she said.

"Yeah, I know," I answered. "Nevertheless, they'll be asking all sorts of things, and a lawyer might at least keep them on the topic of the investigation. You'll probably want to contact a lawyer anyway about your mother's estate, whether she left a will or not. The police will literally be trying to piece together every step you and your mother have taken over the last few weeks, including everyone you've seen, talked to. Friends, boyfriends, girlfriends, whatever."

She nodded, just signaling that she heard me, I thought, not that she really understood. "I feel a little bit responsible," I said, thinking it was time she probably ought to go. "At least until this is all wrapped up, feel free to call me up or stop by here, if you need to talk about any of this. Unless something comes up, I won't be too busy to talk, and talk is free."

"I will, Mr. Foote," she said, giving an odd human kind of smile. "Thanks."

"Call me Big," I said. "Everyone does." I had no idea what to make of the look she gave me then. But she stood up, putting on her coat to leave. She turned back at the door. "So," she said slowly, "I guess I'll have to make arrangements for a funeral and everything, huh?"

"Yeah," I answered. "I expect that's right." Seth Jones was

probably doing much the same thing, I realized. I knew two young people, both recently bereaved: I wouldn't be a bigfoot if I didn't think maybe they'd get along with one another, have something to offer one another. Well, maybe they would. But I didn't need to do anything about it.

"I can't do any of that stuff!"

"You can, I am sure. You'll get a call, in the next few days probably, from the coroner's office, and they'll want to know who you'll want the body released to: just have the name of a funeral home ready; you should call them up in advance to let them know you want them to collect her. They'll take care of almost everything, I'd imagine."

"Yeah, yeah," she said, and I could see that her mother's death was really sinking in now. Such a difference, I knew, between missing, feared dead, on the one hand, and dead indeed on the other.

No doubt, I thought to myself when she had gone, I could have handled that better. But I couldn't worry about it: I'd done what I could. She was going to have to deal not only with the funeral home and its expenses, but probably also with probate, unless there actually was a will, which would make things simpler. If there wasn't a will, she might even have to take out a loan to cover the funeral. The human way, I thought once again, is a strange way to be in the world, and a stranger way to leave it. When my own mother died, we simply burned the body: fire was an old, old enemy, and it took us all in the end. Martha had taken up my mother's place in the Homeland, the role of being the person everyone else turned to, the honorary mother to everyone, in a way. Maybe I could have taken on that role if I'd wanted it. But I hadn't, preferring to live down here.

I didn't really know whether the sheriff's office would be able to find the shooter or not; after all, a lot of time had passed since the shooting, and it wasn't easy to trace anyone's movements of a month ago. Even I'd have trouble with that and I was a bigfoot; when I'd seen the body, I hadn't seen anything that could have started me on a trail. Maybe there was some new high-tech science that I didn't know about they might be able to use.

It did seem as if I wouldn't need to bike up to Point Marion tomorrow: surely the police would follow up with Diane Smart's old coworkers. Well, the bike had needed the tune-up anyway, and I was sure it was the right thing to do—get it done now— while I still had the rest of Emily's hundred bucks in my pocket.

I thought that I probably should have told her it wasn't only her mother's secrets she needed to worry about. The flip side of every secret, I've always understood, is a lie. Nobody wants to learn that their mother has lied to them, or that their mother has died for someone else's lies. I'd be a fool, I knew, to think that there weren't some lies running around in this business, and dangerous ones at that. I'd been on the case for less than a week, and I'd told my own share of lies already—harmless ones, I hoped.

I picked up my phone to check the time. No new messages or texts, apparently. Huh. I sent off a brief text to Deb Armstrong: if the cops had called Emily Smart, Deb really should have had plenty of time to get hold of me. Sure enough, I hadn't even put the phone away before it rang with Deb's number showing on the screen.

"Big?" she asked, when I answered.

"Yeah, it's me."

"I'm glad I caught you. Looks like you're off the case."

"Yeah, that's just what I was telling my client."

"The coroner said it wasn't accidental." No kidding, I thought: accidental gunshot wounds got reported; people called 911.

Sometimes murders even got reported that way by people thinking they could make the cops think it was an accident.

"So you're on the case, then."

"You got it," she said. "Liaising with the county."

"Good luck with it," I told her sincerely. "I really hope you find the guy."

"I really think we might," she said, and she actually seemed hopeful. "We've already got one good piece of evidence." I don't think I've ever heard a real investigator use the word "clue."

"Anything you can talk about?" I asked. I don't know why I asked it, but I did.

"Yeah, it's all over the office; I don't think there's gonna be any secret about it. Probably be in the paper tomorrow, and it's a good one, anyway. She was shot with a muzzleloader; the ball was lodged right up against her spine."

"Huh," I managed. "That's unusual."

She laughed. "You can say that again! And it really suggests premeditation, if nothing else."

"Yeah," I said. "Well, thanks for calling me back. And of course, if you guys have any more questions for me, don't hesitate to ask: I'd really like to see this one brought in."

"I'm sure we will," she answered. They'd need to check up on Emily Smart's story, if nothing else.

"Okay, talk to you soon, then," I said. "Bye." I hit the icon to end the call.

I was back on the case.

CHAPTER 5

WEDNESDAY, INTO THURSDAY

———

I first came to Morgantown shortly after the humans had finished fighting World War II. That first time I walked down from the mountains, Morgantown seemed to me like a smoky, black inferno: every house was burning coal or gas for heat and even for cooking; every car and truck was spewing out petroleum smoke. The electric plant burned coal, and the glass factories, of course, kept their furnaces burning day and night; the new diesel trains hadn't yet cleared the tracks of the old steam locomotives. Even now, after decades of rain and snow, you can still see the greasy black residue clinging to some buildings in town, never scrubbed away.

Bigfoot, you see, are a long-lived clan; my own pappy lived more than a century and a half. I'd been born too late to know anyone who'd seen the American Revolution, but an oldster or two I'd known had talked to some of the men who'd been behind the Whiskey Rebellion up in Little Washington. I always tried to take that piece of history as a lesson: the very humans who'd named their town Washington had rebelled against the Eastern establishment, barely a decade after their Revolution had ended. So short were human lives that they turned and turned again within them, moving, changing, forgetting the past as soon as it happened, always trying to make room for a future.

I myself had seen a lot in the hundred years or so I'd been roaming the world, and I knew well enough just how thoroughly we bigfoot relied upon that human forgetfulness. The last big glass factory in town had been converted into a kind of indoor shopping mall, with a restaurant in the furnace room. The coal-fired power plant on the river bank was something most people just seemed to ignore. Morgantown glass was a collectible now, even an antique, they said, and the tales of bigfoot were mere folklore.

And that was all just the way we liked it. We'd had trouble enough in the nineteenth century, protecting the Homeland from the loggers who had clear-cut most of the mountains, and we'd managed it, in part, by always making sure that a few bigfoot here and there lived out among the humans, laughing at the stories of wild men in the woods, sometimes even telling a few tall tales of their own. Human attention spans were short, and it usually wasn't all that hard to point their attention somewhere else.

Of course, we'd had thousands of years of experience living near the humans in these parts while living apart from them and making our own way in the world, but we helped them out now and then and tried not to need their help in turn. There's never been a time, as far as I know, when the two peoples haven't lived side by side. The coming of the Europeans changed things for us, in some ways, but not as much as you'd think—though what they did to the Native Americans was another story. What I did now—living right among the humans—had long been part of the bigfoot way. And I laughed, often enough, when they told their silly tales of bigfoot out in the woods. Most of my job, as I saw it, was keeping a big secret, and so I told a lot of little lies.

At the end of the day, I didn't really think that made me, or my people, much different from a lot of mountain people the world over: independent, even secretive, ready to lend a helping hand when others were in trouble, but too proud to take that helping hand unless there was no other choice. *Montani Semper Liberi*, the motto of West Virginia says. We have shared a lot with the human mountaineers, especially in my pappy's day and my grand-pappy's. We've lent a helping hand or two, and the humans we've helped out have always been grateful; they've been and become good friends who've kept our secrets and respected our places. Sometimes, they've even given us gifts to thank us for our help.

I was thinking of two of those gifts right now, two I knew about, anyway: treasured heirlooms passed down from father to son in bigfoot families I knew well. I was thinking of a couple of old-fashioned Pennsylvania or Kentucky muzzleloaders, true an-tiques and collector's items in the human world, but just as deeply valued up in the Homeland—the only guns we had.

The only proper way to kill a bear, of course, is with a knapped-flint knife, preferably one you've made yourself. I'd done it, even, back when I was a kid. Almost everyone had. But every now and again, everyone agreed, it wasn't the best way, and so we kept these two guns up in the Homeland. They were always kept well wrapped in oily old deerskins; a tiny stock of black powder and balls was wrapped up and hidden with them. I'd never heard of them being used to shoot a human, but of course it was possible. Ezra himself kept one of the guns, a privilege passed on from his own pappy. And Ezra, and a few others like him, watched the border areas around the Homeland, doing something a lot like my job in Morgantown: keeping secrets, and telling lies. It was work that could all too easily move over the line into violence.

I hoped that Diane Smart had been killed in some purely human dispute, something we had no part in. I wanted justice for her, of course, but if anything was more important than justice, it was the sanctity of the Homeland, its secrecy. What I could never allow to happen was for the humans to find us, to know us. Homeland security was the most essential part of my work; some up in the Homeland would say this was the only part of my work that mattered. Even if a bigfoot had done the actual killing, I had to see that they were never found or identified. If justice was to be had, it had just become a secondary concern. For me, at least.

Even if I managed to convince myself that Diane Smart had been killed by a human and not a bigfoot, I also knew that I could not let this crime go unsolved. It wouldn't be good to have the police constantly on the lookout for users of muzzleloader guns: the powder and the lead balls were points of commerce between us and the humans, and the longer the crime went unsolved, the more likely it was that such links might be found and traced. As long as such things were only trickling out to some loners in the hills, no one would ever care, but if those loners in the hills were suddenly potential killers, the police might start to take a closer look at some people here in town—and I was one of them—who might not stand up to the scrutiny. Because, on occasion, even I had purchased some supplies for those guns and had taken them up to the Homeland; doing so was a simple favor that I could easily manage, and I'd never thought it could cause any trouble.

But it was a complication now. Everything I'd told Emily about how the police didn't much like it when they weren't the only ones investigating something was still all true: working cases the police had in hand only muddied the waters, for them and for me. Fortunately, I did have some resources they didn't have: I knew already about two guns that might have been the murder weapon, and I could at least rule them out. Doing so might help me narrow the field of my suspects. Or maybe it would clarify what kind of job I had in front of me.

It was too late that afternoon to accomplish anything real, but it seemed like it was probably time for me to call in a favor or two, if only to let some people know what was going on. I texted Mel for a meeting in the morning, suggesting we meet at Pie vs. Cake, a little micro-bakery I knew she wouldn't be able to resist. Mel was a bigfoot, too, and when she first came to Morgantown, I'd helped her get a job shifting inventory in one of the big box stores. I still thought of her as new in town, since she'd been here less than a decade, and I planned to ask her if she could take a day or two off to run out to the Homeland for me, ask a few questions, and take a message straight to Martha. I'd probably need to get out there myself in the next few days if not sooner, but I didn't want the deputies to find out that I'd headed back out that way so soon; it was safest to assume that they'd be keeping tabs on me.

I fell asleep imagining all the ways this could go wrong. But even as I did, I thought about how I'd been incredibly lucky: Emily had come to me. If she hadn't, who knows how long it might have taken me to realize that I had work to do to protect the Homeland.

I rolled out of the hammock a bit later than I intended the next morning, but I took the time to step into the shower anyway. Shaving was something I couldn't really put off: it always had to be done. I made up a little cup of instant coffee: not good, but easy, and it had enough caffeine to get me started on waking up.

Mel's answering text had come in overnight. She counter-proposed a meeting time closer to lunch, and so in the later part of the morning, I headed over to High Street, Morgantown's old-timey main street. A number of modern commercial zones are on the outskirts of town, catering to automobile traffic, but like the older Appalachian river town that it is, Morgantown also has a downtown area, with buildings mostly dating from the early part of the twentieth century, and with enough foot traffic to keep shops and diners and restaurants open in most of them.

In this respect, Morgantown is lucky. From what I've heard, most towns in West Virginia have similar main drags, but almost all of them have empty storefronts and sometimes even boarded-up windows. The university keeps Morgantown from falling into the urban decay cities and towns in the rest of the state face: nowadays most of the coal money trickles down somewhere out of the state, if it trickles anywhere at all. The only coal money that comes back into the state, it sometimes seems, is destined for the campaign chests of various legislators and politicians.

Pie vs. Cake is a boutique business that only stays open until the late afternoon. Two university spouses run the place: both human. The man makes pies every day, and the woman makes a variety of cakes. A machine, I suppose, makes the coffee. Every day, a big chalkboard behind the counter keeps a tally of how many slices of pie have sold and how many pieces of cake. Maybe it wasn't proper to make a lunch out of dessert and coffee, but there was no law against it, either. I was a pie eater; Mel could never resist the cake.

It is a long-held custom that bigfoot females adopt nicknames that humans might take for male: if they ever come down among the humans, their size, if nothing else, makes them seem like human men, and the facial hair many wear has the same effect.

The double deception is a useful strategy: if anyone sees through the disguise, confessing to being female passing as male is honest and the bigger secret of bigfoot identity goes unquestioned. Usually.

"One slice of pecan and one of the blueberry," I said when I stood at the counter. "And a coffee, of course." Why stop at one slice of pie? I always figured. And there is no hiding the fact that I am a big eater. Mel was already seated at a table, half a slice of some triple-layered cake already eaten.

"Jim," she said when I sat down. "What's going on?"

"I'm sorry to say it," I said quietly, "but I think I need you to run a message up to Martha for me. I'm going to ask her to come down and talk." Martha, if she did come down, would become Marty.

"You can't go yourself?" she asked, understandably.

"Well," I said, even a bit more quietly, "I don't want to stir up any trouble with the police, and they might be keeping an eye on me right now. It's really just a precaution: I haven't done anything."

"I can do it, I suppose," she said with a sigh. "You're lucky I'm not on at the store tonight." She paused again and stabbed at her cake with a grumpy look. "It's too bad you can't just make a phone call. You really do get used to 'em, you know?"

"Yeah, I know. But I do think it was right to keep the cell towers away, and I can't really imagine the Homeland with cell phones, anyway. Everyone would have to carry a bag, or wear a vest or something."

"Yeah," she said. "I can't really picture it. When in Rome, though."

"It's a good rule, I think. I suppose you want to hear all about it."

"That's the price you pay. It's an all-day trip, after all."

So I told her all about the body that Martha had found and shown me, and about Emily Smart and her mother, and finally I got around to what Deb Armstrong had told me, about the murder weapon being a muzzleloader.

"You think it was one of ours?" she asked, seeing right to the heart of the problem.

"Don't know," I said, seriously. "It might not be. But if we don't solve this one quickly, there might be trails the police could trace—sales of black powder, shot, that sort of thing."

"Yeah. Martha will need to know, and you're right, she'll probably want to talk to you in person, even though she hates the hassle of coming down here."

"Tell her I'll take her out for hot dogs at Jean's." Martha may hate the hassle of coming down here, putting on human clothes and all the rest, but even she has found things in town to love, including some of the food.

"I'll do that!" she said, smiling. "Say," she added then, "maybe it was the Moonshiner!"

The Moonshiner is the university's mascot, but the whole state seems to treat the Moonshiner as a mascot, too. From what I've heard, the Moonshiners themselves have always said they aren't mascots at all since they don't wear big foam heads and they aren't anonymous. They see themselves as spokespeople. In recent years, the Moonshiner has come under a certain amount of fire at both the university and in the state: some folks say the mascot plays in to all sorts of negative stereotypes about the state. Others say the mascot is a piece of their heritage, and it should never be changed. Some folks at the university have been starting to say that they are worried that the continued use of the Moonshiner as a representative of the university encourages students to partake in underage drinking and other illegal activities. But just as strongly, there is a growing respect for the image of the Moonshiner as being a kind of noble figure of rebellion and resistance, someone who refuses to play by the government's rules, a buckskin-wearing outsider with a gun—a muzzleloader, to be sure—who embodies the recent devotion to Americans'—human Americans, that is—celebrated second-amendment rights.

"Ha!" I said laughing. "I hadn't thought of that."

"Those guns really do shoot."

"Oh yeah, I know," I said. I had been thinking that the list of suspects would be very short: a few collectors and reenactors, maybe a few hunters who liked the longer season. But there were more. "You're right: every Moonshiner for the last fifty years has had a gun: they'll all be suspects, at one level."

"Could be a real moonshiner, too, if there are any of them left," said Mel. "Or a marijuana grower."

"Yeah, I thought of that. But I expect most of them to have a more up-to-date gun," I said.

"Sure," Mel answered. "But this is West Virginia, and a lot of hippies are still around, with their faith in the so-called old ways."

"Yeah. Like I said, I'll need to talk to Martha."

"Well, I guess I can head up there for a day or two. It's always nice to spend a night under the stars." She paused, and it looked like she was going to say more. "Maybe you could do a favor for me while I'm gone."

"Of course," I said, guessing that I'd probably regret it. "What is it?"

"Well," she began. "I know you don't always get along so well with Horatio, but you know he's limping along pretty roughly right now. I don't know if it's just age, or some kind of injury, but he's hurting. I know you've had someone to help you, when

70

you've been hurting, so I thought maybe you could find some way to help the old guy out."

Horatio is from my mama's generation, maybe even a bit older. He helped me out, in his curt and unfriendly way, when I first came down to Morgantown. He lives in a little house in Sabraton. I often think that he only gets grumpier and unhappier as he grows older. Maybe he has not spent enough time up at the Homeland. There are some, I can't deny, who say the same about me. "Yeah, I'll talk to him," I promised. "I'll see what I can do."

When we left, I looked at the chalkboard: pie was edging cake by a handful of slices. I felt like I'd helped to accomplish some small good in the world today already.

Mel told me she'd need to stop by her place, and then she'd head right out. "Thanks for the cake," she said. I turned right out of the restaurant and walked down to the bike shop to pick up my bike; they'd told me they needed to replace one of my tires. I paid with plastic, since what I owed was more than I had in cash. I wasn't concerned about paying the eventual credit card bill because I could get spending money any time I needed it—we'd actually had some good financial advice over the years and not too many bigfoot trying to live off it. I always try to live off my own earnings, though, or come as close as I can.

I stepped over the bike and started riding. Checking on Horatio was something I could do right away, so I hopped onto the rail-trail and headed to Sabraton—I'd seen enough car accidents over the years to keep off the streets whenever I could.

While I rode, I reminded myself that Deputies Evans and Bowling must be busy on their investigation. They must have interviewed Emily Smart pretty thoroughly by now and were going on to pursue other avenues. If they hadn't yet looked up Emily's mother's surveying partner, they would soon, so, I thought, I probably needed to stay away from him. They had probably begun checking out the muzzleloader scene—if you could call it that—too, so I'd need to be careful there, as well. If I was too obvious about following their investigation, they'd wonder what I was doing, and that wouldn't be good. I'd have to be careful and clever and think about angles they might not cover.

Horatio's little place looked like it had started out as a coal camp house, a little two-over-two clapboard structure barely as big as my office. When I'd first come to town, places like this still had outhouses in the back, but somewhere along the way, this house and many of the others had been put on the water and sewage lines, like everywhere else in town. That hasn't made that much difference to Horatio: the house is on a dead-end street on the side of a hill, as close to the woods as he was able to get.

I leaned my bike against the little porch, then knocked on the door. In a moment, I heard some scraping and other sounds, and then the inside door opened. "Jamie is it," he said, using a name I was sure he knew that I had put aside many years ago. "What brings you out to visit?"

"Just a social call. You think I could come in for a bit?"

"Huh," he said, looking like he was none too happy to consider it. "Yeah," he finally grunted. "Come in and talk to an old-timer for a few minutes, if you can spare the time."

"Thanks," I said, opening up the screen door and stepping past it. He looked like it would actually hurt him to say, "talk to an old friend," though I'd known him for at least seventy years. He'd always been prickly, and from what I'd heard, he'd always said the same or worse about me. I suppose he'd have described whatever he was wearing as pajamas; at least he had the sense to be wearing a big old floppy pair of house slippers. Even as he moved across the tiny room to the couch, it was clear that he was in pain; his hips canted painfully and his footsteps were uneven. I heard a grunt, or a groan, when he sat down.

I figured I'd get straight to the point. "Mel told me I should look in on you, Horatio."

"She's a good kid," he said. "Brings me groceries, and some real food sometimes, too."

"She's worried about you," I said, knowing he wouldn't want to hear that I was worried about him. He wouldn't believe it, actually, although now that I saw him, I couldn't help sharing Mel's concern.

"She just feels sorry for me 'cause I'm getting old and fixing to die."

"Well, I suppose you can look at it that way if you want to," I said, unable to keep irritation out of my voice. "She asked me to see if there was anything I could do to help you with the pain."

"Like what?"

"I don't know. Medicine maybe?"

"Hah! Human medicine. Fools and scoundrels, the lot of them."

"Well, yeah, that's what you always say. But you've lived among them for a hundred years, Horatio. They're not all helpless fools. And it might help, you know." I was pretty sure that Horatio had never seen a human doctor in all his long life: we didn't as a rule, considering it far too risky. A couple of people up in the Homeland—Martha was one of them—had some experience setting broken bones and the like, and they knew a little about herb lore, too, but I didn't think Horatio would have any patience with them, either. He had always seemed to get along better with the few human friends he had than with other bigfoot. But he'd outlived most of his human friends by decades now. I'd always suspected that he thought of himself as a fool and a scoundrel, too, and that was why he preferred living among the humans. Or maybe it was just his nature to be as cantankerous as a goat.

"Well, maybe."

"Maybe, what?" I asked.

"Maybe if you can find something that helps, I'll try it. I been taking aspirin that Mel brings me from the store, but it doesn't help much at all."

"If I can find somebody who'll look at you, will you let them?"

"No."

"What do you mean, no?"

"I mean if you can find me something to help with the pain, I'll be willing to give it a try, but I don't need any doctor, human or bigfoot, to tell me that I'm old and that I'm dying."

Before I left, I asked Horatio if he needed anything from the store. Nothing in particular, he said, but if I was going to go, he could use a little bread and maybe some peanut butter. And then he asked me to bring him a bag or two of the cheese puffs I liked so much. It was something we had in common. Oh, and some pop, and maybe some toilet paper, too, he added.

"I'll try to bring all that stuff tomorrow," I told him, and though I was sorely tempted, I managed to keep from laughing.

And it wasn't really funny, after all: he holds so dearly to the idea that he is independent, still living alone here, so very far from the Homeland. In his mind, he still doesn't need a thing, and certainly not any favors from anyone. But he is still sharp enough to know that sometimes he actually does need both, even if he doesn't want to admit it.

Eventually I managed to scoot out the door, and as I biked back down to the trail from Horatio's little house, I did a little thinking about what he'd said. It was true enough that he was old, and maybe he was even dying. Bigfoot lives are long by human standards, but still, they are all too short for bigfoot. In my case, I probably have another forty or fifty years before I'm in as bad shape as Horatio. I've been living in Morgantown for seventy years, and I've seen almost every one of the humans I'd first known here die away, one by one. Some bigfoot, seeing that happen, come to think of human life as cheap, and some have always said humans are a kind of vermin on the earth. But I've known enough bigfoot and humans to know that both peoples are made up of individuals: good and bad runs right through us all. I didn't have to like the old guy to think he didn't deserve to live—or die—in pain.

Somehow, thinking about the possibility that Horatio was dying brought Diane Smart to my mind. I knew it was perfectly possible that some bigfoot up in the Homeland had killed her with no more worry or concern than they'd have for killing a bear. People like Martha have been trying to shut this attitude down for a long, long time, but some bigfoot still think that killing a human is an even more potent coming-of-age ritual than killing a bear—although it seems to me that any of that sort wouldn't think that using a gun would be quite right. But killing a human in the first place isn't quite right, either, and I really don't know what would be out of bounds for that sort of person.

I couldn't do much at all in that direction until I either went out to the Homeland myself or until Martha came down for a talk. So when I got back to the office, I parked the bike back in the shed. Inside, I tried to get on the internet, but my ISP seemed to be down. I know better than to rely on it, but still, it drives me crazy when I can't just look things up immediately. I turned the router off and then back on again and breathed a sigh of relief when that seemed to work.

Now, I thought. What to look for? I knew that during every hunting season, a special time is set apart for bowhunters and muzzleloader hunters, before the guys with more modern weapons take to the woods. So I was sure plenty of information would be available online about muzzleloaders and that maybe I could even find some names. It wasn't exactly practical to think of every muzzleloader hobbyist in the region as a suspect, but I had to start somewhere. At the very least, I could start looking for connections. The police must be doing the same sort of thing.

I decided I should probably look into the collectors' market, too: the Homeland guns were authentic old guns, and they still worked, so maybe the humans who collected such things occasionally fire their own antique guns. Hunters probably used modern-made guns, replicas of one sort or another, but until I knew that Emily's mother had been killed by a modern gun, I couldn't rule out that she'd been killed by an antique.

It didn't take long to realize that these two groups showed surprisingly little overlap. Plenty of information about auctions and sales of vintage and antique firearms was available, but individual collectors seemed to keep a low profile: it was easy enough to compile a list of dealers who might be interested in old guns, but I couldn't find any obvious collector's club, especially for a subspecialty like pre–Civil War American handmade long guns. The guns were so rare and valuable that the few people who were actually in the market for them probably all knew each other anyway.

On the other hand, there was a Facebook group for local muzzleloader hunters and a different one for bowhunters. I signed up for the muzzleloader one right away. It couldn't hurt, especially if I had questions they could answer at some point. There was no telling what the internet search aggregators would make of this new wrinkle in my online identity.

Of course, at the moment, it looked like the police would have an easier time of it than I would: they could start with Diane Smart, her circle of friends, acquaintances, coworkers, enemies, and so on, and then filter those people against the tiny little group of muzzleloader enthusiasts: they'd narrow their list of suspects down to one or two people in no time, I thought grumpily. I, on the other hand, felt like I was stuck going the other direction. My first priority, obviously, was to answer the question of whether a bigfoot had shot her: everything else I did in this case would depend on the answer to that. And that question, I knew, was one the police would never even consider.

They had better not. It was my job to make sure they never did.

I went to sleep thinking about old Horatio, and how, in his grumpy and irascible fashion, he'd helped me find my way when I'd first come down into Morgantown. In those days, he'd done a similar job to the one I was doing now, standing between the Homeland and the humans, keeping the two separate, and—when needed—looking out for those of us who came down here to live, keeping us out of trouble, mostly. I'd done what I could to repay him—more than once—in the seventy years since, so I knew him well enough to know he wouldn't thank me, even if I did manage to find him something that would help. But some things you just don't do for the thanks you hope to get.

CHAPTER 6

FRIDAY

————

After I woke up and had a cup or two of coffee, I made a quick check on the internet for Professor Sarah Lloyd's morning office hours and biked over to campus. Sarah teaches anthropology at the university, and, some years before, I'd been foolish or wise enough to enroll in a cultural anthropology class she taught: I had figured that it'd come in handy trying to understand the humans; understanding humans was a constant challenge for me and something I always needed to improve on in my work as an investigator. And in my ongoing impersonation of a human.

For the final project in the class, I was supposed to have engaged in a lengthy fieldwork study of a community I was a member of. I had started out planning to write about the Homeland community as if it were just an isolated family of human mountain folk, which were still plentiful enough in the various remote hollows and valleys of the state. Unfortunately, I'd never done anything like writing a college paper before, and when it came time to do it, I had not been able to. I just hadn't been able to put enough words and sentences together to make anything coherent at all. I had realized then that I should have just audited the course, but that's not what I had done. I hadn't been an eigh-teen-year-old kid, though, and I had figured it would not be polite to just drop out of sight, so instead I had gone to Sarah's office hours and had told her I couldn't do it.

To her credit, she had not tried to persuade me to do what I knew I couldn't, but she had told me she thought I'd been a valu-able member of the class, and that she hoped to get something in writing from me for a final project, even if it wasn't quite what I thought it should be. Before I knew it, we'd gotten to chatting about what I thought—what I thought I could do for a final proj-ect, and what I couldn't. And then I must have said something that had made her suspicious.

"These people are breaking the law," she had guessed about my community. "Growing marijuana or something. Of course you can refer to them by pseudonyms," she had said then. "I am not in the business of turning anyone in."

This was, perhaps, a generous interpretation of the mandatory reporting requirements that many states and schools had insti-tuted after the whole Joe Paterno situation up at Penn State, but I hadn't pushed her on it.

"It's not marijuana," I had said, "but, yeah, there's a secret that we keep."

"We?" she had said.

"Some hu—you know, outsiders—keep it, too," I had said. And then I had made one of those quick judgments that have hounded my sleep for all my life, where I make a guess about someone for reasons even I don't really understand. "If you want, I'll tell you, if you give me a pass on the paper."

"I can't really do that," she had said. "You can't ask me to prom-ise to keep a secret and tell a lie all in the same breath." I hadn't pointed out that that's what keeping a secret always boiled down to. But I had told her anyway: she had just seemed trustworthy, and that was all there was to it. And as events turned out, I was right, and she'd never told anyone but her husband.

I never did write the paper, but she said she could give me a perfect score for attendance and participation, and between that and my exam scores, I had managed to squeak by with a passing mark in the course, even with a zero on the paper. Besides Kenny Hetrick and the various members of the Lovingood clan, I thought that Sarah and her husband were the only humans still living who knew I was a bigfoot.

Today, I timed my arrival at her office to the very end of her official hours. "Jim!" she said. "I wasn't expecting you!"

"Yeah, sorry," I said. "I probably should have emailed or called. Do you have some time to catch up a bit?"

"I've got class in just a few minutes," she said, glancing at her phone, "and a department meeting this afternoon. I'll tell you what: could you stop by the house for dinner tonight? I'll text Nathan, and you know the twins would love to see you."

"Perfect," I said then. "But I'll want to have a real talk with you, and maybe with Nathan, too, after the kids are asleep."

So I had most of the day free, then. Before I got busy with anything else, I biked over to the grocery store, picked up the list of things Horatio had wanted, and dropped them off at his house. "Thanks," he'd managed, which was more than I'd expected. "I'm looking," I said, when he asked if I'd found anything else for him yet.

Most days, I'd have headed over to the Cottonwood Café at this point, but I decided that I'd try the Jackalope's bagels and coffee again. It wasn't good, probably, to fall into habits too deeply, I thought, and hopefully Emily Smart would be working.

She was. "Mr. Foote!" she said in surprise as I walked in.

"What can I get you?" Probably she felt like she was too young—or I was too old—-for her to ever call me "Big," or "Jim."

I gave her my order and paid. "I'll bring that out in a minute," she said. I grabbed a copy of the little daily paper the university kids put out from the stack by the door and sat down at a booth under the window. A few minutes later, I saw Emily talking quietly to a coworker, and when she brought out my food, she had a cup of coffee for herself and she sat down at my table. "I had a break coming," she said, "so I thought I'd talk to you."

"How's everything going?" I asked, figuring if there was anything in particular she needed to talk about, she could bring it up.

"I'm exhausted," was what she answered. "I had no idea how tiring it would be to answer the cops' questions. Or how many questions there would be."

"Yeah, well, they need to know everything. Or at least it always seems that way to them."

"I suppose. But I've got to clean out Mom's apartment, too, and deal with the coroner and the funeral. I know you told me, but still, I had no idea!"

"I'm sure you'll manage everything," I said, because what else was there to say? "The police are all done at your mom's place?" I asked.

"Yeah, I think so. They said that I could take the tape off the door, at least."

"I'd like to have a look around, if you don't mind."

"You think the police might have missed something?"

"I doubt it," I said, "but you never know. I'm off the case, anyway, you know, but an extra pair of eyes might notice something that could be helpful."

"Sure," she said. "I might ask you to help me with some of the hauling, too," she said.

"You probably should get someone younger to lift the furniture," I said, laughing. "But I'll help where I can." I sipped my coffee for a moment.

"Would next Thursday be all right? Or Friday? I've asked my boss for both of them off next week."

I thought about the various things that were piling up; but I had nothing that needed to be done on any particular schedule. I did briefly wonder whether she didn't have some human friends who could help her. Not that I begrudged her the help. "Sure," I told her, "either afternoon. Anyway, did the police say if they had any suspects?"

"No. Not to me," she said, and I reminded myself they were probably still considering her a suspect. "Do you have any new ideas?"

"Not a one," I said, figuring that nothing I'd thought of so far could even be counted as a suspicion. "But I am sure they'll find someone. Someone did it, and they must have left some kind of evidence." Even as I said it, I knew that nothing could guarantee that either the police or I would recognize either the evidence or its importance.

"Well, my break time's up," she finally said. "Thanks for stopping by." Was the look on her face an unhappy one? I wasn't sure, but there was nothing more I could do.

A few minutes later, I bused my own table. I did drop a couple extra bucks in the tip jar on my way out. I hadn't been watching my wallet too closely, but I thought the tip was the very last of the money she'd given me.

I spent most of the afternoon running a couple of loads of clothes through the washer and hanging them up on the line in the back. In between, I kept looking things up on the web. There was a little place on the road to Point Marion where they had a firing range and a candy shop—a crazy combination, I had always thought, but it had opened long before the recent human frenzy for firearms reached such a pitch of intensity, at a time when candy, believe it or not, had been a surer route to profit than guns. I'd actually been up there before, buying black powder for the Homeland guns—one of those loose ends I sincerely didn't want Deputies Bowling and Evans to ever trace. I'd never even shot one of the guns, but now it seemed like it might be worth the effort to see if this place had a muzzleloader I could try out on the range. It seemed like a good idea, just to get a sense of what Diane's shooting would have involved, so I called them up and asked. They said I could drop in any time but warned me, "Just so you know, you might have to wait if there are a lot of customers."

"Well, I'm sure I can find some candy to pick up while I wait," I said.

Around suppertime, I bought a couple of fresh baguettes from the one decent downtown bakery that was still in business and carried them over to my dinner at Sarah Lloyd's house. Nathan opened the door, the eight-year-old twin boys pushing past his legs to greet me. I bent down to shake their hands, as serious as I could be, the little ritual we had developed. "Sarah's in the kitchen," Nathan said. "Can I get you anything?"

I handed him the bread. "Water's all I need," I said. "Thanks." The boys knew me a little: I visited the house two or three times a year, maybe. From their perspective, I was a fascinating figure, taller than anyone else they knew, and they led me into the living room with many a glance up at me. I looked around at the low antique loveseat and the cane-bottomed chairs, and I figured my weight would break right through the chair seats if I sat on them. I pulled out the piano bench and sat there instead.

When dinner was served, we sat at the dining room table and

made our way through small talk and a pleasant dinner of salad and lasagna: the bread had been a fortunate choice. A human would have probably brought a bottle of wine, but it never seemed right to me to bring something that I knew I wouldn't share. Eventually, Sarah brought out dessert, and then Nathan took the twins upstairs to put them to bed. Sarah glanced at me, pouring a bit more wine into her own glass, and then asked me finally why I wanted to see her. "Homeland business?" she asked.

"Sort of," I answered. "A medical question; maybe a physiological one." And without mentioning any names, I described an older bigfoot friend of mine, very probably at the end of his life, in more-or-less constant pain, and asked her what might ease it.

"You don't mean euthanasia, do you?" she asked.

That hadn't even occurred to me. "No," I said slowly, "I don't think so. I won't say bigfoot have never practiced euthanasia, but in this case, I think we just have a stubborn old cuss who wants to hang on through thick and thin. But it hurts us all to see him hurting."

"Yes," she said sympathetically. "I know how that is. Is there anything more you can tell me?"

"Well, I guess he's been taking aspirin, but it's not enough anymore."

"Aspirin works for you?"

"Yeah, it does. I've taken it, for aches and pains you know, and it seems to help."

"That's interesting," she said, and I knew I'd managed to really engage her intellect. She wasn't trained as a physical anthropologist, but she had taken some classes, and when I'd first let her in on the secret, it was the physical details as much as anything that had eventually convinced her I wasn't pulling some sort of hoax. "Have you ever tried anything stronger?"

"You mean like prescription strength?" I asked, echoing commercials I'd seen on TV.

"Yeah, I suppose. Codeine, oxycodone, that kind of thing."

"No, never," I answered. "You know that I've never been to a regular doctor, never had a prescription."

"Well," she said, frowning. "Plenty of folks here in West Virginia don't have a prescription, either, yet they still seem to take the pills."

Of course she was right. The West Virginia appetite for illegal prescription drugs was a matter of public record, an open secret, and a public scandal all at once. I'd heard more prescriptions were written each year for OxyContin in the state than there were people living here. It was probably the same in other rural areas around the country, but the mountains had always seemed to be a place where humans looked for escape, literal or chemical, or, I supposed, financial. While I was thinking this, Nathan came back downstairs and picked up his wineglass for a small sip. "Both asleep already," he said with a gentle laugh. "I wish I could fall asleep that easily!"

Sarah and I laughed too, though quietly enough to keep from waking the boys. "Nathan," Sarah said then, turning to her husband. "Do you have any of that codeine left from when you had that root canal?"

Nathan glanced my way, but otherwise he took this question as if it was perfectly normal. "Yeah, there's two or three of them left. Why?"

"Go get 'em," she said with a strange smile. "We'll do a little experiment here, and give one or two of 'em to Jim."

We decided eventually that I should take two: I had a lot of body mass compared to most humans, and there was no point in the experiment if we generated only subtle, uncertain effects. "But I'm not really in any pain," I said at one point. "So I won't really know if it works or not, will I?"

But Sarah just laughed. "I know you're even older than we are," she said. "And I've seen you walk: everybody, once they reach a certain age, has aches and pains that are just there all the time. Don't tell me you guys don't!"

I couldn't argue with that. Yes, I have aches and pains: they are always there, and I always ignore them, or try to. Living hurts, but it's better than the alternative. The problem was that the kind of living Horatio was doing hurt more than it ought to. "Bottoms up!" Nathan said, draining his wineglass when I swallowed the two pills with the rest of my water. For some reason, all three of us were on the verge of laughter.

Quickly enough, that giddiness passed. "I don't feel any different," I remember saying at one point, though whether or not I'd given the pills time to work, I don't know. Sarah turned the conversation to the twins, probably to get my mind off the pills, and it worked. I remember laughing at some joke, and Sarah shushing me with a finger and a nod up the stairs to where the boys were sleeping.

I woke up to the sound of the kids tiptoeing into the dining room; I was lying in front of the little loveseat, stretched out on the floor, still dressed. I must have slept a little more, because the next thing I remember was Nathan shepherding them out the door for their early soccer practice, while Sarah brought me a cup of coffee.

"I figured a big cup of coffee might be in order," she said, laughing quietly as she set it down on the table.

"I'm so sorry," I began.

"It's nothing," she said. "What are friends for? But I guess we got our answer. Two codeine tablets certainly knocked you right out."

So they had, I admitted to myself. "What was I like," I asked, "before I went out?"

"I never noticed it working. We were talking, and laughing, and then at one point you just pretty much tilted over, asleep. Nathan and I got you over here—you weren't quite completely out, yet—and figured we might as well let you sleep it off here."

"I don't really remember," I said.

"That's how we know it really worked," she said in return. "Drink your coffee."

So I did, taking a few minutes to wake myself up and to try to get over the embarrassment of waking up on Sarah and Nathan's living room floor. It was something I'd be able to laugh about, if I gave it some time, but for the moment, sitting there with my back against the loveseat, I couldn't manage that quite yet.

"Well," I said, when I'd made it about halfway through the big cup, "I guess the next step is to see whether the old guy will take them. They might do him some good. What do humans feel when they take them?" I asked with a sudden curiosity.

"I can't speak for anyone else," Sarah said, "but I just get a feeling like nothing matters. Sometimes I know I'm not thinking clearly, too, but then, that doesn't matter either."

"Do you enjoy it?"

"Not especially." She paused. "But then, I'm lucky: I've got a good job, a nice house, enough money. I don't have so many worries that I'd pay money just to make them go away for a while."

"Yeah, me either, I guess," I said. Horatio was another matter. He might well appreciate letting the pain go away for a time. "Are they easy to get, these pills?"

"I was afraid you'd ask that," she said seriously. "No, is the short answer. Doctors and dentists usually just prescribe a handful, enough for a day or two after a procedure." She picked up the bottle from the coffee table. "Nathan's prescription was for a dozen pills, and he had three left over: you took two of them last night."

"So that's where the black market comes from, the leftover pills," I said, knowing the answer already. It seemed like there always had been one illegal racket or another around here. When I was very young, there had been an active market in moonshine; the tradition of putting illegal stills out in the woods had a history stretching back to the eighteenth century. I'd heard it said that the very word *moonshine* had referred to lies people told before it had ever referred to illegal booze. This interpretation made a great story: after all, there was no such thing as legal moonshine, not really. You couldn't really call it moonshine if it didn't taste of lies and lawlessness. And there was something in humans—or perhaps it was only West Virginians—that loved a lie.

"Yeah, there's a black market," Sarah said with a sigh. "You're on your own there, I'm afraid."

"You don't think I could get a prescription?"

"For you? Or for your friend? I suppose you'd just go to one of the doctors who writes all the prescriptions for people who say they have chronic back pain, and you tell him that you have chronic back pain, too."

"As long as there's no examination," I said.

"I doubt there would be. From what I've heard, these guys keep pads of prescriptions practically filled out in advance. You'd probably need to pay in cash, though."

"So where are these guys?" I asked.

"No idea," she said. "Luckily, I know an investigator."

I left before Nathan and the kids made their way back from the soccer field. I had the last of his codeine tablets in its little plastic bottle in my jacket pocket. She didn't need to remind me that I shouldn't have it at all. She trusted me, and maybe the pill would help Horatio. Sarah had promised that she'd give some thought to how or where I might get a supply of the pills, but she said not to expect too much from her. If I had wanted some illegal Adderall, she said she could probably ask just about any of her students, and they could get it for her. And in a pinch she probably knew someone who could set me up with someone who could get me some marijuana. Pills were a bit more serious, though, and the people she knew just didn't talk about it. Still, someone must know, somewhere.

I thought about taking the pill right over to Horatio and letting him try it before deciding whether or not to track down a supply or a supplier. But I wasn't sure just one pill would do any good, and I knew he wouldn't thank me for it. So I kept it in my pocket. I thought about heading back to the office, but I was already on this side of town, and it was more convenient to stop in at the Cottonwood Café for a bite of breakfast than it would have been to go back there.

I got a table to myself. I didn't have my computer with me, so I just picked up a copy of the paper. I was glad I did: it turned out that there was a notice for a memorial service for Diane Smart printed there, so I knew that the coroner must have released the body. I'd have to try to stop by, for Emily's sake.

That was the only thing of interest, though I did see a small item about a prescription drug ring arrest in the southern part of the state. I was folding up the paper when Hobo Joe walked in, stood by the counter, and ordered a coffee. When he glanced my way, I gave him a nod, and then I gestured toward one of the extra chairs at my table. A couple minutes later, he was taking off the big pack he carried, propping it against one chair, and sitting down in the other.

"Big Jim," he said. "How you doing?"

"Not bad," I answered. As always, it makes me a little uneasy to be reminded how quickly and easily people I barely know come to call me by name. It doesn't exactly make me feel comfortable to be reminded so plainly that I am a local character every bit as much as he is: people who know me by name probably think they know something about me. But there is nothing to be done about it.

"I wanted to ask you, man," I said then, "if you've ever been to one of the states where there's medical marijuana."

"Hell, I been to Colorado," he said. Somehow, I had known that Hobo Joe and weed were old acquaintances.

"Yeah?"

"Yeah. You can buy the stuff right in a store: but you can't smoke it in public, or in a hotel room, or anywhere else really."

"I suppose that just means you've got to smoke it somewhere where nobody's likely to see you."

"That's it!" he said, laughing. "Hell, that's where I spend most of my day anyway, hanging out in places where nobody's likely to see me."

I didn't point out that I've seen him all over town. "Before they legalized in Colorado, did you ever go to California for medical marijuana?"

"Once I did," he said. "I got a prescription. A doctor was set up right next to the dispensary. He asked me a few questions, and I said, 'That's right, doc, I got a lot of stress,' and he wrote out a prescription right there."

"Expensive?"

"Not too bad," he said slowly. "But legal, least as far as the state was concerned."

I nodded, holding my tongue a bit. "Probably won't be long," he finally said, "before they legalize it here. They did in Ohio, last November."

"Yeah, I heard. I never tried it," I said, watching him closely. "I'm too law-abiding, I guess."

"Yeah, that's what I heard about you," he said, and I had no idea whether he really had heard that or that he'd heard the very opposite. Sometimes, I had no idea what humans were really saying. Knowing all the words wasn't always enough.

"If it's ever legalized," I said quietly, "you got any idea of a doctor I could see? You know, 'cause I already got a lot of stress."

Here he looked at me with his lips pursed. "No idea," he said. "But I'll give it some thought."

I headed back to the office feeling foolishly proud of myself. I didn't know, of course, whether Hobo Joe would come through for me, but I hadn't actually asked him to do anything illegal in any way, nor had I said that I wanted to do anything illegal. But, I thought, or hoped, he'd know just what kind of doctor I was looking for.

Or at least that's what I thought for a minute or two. When I thought again, I realized that if there was one thing that Hobo Joe must know about me besides my name, it was that I worked as a private detective. It was just as likely that he would think I was pursuing some line of investigation, and that at the end of it, someone would get into trouble. If he thought that, he'd probably never get around to telling me anything. And he might tell other people, including the very people I didn't want to know, that I'd asked. In that sense, I might have done more harm than good by asking him.

But for the moment, I'd have to put Horatio's troubles on the back burner. I had an idea about something I could do, and I even had an idea that it might do the old guy some good, but I couldn't make too many waves too quickly. Best to give Hobo Joe a day or two to think it over, and then he'd either come through with a name, or he wouldn't.

When I got back to the office, Deb Armstrong was standing at the door. She had a little pad of sticky notes in her hand, and I guessed she had been just about ready to write one up for me. "Hey, I'm glad I found you," she said. "Can I come in for a bit?"

"Sure," I said, unlocking the door.

"Just so you know, this is an official visit," she said, standing up behind the chair I would have encouraged her to sit in if she'd said anything else. I stuck my hands in my jacket pockets before taking it off and dumped the various junk in its pockets onto the desktop, and then hung it up on the coatrack. This time of year, the rack had almost every coat or jacket I owned on it, and a hat or two, too.

"Working on a Saturday?" I asked.

"Yeah, I know. But Deputy Bowling asked me if I'd come over here and have a little informal chat with you," she began, a hint of apology in the tone of her voice, I thought. "The county and the city are investigating the Smart case jointly, and I've been asked, unofficially, to head it all up from our end."

"You're doing the work of the city detective."

"That's right; equal to the County guys, in fact."

"They giving you a detective's pay?"

She actually laughed. "No, but the chief says it might be a step toward promotion. Eventually." She finally stepped around the chair and sat down.

"Well, anything I can help with to find the shooter," I said to her, "I'll be happy to do."

"Yeah, thanks. But you need to know you are still a person

of interest as far as we're concerned. Bowling thinks it's just too much of a coincidence that Emily Smart meets with you one day, and you turn up the body in only half a week. And when you throw in the Darla Jones case, which they told me all about, I can see where they're coming from."

"Yeah, well," I said. "I had nothing to do with either one. Just a coincidence. They do happen."

"Yeah, I know. But just be aware." Her hand reached out and picked up something from the trash on my desk: the little plastic bottle with Nathan's codeine pill. "What's this?" she asked.

I could see clearly enough that she knew exactly what it was: all the prescription information was printed right on the label. "I've been having trouble with a toothache," I said, hoping that was good enough. "Nathan Lloyd gave me that, left over from last year."

She grunted: an acknowledgment, I thought. "Best get it taken care of," she said. "You should probably just throw this one away," she said, as she set the bottle down at the very corner of the desk. Of course it was illegal, and it seemed to me she was saying she wouldn't push it. But I could see that she was storing it away in the back of her mind. It wasn't the kind of thing a person of interest ought to leave lying out on the desk.

"You have a dentist you'd recommend?" I figured I'd better ask. She gave me a name, and I jotted it down on a little slip. "Thanks," I said. "I'll see if I can get an appointment."

"Tell 'em you're in pain," she said. "They'll find a way to squeeze you in."

Of course, I'd never do that: teeth were a dead giveaway. And maybe she knew I was bluffing, too, because soon enough, she was gone, never having told me whatever it was that Bowling might have wanted her to say, or ask. Probably that I was supposed to not leave town. But while she'd been here, I'd lied to a police officer on an official visit and I'd been caught red-handed in possession of illegal prescription drugs, and I couldn't help but think that maybe I hadn't done very well today at all.

Maybe I could blame it on the aftereffects of the drug. But for all the lies I'd told in my life, I knew the lies we tell ourselves are the worst.

CHAPTER 7

STILL SATURDAY,
INTO SUNDAY

———

It couldn't have been more than twenty minutes after Deb Armstrong left that Martha showed up, her beautiful mane of hair unrestrained. She was wearing a set of grimy denim overalls with some kind of a long-sleeved sweatshirt underneath. It was a look she might have gotten away with around here once, but not in this century. That was how things worked up in the Homeland: a few sets of human clothes were stored there, just in case, but they were rarely used, and the turnover was incredibly slow, so they were all outdated. I realized I should have asked Mel to take her a change of clothes.

"Marty," I said, making an effort to get the name fixed in my own mind, "I'm glad you made it down. But we'll have to do something about those clothes. And you can wear a pair of my shoes."

"What's wrong with these?"

"You look like a hillbilly from the 1940s," I said. "No one will take you seriously."

"All right, then," she said. "Pick something out for me, and I'll change. And I'll wear the stupid shoes."

I found her some clothes and gave her some privacy in the back room so she could change. I don't know why, really: when I'd visited her up in the Homeland, she hadn't been wearing any clothes at all. But down here it seemed different, somehow. I had tried to come up with things she could wear that were simple and durable; I knew that whatever I gave her would be taken back up to the Homeland and hidden under a rock or something, stored away until the next time she, or someone else, needed a set of human clothes.

"What will you do with these?" she asked, coming back out front with the pile of dirty clothes.

"I should probably burn them," I answered. "But dumpster fires are already too much of a problem in this town. We'll just throw 'em away."

"How do you do it, with the shoes and all? Every day?"

"You get used to it," I said. "We should do something about your hair, too."

"What do you mean?" she said.

"Hair fashions change pretty quickly down here, you know," I answered, frowning in thought. "I think we'll try to give you what they call a man bun these days," I finally said. "At least we can see how it looks."

In the end, I didn't know whether the man bun was a failure or a success, but then I couldn't tell whether they worked on the human males I'd seen sporting them either. When the bun seemed as good as I could make it, we walked over to Jean's, since Mel had told her I'd buy her as many hot dogs as she wanted. It was a bar, really, over in a part of town that was mostly residential and cheap: half student rentals and half locals. It hadn't changed in at least fifty years, I think, and I'd been going there even longer than that. The hot dogs were presumably made of actual meat, but you couldn't really prove it by their taste. As far as I was concerned, that was the true beauty of human cuisine anyway—the way it offered you tastes or combinations of tastes that you'd never encounter in nature.

There was nobody else in the place though it was Saturday; later in the evening, there'd be a small crowd of semi-regulars. "Big Jim," said the owner-bartender, son of the original Jean, from the corner of the bar. "And who's this? He's even bigger than you!"

"My cousin Marty, just visiting from Uniontown," I answered. I always told humans that my visitors from the Homeland were from much farther away, just because they came to town so rarely and it wouldn't make sense to see them only once every couple of years if they were local. As it happened, there really was another Homeland over in the Laurel Highlands, not all that far from Uniontown. Some of the humans up in Pittsburgh refer to our cousins over there as Yinz-foot.

"A couple of beers then?"

"Just a Sprite for me," I answered. "And some hotdogs: four, with everything."

"Same for me," said Martha. "Sprite and four dogs."

"I think maybe you've been here before," said Jean II, "though it's been a few years."

"That's right," I said. "We'll be over in the corner booth."

The two of us pretty much filled up a booth intended for four humans, and here we wouldn't be bothered much by anyone else. We chatted about nothing whatsoever for a few minutes, until Jean brought us out the food. I handed him a twenty and a ten, and he came back a minute later with the change. I let it sit on the table. "We might want a couple more, in a bit," I told him. "But I'll come to the bar and order 'em, if we do."

"Sure enough," he said, nodding as he went back.

Now Martha and I could get down to business. "You got anything you can tell me?" I asked, unable to put it off any longer.

"Ezra told me that one of those guns had been given to his grandpappy by somebody called Davy Crockett. That mean anything to you?"

"Yeah, it does," I said. Now that she'd said it, I remembered that I'd heard Ezra say it before. It was possible that it was even true. "Davy Crockett was a human woodsman," I finally said, "and he died, I don't know, maybe 180 years ago. He came from Tennessee, I think." I didn't know all that much about Crockett, and if he'd ever come up here from Tennessee, I didn't think I'd ever heard of it from the humans. The Lovingoods had come up from Tennessee right around the same time, however, and there was probably some connection. But this was all more historical detail than Martha would need. "There was a TV show about him, and a song on the radio, too, just a few years after I came down here."

"Huh," she said.

"He's a famous hero to the Americans," I said. "Kill't a bar when he was only three."

"Three years old?" Martha was incredulous.

"It's what it says in the song, though I doubt it's actually true. But Crockett is so famous that if a human had that gun, and they could prove it was Crockett's, there'd be people who'd kill for it, probably." Martha had only the vaguest sense of the value of money: she knew I used it to do things like pay for the hotdogs. A lot of money or a little was all the same to her, but she knew the value of a life.

"I guess Ezra knows that, then."

"Yeah. He used to hang out with the youngest of the Lovingood boys, you know." Even as I said it, I realized that the boy I had in mind must be something like forty years old by now, Bill Lovingood's little brother. Of course there were even younger kids now; I'd seen some of them at the ramps festival. Time passes, quicker than you think. "But I doubt that Davy Crockett has anything to do with Diane Smart's death."

"No, I suppose you're right," she said.

"Could you find anything out about whether the guns have been fired recently, or any rumors about an initiation killing?"

She made a face of distaste, her moustaches curving to one side. "Plenty of rumors," she said. "There always are. But nothing I can be sure of. I looked at the guns myself, but I have no idea whether they've been fired or not. I've just never had anything to do with them."

"Yeah, well, thanks for asking, And thanks for coming down to tell me. I don't think the police would be happy with me if I disappeared for a couple of days right now. I'm too much of a suspect already."

"You?"

"Yeah, of course. They think it's far too much of a coincidence that I found the body. It's nothing, but I can't do anything to draw even more attention to myself on the off chance that it will lead them up to you." There didn't seem to be any reason to mention Darla Jones. I didn't want Martha to think I was in more trouble than I was.

"Oh," she said, obviously thinking. "I see what you mean. It puts you in a bit of a spot, doesn't it?"

"Nothing I haven't handled before," I answered. "And more than once. Say—you want another dog or two?"

"Two, please," she said with a smile. "And another Sprite."

I looked around the room and saw that it was at least half-filled now. "You be all right if I go to the bathroom while I'm up?" I asked.

"This ain't my first time in the big city, you know! I'll be all right."

She was as old as I was, more or less. Of course she'd be all right. I stood up slowly and met Jean at the bar where I ordered more for Martha and myself. I then went into the men's room at the back.

I should never have left her alone, even for a short time. When I came back from the restroom, Martha was standing up at the bar, two or three human males standing around listening. She loves to tell a story, and she never seems to understand the notion of keeping a low profile when she comes down here. So I hardly knew what kind of tale she'd have dug up to try out on these guys. When I got to the bar, I reached for one of the hot dogs that Jean had set out for me, and she barely gave me a glance.

"Anyway," she was saying, "this old girl seen a painter up there, and she knew it was more'n a mile back to her cabin. She didn't have a knife, no gun either, and all she could think to do was run. But that painter had seen her, sure enough, and soon enough the painter had her scent.

"So then she was running along, dodging between the trees, and the painter was a-gaining on her. So then she thinks she needs to distract that painter, and the only thing she can think to do is to take off her jacket and throw it on the ground. Sure enough the painter stops and checks it out, distracted by the scent. But he's not distracted long, and soon enough that painter jumps up and he's chasing her some more.

"Well, that old girl ran some more, and she stripped off one piece of clothing after another. Each time, the painter, he stops and he sniffs, but he's up and running again faster every time. By the time she shut the cabin door on that painter's nose, she was naked as the day she was born!"

She looked at her audience, obviously expecting laughter. They gave a chuckle or two, but even I could see that they hadn't understood the story at all. They were just humoring her. Even Jean seemed not to get it. So I spoke. "Panther," I said. "A painter is a panther."

Then, of course, there was laughter, loud and rough. "A painter!" I heard Jean say, while the others were laughing. "Of course."

"He's from Pennsylvania," I said to the guys at the bar. "That story kills, up there." It was always a good idea to point the laughter at someone from somewhere else, though Martha probably wouldn't thank me for it. "Come on, Marty," I said, "Time for us to get you home."

"They'll think you were drunk, don't worry about it," I told her as we were walking back to my office.

"They were laughing at me!" she said, still indignant.

"Yeah, well," I told her. "When was the last time you saw a painter, or a panther?"

"It's been a while, I suppose. When I was a youngster, I guess."

"Okay. Now how old were those guys, do you think, when you saw that painter?"

"Oh."

"Yeah, 'Oh.' They know panthers well enough: they've seen 'em in the zoo, or they watch Pitt football on the TV. But there hasn't been a painter, or a panther, seen in this part of the state since before those guys were born. Maybe since before their grandparents were born. They probably thought you were talking about an artist or a house painter."

"I don't know how you get used to it," she said.

The different ways time passed, I knew she meant; the change in the language was only a piece of the bigger issue. "It helps that I'm down here every day," I answered. And it does, I know. The way things change quickly in the human world is one of those things that I know, and I keep it in my mind more or less all the time, and still I don't know how it must feel to a human. I learned, over the years, to stop worrying about how to feel about it myself: humans just have shorter lives, and their generations rush past in the span of a bigfoot lifetime. Of course the bigfoot way seems normal and natural, to Martha maybe even more than to me, but the human way must seem natural to them, even more so since they know nothing of how we live. Obviously, if humans had lived to see the changes in the world that I have seen, maybe they'd be more hesitant to build, and change, and pollute. By the time a human is old enough to see what they have wrought, most of them are beyond any age where they can even think about changing their ways. And so every generation's problems are passed on to their children. Diane Smart, even, seems to have passed her problems down to her daughter. More than anything else I've ever been able to figure, this is the human way.

"Where can we go to hear some music?" Martha asked, her irritation at the drinkers' laughter already gone. Whenever she comes to Morgantown, she always wants to make it into a real night on the town. I can't blame her.

"You won't hear any of your old favorites," I told her. "But we can see what's going on at the Burrito Pit."

"Then I'll hear something new," she answered. And off we went.

I woke up in the morning to the sound of Martha in my shower. I had given her the hammock to sleep in, and I'd spent an uncomfortable night in my office chair. She was probably in there, using up most of a bottle of shampoo and all of the hot water. I couldn't blame her; I had my own set of vanities, never doubt it. I knew that when she finally came out, her coat would be looking better than ever.

While I was waiting, I took a quick peek at my email. I was surprised to see a notice from the muzzleloader group I'd joined online; it was a reminder that there would be an event or two of interest to the group at the reenactors' encampment at Prickett's Fort in Fairmont on Wednesday, and a campout was scheduled for the reenactors on Tuesday night. Mike Merrill had told me that he'd been organizing the concessions again this year. He'd never asked me to work security there since Prickett's Fort was one of the state parks that actually had a staff, but I wondered for a moment if he might be there running things or if Deputy Bowling had him locked up.

This year, they were planning to reenact the disastrous Battle of Jumonville Glen, which had happened a little way north of the border, near Uniontown, on May 28, 1754. It was the skirmish that first brought George Washington to international attention, even before the events at Fort Necessity. Although Washington was from the eastern part of Virginia, his early exploits in what was then still known as "the West" made many of the locals treat him like a native son, and it was apparently more fun to reenact something like this than it was to stick to historically accurate geography. "Holy cow!" I said to myself, when I read it over a second time: the reminder had been posted by Harlan Stephens, Diane Smart's old surveying partner. I didn't want to run into Mike at all, but it might be worth the risk to get a chance to check out Harlan Stephens. I wrote myself a little note and stuck it on the desk drawer, a reminder.

When Martha finally came out, I had a coffee ready, not instant this time, one for her and one for me. "You heading back to the Homeland today?" I asked her.

"Yeah," she said. "I know I haven't brought you much that's of any use. Maybe you would find out more if you came up yourself. You know Ezra and those guys: they don't think they owe me a thing, not even the truth."

"But you don't think they shot Diane Smart, do you?"

"I don't believe so," she answered, hesitating. "But like I said: you know some of those guys. They're secretive at the best of times. And they can be mean."

"Yeah. Maybe I'll be up in a couple of days," I said, though the week ahead was already getting mighty crowded. And I'd have to tell Deb Armstrong, at least, that I'd be out of touch for a bit. I thought she'd let me do it. Probably.

We chatted for a while before she stood up and said she'd better get going. "Thanks for the hotdogs and everything," she said. "I'll have to come down for some more sometime."

"Any time," I said with a smile. "Keep the shoes, though. Take them with you, and you'll never have to worry about leaving tracks again."

She looked down at the shoes I'd lent her, sitting empty by the door. "I wouldn't want to lose my edge," she said. I clamped my mouth shut, having nothing that I wanted to actually say.

I spent a good part of the rest of the morning in a foul mood. Martha would never say outright that she thought I was losing my edge, but she might well think it, even though she knew perfectly well that someone needed to be here in Morgantown, keeping an eye on things. She'd know it even more once she'd stopped by and visited Horatio. I had told her, last evening at the Pit, that she should drop by his place, just to say hello. I knew she'd be worried about him. She'd probably even try to get him to move back up to the Homeland, but I knew he'd refuse. It sometimes seemed like refusing had become a way of life for Horatio.

Even if she wouldn't want me to say it, Martha is the closest thing we have to a leader in the Homeland these days. Mostly this just seems to mean she is the one who takes responsibility for the stupid things other bigfoot manage to do. She tries to make sure guys like Ezra are keeping an eye on the borders for wandering human hikers, and she rides herd on the youngsters who act bored by their woodcraft lessons. She teaches what she knows to anyone who'll listen. But we bigfoot tend to be solitary souls, every single one of us is all the government we ever needed. Or so we like to think.

I know how much they really need her up at the Homeland. Although I probably wouldn't say it to her face, I think she is the wisest female of my generation. She keeps the whole Homeland together, and everyone up there knows it. She is the one everyone else owes favors to. I wouldn't want to do what she does, although, as Martha had once pointed out to me when she'd visited Morgantown a few years ago, I pretty much serve the same role for the bigfoot here in town that she does in the Homeland, which hadn't made me exactly happy, although I couldn't deny it, either.

After I sent Martha off to see Horatio, I returned to thinking about what I could do for him. I hadn't seen Hobo Joe since I'd hinted so clumsily that he could maybe help me out, and I'd heard nothing from Sarah Lloyd, either, though she'd told me not to expect to. From the frequency with which stories about the traffic in prescription drugs appeared in the news, I knew plenty of people around here must know something. But they wouldn't be any more eager to talk about it to a stranger than I was, presumably. No matter how long I may have been a fixture in Morgantown, I couldn't really count on many humans for that kind of friendship. Well, there was no use worrying about it now.

I glanced down and saw the note I'd made about Harlan Stephens and the Prickett's Fort reenactment. I dug around in the top drawer until I found Seth Jones's business card. I was a little uncertain about calling him out of the blue, but I remembered that Mike Merrill had told me Seth would be working as a vendor at the reenactment. I dialed his number.

"Seth Jones speaking," he answered.

"Seth, this is Big Jim Foote." We exchanged greetings, and I asked him how he was managing these days. Talking to him reminded me again of how I knew two young people now, both of their mothers recently lost. I felt a powerful protective urge toward both of them, and I wondered again if they'd want to meet each other.

"I wanted to ask you a couple of things about the reenactment this week down at Prickett's Fort," I finally said. "You still going?"

"I can't," he said. "That's Mike Merrill's gig, you know? I won't give him my money. I'd ask the bastard for my deposit back, if I thought he'd send it."

"Will he be there?"

"I don't know. He might be, if he's out on bail or something. I know I won't be."

Too bad, I thought to myself, though I certainly couldn't fault his reasons. I wouldn't want to see Mike either, if I were him, much less pay him for a rental space.

"Do you suppose," I said to him then, "that you could come down to Morgantown on Thursday afternoon or Friday? A friend of mine could use some help, and I wondered if maybe we could use that pickup truck of your mom's?"

"Somebody who's moving?" he asked.

"No," I said, hesitating, "someone else who's just lost her mom. She needs some help clearing out her place."

"Oh," he said slowly. "Yeah, yeah, I can be there."

"I'll let you know which day would be better," I said. "I'll text you."

"And tell me where to meet."

"I will," I promised.

In the late afternoon, I made my way over to Diane Smart's memorial service. There was, thankfully, no dolled-up body to be maudlin over, which I have always found to be one of humankind's strangest customs. "There was a cremation," the notice in the paper had said, but a quick glance around didn't show any tasteful urn, either, which was fine by me. I spotted Emily right away, sitting with a small group, talking quietly. Here and there, some mementos of her mother's life had been placed around the room, and I saw a couple of other people milling around. I was afraid I stood out conspicuously and knew I would have even in a bigger crowd.

I spent some time looking over what the funeral director probably called a photo montage. Mostly it was made up of pictures of Diane Smart alone: hiking in the woods, sitting at a dining table. A few had Emily in them. Generally, they looked like the kind of pictures you'd find on someone's online profile, and most of them had probably been taken by her daughter. After a few minutes, Emily herself came over. "Mr. Foote," she said quietly. "I am so glad you came."

"I didn't know your mama," I said, "but I was happy to do her a good turn in finding her, even if it was too late."

"I know you were. It's nice to see so many people here who loved her and cared for her."

I didn't really know how to answer, especially since I hadn't known her at all, so I just nodded and let my gaze move back to the photo collage. She didn't move off right away, though, so I decided I'd better speak. I almost told her I'd found someone to help with the hauling, when she cleared out her mom's things, but it didn't seem kind to remind her of that. "Well, keep in touch," I finally managed. "Let me know if you need anything." Maybe there was something better to say, but I couldn't find it.

"I do need your help, I think," she said, bailing me out. "Can I talk to you when this is over?" She gestured vaguely with her hand, and I gathered that she meant when the memorial gathering was over.

"I'll come back," I said. "Will that be all right?"

She smiled a fragile little smile and nodded. "Thanks."

On my way out the door, I checked the schedule: the memorial was scheduled to last until six, so I had nearly another hour to fill. I checked my phone, but nothing was of interest, and the weather was nice, so I headed downtown. Even if it is doing better, economically, than many other West Virginia towns, downtown Morgantown still doesn't really offer much to the wandering pedestrian. I hoped maybe I'd run into Hobo Joe, or someone else. Mostly, though, I saw undergrads scooting into various bars and nightspots; apparently five o'clock on a Sunday was not at all too early to start drinking.

I sat for a while on one of the benches along High Street, just people-watching. Probably, Emily just wanted to make sure I could still help clear out her mama's apartment or something; if that was it, she'd be glad to hear I'd already found someone with a truck. I couldn't figure out what else she might want to talk about. Maybe she was still getting some kind of flak from the police and she thought I might have some insight into what was going on or how to handle them. That seemed as likely as anything else I could come up with. Maybe she had some secret she needed to come clean about.

Even while I was thinking through these things, I knew in the back of my mind that something odd was happening. I made a conscious effort to look around, to really observe. It wasn't long before I realized what it was: pedestrians—not all of them, but some—were stepping around me, going just a little bit out of their way to avoid me, even though I was just sitting quietly on the bench. With some chagrin, I remembered that this particular bench was often occupied by one or another of Morgantown's homeless population. The folks going by were probably thinking that if they stepped a little bit out of their way, they wouldn't be able to hear me if I asked them for small change. Apparently, there was something about my look that wasn't really working. I laughed ruefully, remembering how I'd made Martha change clothes. I got up and walked some more.

A few minutes after six, I finally made my way back to the funeral home where the memorial gathering had been. I figured that Emily would not be free immediately at six, but there she was, on the steps, outside a door that was already locked when I got there. "Sorry I'm late," I said from the bottom step.

She stepped down toward me. "That's all right." She took a moment and looked me up and down, and I saw her eyebrows pinch together, in puzzlement or irritation, I thought.

"That was rough," she said then. "I need a drink. And maybe some food."

"Um," I said, growing even more uncertain about what she was thinking.

"Just walk with me over to The Station, Mr. Foote," she said. "And then you can decide whether or not you'll let me buy you dinner."

"All right," I said, and we began walking. The distance was about three blocks. Like I said before, downtown Morgantown is not all that big.

"You didn't know my mom," she started, "so let me tell you a little about her. She grew up out in Preston County, lived around here all her life, went to the university here, and finished her degree while she was raising me. It was always just the two of us, me and her, and I don't think she ever once did wrong by me. We might have had a shouting match or two, but if she took a stand, it was always the right one. Even if I didn't know it at the time." She paused, and I just nodded when she looked at me. "She was mother and father both to me, I guess."

Another pause while we walked a few steps. "She loved to read, and she thought that explosions in movies were overrated. She got me a library card even before I could read myself. She never drank anything stronger than wine, and she ordered her coffee with cream. She was raised by her mother, just like me, and her mom died when she was in her twenties. Just like me."

"Oh," she said, the anguish in her voice clear, "I don't know why I'm telling you all this."

"I know why," I said. "It's because you want me to know that she was more than just a body I found in the woods. She's what made you who you are."

"I guess that's it, Mr. Foote. Something like that."

For a while after that, neither of us said a thing. Maybe she was struggling to hold back tears. But I also thought she had something more she wanted or needed to say. I figured she would either tell me what was going on with her, or she wouldn't, and I remembered thinking the very same thing when she'd first stepped into my office. Now it was something she guessed I wouldn't want to hear. She couldn't fire me, of course: I wasn't working for her anymore. But it was something like that, and I couldn't help but think it was something that might be unpleasant.

We stopped and waited at a crosswalk, and she looked around to see if anyone was nearby. There wasn't anyone close. "Look," she finally began. "I don't know how to say this, so I'll just say it. You're one of them, aren't you?"

This seemed like a risky direction for our conversation to take, so I hesitated. "One of who?"

"A sasquatch," she answered. "Or whatever you call yourselves."

I decided to play for time. "Wow. Whatever could have given you that idea?" I said, neither confirming nor denying anything.

"I'll tell you all about it, if you'll come in for a bite to eat," she said. "I owe it to you, for lying to you."

This was hardly the most appealing invitation, but I thought she meant it as a kind of apology. I couldn't just let this go: I had damage control to do, one way or another. So we went through the routine of letting the hostess at The Station find us a suitable table, ask for our drink orders, and tell us the name of our server. "Iced tea for me," I said. Emily Smart ordered a glass of red wine.

"I lied to you," she finally said, once we'd been left alone for a bit, "when I told you that my father lived in Texas. He doesn't. He lives right here in West Virginia." I said nothing: I wasn't happy she had lied, but she hadn't yet gotten to the heart of her confession. "His name is Bill Lovingood."

"Oh," I said, completely surprised. "I know him. Not as well as I know his uncle, but I do know him." I didn't know he had any daughters Emily's age, but it was possible. She had all my attention now.

"When I was young," she was saying, "my mom would take me up to the hollow in the mountains where he lives. They were never really married, I don't think, but that was one of the calls she made: she thought I should know who my dad was, get to know him a little, you know, get to know his people. He took me over to visit with some of your people—the biggies, he called you—when I was about five. When Mom found out, she swore she'd never take me back up there. And she never did."

"Wow," I said. "This is quite a story." I was pretty sure that there was nothing she could remember very clearly from when she was five. "So you told me your father lived in Texas because you figured there was no chance he had anything to do with your mom's death."

"Yeah," she said. "That's what Mom always said whenever anyone asked about my dad. 'He lives in Texas,' she'd say, and so did I. It was just a habit."

"And what did you tell the police?" I asked.

"I told 'em he lived in Texas, too."

"Hmmm," I said. "I guess you've had a lot on your mind these last few days."

Here our server—"I'm Sean," he said as he walked up—took our orders. I thought about telling him we'd be on separate checks, but I chickened out at the last second. She could buy me dinner, I thought. Accepting that didn't mean I'd accept her apology.

I was angry, but already I could see that there wasn't much I could really be angry about. True, she'd lied to me, but she'd told the same lies to the police, and what she really wanted from me was probably for me to tell her how to handle that lie with them. As for figuring out I was a bigfoot, well, she wasn't the first to figure it out, and maybe she'd keep the secret. She'd have to.

I could see that she was asking me to confirm that I'd told her a lie, too. A lie of omission, or worse, for not being open about not being human.

"We almost never talked about it, after that," Emily started, once Sean had gone away again. "It was like a secret between the two of us, one so big that we didn't even need to mention it. But it marked us, maybe it even scarred us. It was the biggies that broke my mom and dad up, but they held her and me together some-how, too."

"Bigfoot," I said, giving in. "Not biggies. Not sasquatch."

"Oh," she said, looking like she'd swallowed something wrong. Probably she figured I'd never admit it, or maybe she thought that she or her mother had made the whole thing up. "Okay. I guess."

"It would be just like some of the Lovingoods to have a name like that for us. It's not right, though that wouldn't ever stop them. What you remember is true," I went on, figuring it wouldn't help her now for me to deny it, "there's a whole bigfoot community up there. My family's up there, such as it is. Your mom was right: it's a secret, one you can't tell anyone."

"Yeah, I know," she said. "I don't want to tell anyone, really. Live and let live, I guess." There was something more, but she didn't say it. "I didn't realize it right away, but it's a secret you and I share."

I nodded a grim agreement. "I know that doesn't mean you owe me a thing," she went on, "just because I know your secret. But, you know, all the time I was growing up, it was just me and my mom, just my mom and me. I didn't know any different, of course: that was my whole world. She never had any real friends, and neither did I somehow. We had a secret, and it made us into a little two-person world. I don't think it's like that for everyone."

I just looked at her. What she was describing was a way of life among the bigfoot, almost as exactly as if her mother had done it on purpose. A female bigfoot had a child, male or female, but the male parent just wasn't part of the child-rearing. Everybody knew who their pappy was, of course, or most of them did, anyway.

Bigfoot got to know their pappies later in life, that was all. If they were worth knowing, that is. Not all of them were. But bigfoot, in general, are a solitary folk, and the males most of all. Horatio wasn't all that unusual when you got right down to it. Human families were often a mystery to me, but not Emily's. It was like she was one of us, and I knew, so very well, just how alone she must be feeling. "What is it you want me to do for you?" I finally asked.

"Could you take me to meet my father?"

CHAPTER 8

STILL SUNDAY, INTO MONDAY

———

"Look, I'll take you out there," I told Emily later, while we were waiting for dessert. "But you must know there's got to be a reason why your mother never married him, a reason she decided to raise you all on her own."

"She didn't talk about him too much," Emily answered. "She said his whole family was pretty old-fashioned."

"I guess that's one way to put it. A pretty good way to put it, actually. But it probably hides as much as it tells, even so." I thought about how to put it myself. "A lot of humans," I finally tried, "think being 'old-fashioned' is a good thing. Closer to nature, maybe, true to traditional values, authentic in some important way. I guess it's all true, as far as it goes, but 'close to nature' sometimes means having a lot of familiarity with blood and death and killing animals for food, and also it usually means knowing the—the gnawing desperation of real hunger. 'Traditional values' should probably include racism and sexism, and probably even the willingness to back them both up with violence. 'Authentic,' I truly, deeply hope, doesn't have to mean that being a violent racist or sexist killer is what real human nature involves."

"So there's a reason you live down here yourself," she said.

I grunted out a surprised laugh. "Yeah," I answered: everything I had just said was as true among the bigfoot as it was among the humans. "The modern world has its problems, for humans and bigfoot alike, but one of the things it succeeds at best is not being too old-fashioned."

She smiled, with a sadness I couldn't quite parse. "So you think my dad is probably a racist, sexist jerk," she said.

"Maybe," I answered. "I've known him all his life, but I can't say I know him very well. I know that family: some of 'em are great folks, and I'd trust old Sut Lovingood with my life. The rest of 'em are friendly enough when they come up to the Homeland to talk, or hunt, or whatever. But I've heard that some of them think of us as animals."

"They are speciesist."

It was a word I didn't know, but it seemed to cover it. "Probably. I should probably add that some bigfoot are, too. One of the things I am worried about with your mother's death is that some bigfoot killed her, one who thinks that humans are the animals."

"That's terrible!"

"Yeah, well, there's a lot of traditional family values up in the Homeland, too. And you tell me whether you think I should keep living incognito down here or whether I should just tell the whole wide world what I am."

She thought about this a bit, nodding. "But 'Big Jim Foote'?" she finally said.

"Hiding out in plain sight," I answered. "Sometimes when you're telling a lie, it's more believable the closer it is to the truth."

In the end, I let her pay the bill, even though I probably shouldn't have. She knew, now more than ever, that she was on her own, and if she wanted to pay for my dinner, I could find a way to resist the urge I had to take that away from her. Condescending paternalism is a kind of traditional value, too, as I knew well.

"There's so much I feel like I want to know," she said, as we stood outside the restaurant door.

"There's even more that I need to know," I answered. For one thing, I was almost certain that the Lovingoods must have a muzzleloader or two in their collection, and while I didn't really suspect that Bill Lovingood had shot his daughter's mother, I knew that old clan feuds could boil up in ways nobody really expected. If Diane Smart had been caught in one of those, anything might have happened. And although we had talked about a lot, I still hadn't given Emily any good ideas on how to deal with the fact that she'd lied to the police. Standing here on the sidewalk didn't feel right for bringing up such a topic. "Any chance you'd like an after-dinner coffee or something?" I asked.

"To tell you the truth," she said, "I could use another drink. That memorial thing was harder than I thought it would be."

We ended up at The Pharmacy, which I always figured had been named by the owner in anticipation of the day when legal recreational marijuana might make it to West Virginia. It had only been open a couple of years, but it was known for being a place that served Belgian beers and made room for people who really wanted to sit and talk. I ordered beers for both of us. "And water, too," I added, knowing that I'd be drinking far more of the water than the beer. There are times when I just can't pass as human without having a sip or two of beer, and I've seen how much humans seem to enjoy it over the years. Sometimes there is a real price to pay for seeming to fit in. Sometimes it is the right choice to pay it.

"This is good stuff," Emily said of the Chimay. "Thanks."

I took a tiny sip. "It is good," I lied, and then I jumped right in to business. "Look, if I know anything about Deputy Bowling, it's that he's not going to be too happy to find out you lied to him about where your father lives."

"Maybe I should just tell him. Tell him I forgot."

"You could do that," I said. "But it's still going to look suspicious."

"Like he'll think my father shot my mother?"

"Maybe. Or at least that you were hiding something."

"Me?"

"Sure. Family is always the first place to look in a murder case. You'll both be suspects, and even more so if they figure it out themselves."

"You mean we don't have to tell them?"

"Well, you probably should tell them. But if you don't, and then they find out that you went up into the hills to visit Bill Lovingood, they'll really suspect you've got something to hide."

"So you think I shouldn't go up there until the police find my mom's killer."

"Maybe. Maybe not. It won't hurt anything if we keep trying to help the police out, especially if it starts looking like they're not going to find the shooter."

Emily was quiet for a minute, thinking things through. "I thought you said you were off the case."

She was sharp, there was no doubt about it. I had a sip of water, while I thought about it. "Well, I am off the case. And I let you buy me dinner, but I won't take any other money from you. Let's just say that I've worked with the police and the county often enough to know that it's probably best to keep an eye on what they do." That was vague enough, I hoped, to cover it.

"Well, thanks for looking out for me, then," she said. I could tell she wasn't completely convinced. Something still seemed to be missing for her, and of course something was missing: I was lying to her, even if she couldn't quite figure out where the lies began. Yet.

I took another small drink of the Belgian beer. I'd pay for it, soon enough.

"You have a car?" I asked her.

"Yeah, of course."

"I'm not sure I could make my way up to the Lovingoods' hollow by car. I've never gone that way."

"I've got a GPS," she said.

"Yeah, but I think that's only good if we have an address to plug in, right? I'm guessing that you don't send Bill Lovingood any Christmas cards."

"No, I suppose you're right."

"Well, I might be able to figure something out. What's your schedule like over at the Jackalope? When will you have a day or two off?"

"It varies, week to week, but next week I've asked for Thursday and Friday," she answered. I remembered that those were the days on which she had asked if I could help clear out her mother's place.

"Okay," I said. "We'll go on Thursday. You'll have to drive." She nodded, sipping at her beer. "And are you sure the police are done with your mom's apartment?" I asked her again.

"I think so. They told me I could go in, and the landlord told me I need to get it all cleaned out by the end of the month. I don't know what I'm going to do with all of it."

"I really would like to look around before you take everything away," I said. "I found somebody who might be able to help us clean it out, probably on Friday, if you still want to."

"Is there anything you're looking for in particular?"

"No, and I'm sure the police probably didn't leave anything crucial behind, but like I said before, another set of eyes might see something. You never know."

"I suppose." She looked uncertain. "Do you think we'll ever find who did it?"

"I really don't know. It always seems to me that if it's not obvious who has done something, it's pretty hard to find any kind of proof. It's not like on TV."

She still seemed uncertain, as if there was something she needed to ask. "Go ahead," I told her. "I see there's something still on your mind."

"Okay," she said finally. "I'll just tell you, and you can tell me if you think it's something I need to worry about. There was only one person at the reception who was a surprise to me: Merle DuPont."

The name seemed familiar for a moment, but I couldn't quite place it. Then it clicked: "The PaVaMa boss? The guy who's always being indicted?"

"Yeah. I mean, I know my mom was working for his company when she died, but I didn't expect him to be there."

"Did he say anything to you?"

"Not much. He offered his sympathy and said my mom had a good record with the company. He said he'd known her a long time. It seemed very odd, I thought."

"Yeah," I said. "It does seem unusual. Did he stay long?"

"No, although I saw him talking to Harlan Stephens for a bit. But Harlan works for PaVaMa, too."

"Yeah, but I bet not everyone who works there knows the CEO."

"That's what I thought, too."

Before we parted, we settled on the next day, after she got off work, as a time I could go in and look around her mom's apartment. She swore she'd be all right making her way back to her own place alone, and so we split up at the door of The Pharmacy.

When I got back to the office, I almost didn't notice the sticky note on the door. I saw it had only three words on it once I'd gotten inside and turned on the light. "Big. MacDonald. Joe."

It didn't make much sense to me. "Big" must be me, of course, but who was Joe? I finally decided it must be Hobo Joe, which seemed obvious, once I'd figured it out. The alcohol headache wasn't doing me any good at all, I decided, even though I'd had only a few sips. But what did Joe want? Was he trying to say I should meet him at McDonalds? And when?

There are no McDonalds restaurants in downtown Morgantown, though there are a couple on the outskirts. The city has been fairly good (though far from perfect) in keeping the downtown area filled with local businesses rather than chain stores and restaurants. How they have managed it, I don't know: fifty, sixty years ago, I'd have put it down to influence trading or inside interests on the part of the council members. But one hoped that we were past that part of West Virginia politics.

Well, I wasn't about to go out again tonight, regardless. If Hobo Joe wanted to meet me, it could wait until tomorrow.

In the morning, I woke up, rolled out of the hammock, and made some coffee; I didn't always use it, but I had one of those little pour-over contraptions, so all I really needed to do was boil water and spoon out some grounds into a filter. It made a pretty good cup of coffee, and after I'd drunk a few swallows, I took the one half-formed idea I had and pulled out my old-fashioned paper phone book. There was one physician named MacDonald listed, seeming to be in general practice. I looked at the business address, and it didn't make any sense at all. It was no place I recognized, so I looked it up online: it was ten miles or more west of town, and it looked like it was the middle of nowhere. Maybe Hobo Joe had come through with exactly what I hadn't actually asked him for: the name of a doctor who could help me out with my chronic back pain.

I tried the number listed, but there was no answer. Maybe nine o'clock was still too early. I checked the weather and decided I'd need a jacket. Before I put it on, I pulled open another drawer and found the old manila envelope where I always kept a few hundred bucks. I took it all and put it into my billfold. Then I went out back and got the bike out. I usually preferred to take the trails when I could, but I could ride the roads when I had to. An hour later, I was at Dr. MacDonald's office.

The "office" turned out to be a mobile home. There was a small sign by the door but nothing by the road: if I hadn't been looking for the place, I'd have never known it was anything other than someone's house.

"Jeez, you're a big one!" said the guy inside when he opened the door. "Come on in."

"Hi," I said. "I'm looking for Dr. MacDonald?"

"That's me," he said, though he wasn't dressed any more like a medical doctor than I was: blue jeans, flannel shirt, Birkenstocks. He showed me into a little office not far from the door. I didn't see any kind of medical equipment at all. "You got an appointment?"

"No, sorry: I called, but there was no answer. I got your name from a friend of mine," I said, figuring that I needed to offer some sort of explanation for showing up at his door. "I've got a lot of back pain."

"Tall guys often do," he said. "Especially if they're a little on the heavy side."

There was nothing I could say to argue with that, I figured, but it wasn't the kindest way to phrase it, either, I thought. "What's your name?" he asked. I told him, and he opened up a file folder and started asking me for information and filling in some blanks on a single sheet of paper that was inside. Name, address, email address, stuff like that. "Insurance?" he finally asked.

"No. I'm self-employed."

"You on the Obamacare, then?"

"No," I said. "I try not to see any doctors at all."

"Well, I'll let you fight it out with the IRS, then. Tell me about your back pain."

So I did. He asked if I biked everywhere, and I told him I didn't drive and it was the only way I could get around. "Bending over the handlebars on that thing isn't doing your back any good," he said, finally, making a note at the bottom of the page he was writing on.

He reached out to a shelf behind him and pulled down a prescription pad. Before I knew it, he'd ripped off the top sheet and handed it to me. "A hundred and fifty bucks—cash—for the office visit," he said. "No refills on that: they're dangerous drugs. But if you need any more, you come on back and see me again." And pay another one-fifty for another office visit, I saw. It wasn't hard to figure how this worked.

I gave him the money. "Thanks, doc," I said as he walked me back to the door. Another patient was just driving up as I got on the bike again for the trip back into Morgantown.

While I pedaled my way back into town, I thought some more about Emily and what I could do for her. It didn't happen often that a human recognized me as a bigfoot; it was even less often that I didn't deny it when they said it. But if she'd been out to the Homeland, even when she was only five, there was no point in denying it. She might want to reintroduce herself to Bill Lovingood, but I wasn't exactly hopeful about the reception she'd get from him. The Lovingoods had always struck me as clannish: if you didn't live out there in their hollow, you weren't one of them, and you never would be.

Human motivations are always tough for me, and I certainly could have been wrong about it, but my best guess was that maybe she was just telling a kind of truth: she really was looking for someone to be a kind of parent figure for her. Maybe, as far as she could see it, she had two choices in front of her. One was Bill Lovingood, who might actually be her father, though she hadn't seen him or even talked to him for the better part of twenty years: almost her whole life. The other person, as far as I could figure it, was from an older generation, someone who might help her out when she needed something, who might give her advice, who might be willing to introduce her to someone who might play a role in her life—that was me. She was looking for someone to latch onto who wasn't just one of her peers. At least that's what it looked like to a bigfoot.

I'd have to be careful. It wasn't entirely crazy: she already knew a secret about me—a secret she and her mother had shared—and there was every chance that I might know a secret or two about her before this whole mess with her mother's murder was cleared up. Maybe this wasn't a really solid basis for trust, I thought, but secrets are intimate things. If she stayed in Morgantown, we'd be sure to run into each other from time to time, and every time we did, the secret would be there, between us, either as a bridge or as a barrier. I didn't know her well enough to know if I wanted that bridge, but nothing she'd done or said made me think I needed a barrier, either. If I was honest with myself, I'd seen that she was as smart as her name implied, and I knew well enough how that could make it tough to fit in. It was something I respected, in her or in anyone.

Well, we'd have to see.

When I got back into town, I rode right onto the rail-trail and headed to Sabraton. I took the prescription I'd gotten straight into the grocery store's pharmacy. The pharmacy tech at the counter looked at it and looked me over, perhaps just to make sure I was eighteen, but he said nothing. My guess was they did a good business with similar prescriptions and didn't ask too many questions. "It'll be a few minutes," he said.

I did a little shopping while I was waiting, picked up a few things Horatio might want or need, and finally made my way back over to the pharmacy counter, where the tech had me sign my name in an old-fashioned paper ledger. "Cash," I said when he handed me the little bag and asked for the payment.

"No problem," came the answer. I wondered if there ever was a problem with cash.

A few minutes later, I leaned the bike up against the porch rail at Horatio's little house again. I knocked, and I said loudly, "Hey, Horatio, open up. It's me, Jim."

It took a moment or two, but he did manage to shuffle to the door and open it up for me. "You again?" he asked. "What's this all about?"

"I brought you a few things from the store," I said, lifting up the bag to show him.

"Mel's looking out for me fine," he said. "I don't really need anything else." But he opened the screen door for me, anyway.

"I'll just put these groceries in here," I said, setting the bag down in the little kitchen. Then I came back out and pulled the prescription bag from my jacket pocket. "And I've brought you something for your aches and pains, too. Do you have a little bottle or something I can put these in?" Of course the bottle they'd given me had my name right there on the side. I didn't think there was any reason to think they'd be traced back to me if Horatio took them, but there was no point in leaving loose ends when you didn't have to. I remembered when Deb Armstrong had caught me with Nathan Lloyd's bottle.

"Yeah, I can find something," he said, heading over to a little glass-fronted china cabinet near the table. He came back with a little stemmed piece that he must have gotten when he still worked at the glass factory downtown. "Just pour 'em in here." There was something strange, I thought, strange but sweet, in seeing big old Horatio carrying a delicate little piece of blown glassware.

"You know, that was the first paying job I ever had," I said to him, "when you got me hired on in the packing department there at the factory."

"Yeah, but you didn't stay long," he answered. Some people look for the silver lining in every cloud, but there was never a day so clear that Horatio couldn't find the cloud in it.

"It was still a big favor you did me," I said. "It made the transition a lot easier than it would have been otherwise."

"It wasn't nothing," he said gruffly.

He didn't want me to say thank you, and there was no point in trying to say I wanted to pay him back for old favors: he wouldn't take either thing with any kind of good grace. "Just take the pills," I told him.

"Human pills?"

"Well, yeah, Horatio," I said, probably with some irritation in my own voice. "That's all there is, you know, unless you want me to boil you up some willow bark tea, and if that's all you have in mind, you might as well just take the aspirin Mel's been bringing."

"They probably won't work, then."

"They'll work: I've tried 'em."

"Huh," he said, peering into the little glass at the pills it held.

"I took two," I said, "and they knocked me right out. Maybe you should try out just one, at first. That's what the directions say. One tablet, every six hours, as needed." I held up the empty bottle for him to look at.

"You got a prescription? You saw a doctor?"

"He never even touched me," I said.

"You're breaking the law, giving these to me. That's a risk."

"Yeah," I said, "it's a risk." Old Horatio never could resist the temptation to lecture me on how to get along among the humans, as if I hadn't been doing it now, off and on, for the last seventy years. "A small risk," I admitted. "But if the cops come knocking on your door and ask you where these pills you're taking came from, just don't tell them. Tell them you had them left over from some dental surgery or something. There's nothing they can do: and they'll never come in here anyway, and you know it."

"You're probably right," he said, grudgingly. As if every day he lived down here wasn't a risk.

"Take one now," I suggested. "Let's see if they do help, or whether maybe you need to take two at a time."

He swallowed the pill easily enough, fetching a glass of water from his little kitchen. I helped him put away the bag of groceries, and we sat out in the front room for a while, talking now and then. "How are you feeling?" I finally asked, maybe forty minutes later.

"I don't feel much of anything," he said.

"You mean, like the pill hasn't had any effect, or like the pill has taken the aches away?"

And he gave a little half-smile. "Like maybe it's working!" he said. "I'll give these a try."

For a moment, I dreaded the possibility that I'd have to go through the whole business—doctor's visit, trip to the pharmacy—again and again. I'd do it, though, if it really helped him. I probably shouldn't have expected him to say "thank you" before I left, and of course, he didn't. But, I told myself, he meant to. Like I said, sometimes I'm not above telling a little lie, even to myself.

Back at the office, I made myself a sandwich. The bag of lettuce I had in the minifridge had gone slimy, so I threw it out without using any of it. Apparently I should have gotten some things for myself when I was at the store.

I felt odd, somehow, and it took me a while to decide that I felt uneasy with how quickly I'd found myself in the illegal prescription drug business. I wasn't selling them, though; and Horatio really needed them. But even so, he was right, it was a risk. Just a small one, I told myself: all I'd done was lie to the doctor. He'd written the prescription, and that was perfectly legitimate. Even if he was in the habit of writing prescriptions a little bit too easily, the only way it could possibly come back to me was if he got raided or something, and they went through his files and found my name. I might as well worry about the fact that Deb had seen the pill bottle with Nathan's name on it in my office. This stuff must happen all the time.

I spent most of the rest of the afternoon uselessly worrying about whether I'd taken too big a risk. I supposed, if it all blew up, I'd have to disappear. I'd be sorry to give up the Jim Foote identity, but all the same, a part of me always wanted to find a good excuse to go live in the Homeland again, even if I would have to give up almost all my stuff. Not that I could just drop everything and go. I had a job to do down here, and someone else would have to do it if I couldn't. But there wasn't anyone, really, ready to do it. Mel, maybe, though she wouldn't be happy to hear it. I was stuck with it for now, and I shouldn't be taking any risks that were too big. Well, I'd just do what I had to do. As always.

I met Emily at The Jackalope just as her shift was ending as we had planned the previous evening. She went into the back and counted out her money drawer and came back with a smile on her face.

"I'm glad you're going to go over there with me," she said.

"You haven't been, yet?"

"I have: I stopped by. But it was so overwhelming. There was all her stuff, and I just couldn't face it, really. It's so hard."

"Yeah," I answered. "Where are we going?"

"Oh," she said, stopping on the street. "She lived in a little apartment building out near the airport. I thought I'd drive. Do you need a ride?"

"I could bike over," I said. "I just figured she lived downtown. But, yeah, I could use a ride, or else you'll get there way before me."

"I'm parked over here," she said, and we started walking. There was a thoughtful look on her face. "You don't drive at all then?"

"No."

"Let me guess: no driver's license, no Social Security card, no birth certificate."

"Not ones you could really rely on. Officially, I don't exist. None of us does."

"You're off the grid! I didn't know it was even really possible."

"Well," I said, hesitating. "I have a bank account, and I have bills to pay, so I'm not really off the grid. And I'm leaving a real-enough paper trail. Well, mostly an electronic one these days."

Emily's car was barely big enough for me to squeeze into, even after I'd put the seat all the way back. But soon enough, we were headed up to the Mileground, as the area near the airport was called. It was natural enough, I told myself, that she had been thinking about me, and how I'd lived incognito. Still, I wasn't exactly comfortable going over the details with her.

"I'm heading down to Prickett's Fort tomorrow," I told her. "To the big reenactors' encampment down there. I'm hoping to run into Harlan Stephens."

"He was at the reception last evening," she said.

"Yeah, you said that. What's he like?"

"Are you investigating him?" she said, either in eagerness or surprise. At least I thought those were the two most likely possibilities.

"I haven't narrowed anyone out of the picture yet," I said. "Even you."

"Me?"

"Oh, I don't think you shot your mom," I said. "But I haven't found any proof that you didn't shoot her yet either. That's all."

"Hmm. I guess I can see that. Mr. Stephens seems like a nice enough guy. He said he liked working with my mom." She pulled the car into a parking space outside a three-story apartment building, one of the ones that might cater to the college student crowd if it were a little bit closer to campus.

I levered my way out of the car and stretched a bit. Emily got out and led me up the external stairs to the second story, opening a door about halfway along the building. There was no sign of any police tape, so she'd told the truth about having been here before. "Here we are," she said.

The apartment was filled with all the stuff that a person might own: clothes, pots and pans and dishes, a computer desk, three televisions, games, books, papers. Posters on the wall in cheap frames. "I'd log you onto her computer," she said at one point, "but the police took it."

"I doubt that I would have found anything useful there anyway," I told her. I wondered for a moment who'd done the searching: Deb Armstrong and the city police or the sheriff's deputies. Here in town, it could have been either. "I'm sure the police investigators have found everything that I would have found and more. Their experts are better at computer stuff than I am."

"What are you looking for, then?" she asked.

"I don't know. Really, as much as anything, I'm here to help you. What is it you want to get started on?"

"I don't even know where to start," she said, and I thought she seemed on the edge of breaking down. I didn't know whether I'd be better off urging her to do the hardest part first, or the easiest. "Let's start with the clothes," I finally said. "Anything you don't want to keep, we'll bag up for the Goodwill."

We worked for a while, and she was able to keep from bursting into tears, for which I was thankful. I really wasn't in a position where I felt like I could offer her any real comfort for her grief. Pretty soon it became clear that she didn't want to keep much of anything. Not much seemed to have any sentimental value to her and not much had any real monetary value either: no sterling flatware, no paintings or art. Even the TVs were older models.

"You'll probably need several trips to take all this stuff away," I said. "But it seems like you've got it pretty much in hand. The help I was telling you about? He's got a pickup truck."

"That would be useful," she said. "Who is it?"

"A young guy I met at the ramps festival," I told her. "He runs a food truck up in Pittsburgh. I doubt you know him."

"What should I do with the medicine?" she asked. "I know you're not supposed to just throw it away."

"Yeah, you can't drop that off at the Goodwill, either," I said, stepping over to the bathroom. I opened the medicine cabinet and saw the toothpaste, the hair products, and the other toiletries that anyone would have. Two or three little bottles of prescription drugs stood there, too. "These," I said, "maybe you can take them over to the hospital and see if they will dispose of them for you." I glanced briefly at the bottles, but I didn't recognize any of the drugs. But I was surprised, and a little worried, to see that all three bottles had been prescribed by Dr. Philip MacDonald.

CHAPTER 9

TUESDAY

———

I had a couple hours while traveling to think things over. I was on the bike again, headed down the rail-trail to Fairmont so I could get to Prickett's Fort where the reenactment was going to be held. If I could've gone in a straight line, I probably wouldn't have been going more than fifteen miles, but the Mon River Rail-Trail follows the river and is close to twice that distance overall. The trail is rarely crowded, except for right around Morgantown itself, and I've never seen a bear on it. At some times of the year, though, you have to watch out for the Canada geese. For most of its length, it is paved in soft cinder or limestone gravel, and you can often see stacks of decaying railroad ties piled up to one side. It was just exactly the right week to see all the wildflowers: dogtooth violets, bluebells by the millions, it seemed, trilliums, Dutchman's breeches. The green of the springtime leaves was nice, but seeing the flowers really made me long to spend more time in the woods. I wondered if I'd be able to spot a jack-in-the-pulpit.

The rail-trail passed by more than one dam on the Mon. I took a break, stopped just downstream from one of them, and watched for five minutes while a Styrofoam cooler, its hinged lid hanging wide open, floated around and around in a circle in the outflow. All the ice that would have still been on the cliff faces along the trail a month or two earlier was gone now. Groundwater oozed from the rocks all year round here and everywhere in the state, clean and pure, with literal mountainsides of filtering. But I wouldn't have wanted to swim in the Mon or eat the fish that came out of it: coal was still king in West Virginia, and in most of the state, the groundwater didn't stay very pure for long once it was on the surface.

I had searched the internet last evening for the names of the drugs we'd found in Diane Smart's cabinet: none of them was anything that was subject to abuse, though I wouldn't swear it had never been tried. One was for hypertension and another was a mild antidepressant; both were pretty widely prescribed. As far as what they were was concerned, the police would have had no reason to ever look twice at them. But what had Diane Smart been doing getting drugs from Dr. MacDonald? He didn't exactly have the kind of practice that I would have expected to dispense drugs that would actually help anyone, but I suppose even a crooked doctor will try to care for his patients.

I asked Emily if the deputies had taken any other bottles of pills from her mother's apartment, and she dug around a bit for the receipt they'd given her: they'd taken her purse and contents; her laptop, iPad, and phone; and an album of old pictures. "They're trying to see if she's got any connections to anyone they think is dangerous," I told her. But unless there had been a bottle of painkillers or other drugs in the purse, there hadn't been any medicines in what they took.

For all I knew, Philip MacDonald and Diane Smart had known each other for years, and she just thought of him as her regular doctor: there was no reason to suppose that she must have been getting painkillers from him the way I had. But it was a loose end and I knew it: if the sheriff's deputies were looking for any connections she had to dangerous individuals, surely this connection was one they'd want to know about, if they didn't already. I decided that I'd presume they'd trace the link to Dr. MacDonald from Diane Smart's phone or laptop.

That very connection, I realized to my own surprise, had now become a connection to me, a tenuous one, but one I rather hoped that the sheriff's office wouldn't actually trace or their tolerance for coincidence would be even more strained. It made me wonder, though, how Horatio was doing with the painkillers I'd given him. I hoped they worked well enough for him, even as I also hoped they didn't work *too* well. The human propensity for addiction was well known, but I knew that it could afflict bigfoot too. I wouldn't want the pills to make their way back up to the Homeland; nothing good could come of that.

But for all I knew, there might be any number of bigfoot painkiller addicts throughout the state. A handful of other Homelands were scattered throughout the mountains, and maybe the under-the-table market for pills was finding bigfoot customers as well as human ones. When you looked at the numbers of addicts published by the state, it was hard to believe how extensive the market was, even if only the human residents were concerned. I realized I should have asked Martha about it; though when she'd been down, I'd had no idea that drugs might be in the mix. Lies, though, ran right through this business. The new moonshine.

Thinking over all this, I hit what must have been the only pothole on the trail, and my front tire went flat. I was lucky I didn't bend the rim, but I didn't feel lucky. I pulled the bike over to the trailside and turned the whole thing upside down. I was able to get the tire reseated and managed to hook up the little foot pump. The thing was a piece of junk, and I practically had to hold it with my hand to keep it together while I pumped it. I probably didn't get a full charge of air into the tire, but by the time I'd had enough of the pump, it was rideable again.

It was nearly eleven when I finally made it to the entrance of Prickett's Fort. Just short of the northern stretch of Fairmont, the trail moves away from the riverside, probably because the railroad bridge over the river here is still in service. The fort is a reconstruction, though it is not too far from where the original fort stood. It is basically a wooden palisade with a couple of rough buildings inside; a real nineteenth-century homestead stands behind it. A modern visitor center, an electrified outdoor amphitheater, and a boat dock make up the rest of the park. A broad field was already filled with a couple dozen old-style canvas tents, and as I rode up the hill into sight of the fort, I imagined that if you could find an angle where the modern buildings and the parking lot and the electrical lines and the paved roads and the railroad bridges were not visible, the whole encampment might look like a scene from the nineteenth century.

The whole idea of historical reenactment must be an exercise in imagination. It is one of the greatest differences, I have always thought, between bigfoot and humans: for most bigfoot, life in the forest is life in the present, in our minds and hearts it is a kind of unchanging and eternal present. For humans, as long as I've known them, and even longer, life in the forest is life in the past. But then, West Virginia itself is a state that now lives in the past. For some humans, the past seems to be a land of endless romantic enchantment, and for some in this particular generation, that romantic imagination comes out in this kind of event: for the next day and a half, they'd be in Virginia, before West Virginia even existed. But even so, they'd probably be re-creating a Virginia without human slavery, historically accurate or not.

In an earlier generation, a similar romantic impulse had brought a whole raft of hippie homesteaders, as they were now often called. Usually these were city folks, moving to the wilds of West Virginia in the grip of a dream that they could get closer to the land to recapture the life they'd read about in Eliot Wigginton's *Foxfire* books. The marijuana many of them grew wasn't exactly a cash crop (though it sometimes was over the river in Ohio), but it was a kind of moonshine in its own way, the kind of lie the whole state seemed to want to tell itself in order to be the kind of place it needed to be.

A big banner was hanging over the entrance to the park, with an enlarged image of Merle DuPont, the controversial CEO of the PaVaMa power company pictured on it. "Corporate Sponsor," the banner said, with an empty little welcome message from DuPont printed below the name of the event and the dates; Mike Merrill's name was there too, in the fine print at the bottom. Somehow the online pages I'd seen advertising the reenactment hadn't been nearly as obvious about the PaVaMa sponsorship, but it was just like DuPont, I thought, to portray himself and his company as a benefactor of local culture and a protector of local history. It was part and parcel of the whole mythology that drove the state and all the local governments: the state—its heritage, its prosperity, its future—was built on coal. And oil. And more recently, Marcellus shale fracking. It was ironic, I thought, that the period being reenacted, before the Revolutionary War, had been a time before coal had ever been mined here. The whole encampment ought to have reminded people of a time before coal was king.

I locked up the bike in the parking lot and crossed the little paved road to the park. I paid the entrance fee, and they told me I would have to get the back of my hand stamped if I wanted to come back tomorrow. Today was largely a setup day for the battle, which would take place tomorrow morning, but since the reenactors wouldn't be fighting today, they were busy in their various roles as educators, as vendors, and as simple enthusiasts. I could see that at least one busload of school kids was already here on a field trip, and I knew that was one reason the whole thing had been scheduled for a weekday. All of us visitors were free to wander around the encampment and talk to the reenactors, go to the visitor center, or explore.

I wandered, along with everyone else. I was looking for Harlan Stephens. I finally found him at a little booth where people could join a real-time muzzleloader shooter's club, although the social-media page was being promoted, too. I hung around for a few minutes, looking over the literature they had lying out, but mostly trying to listen to the talk. Harlan Stephens, the only one behind the table, was talking to a couple of folks who looked like they'd ridden in on a motorcycle.

There was a lull, and then Harlan Stephens spoke to me. "You're Jim Foote, right?"

"Yeah," I said, uncertain about how he knew me.

"I used to work with Diane Smart," he said. "I know her daughter was real happy you found her." Happy probably wasn't the right word, but I knew what he meant. She was relieved that her mom had been found, relieved to have the uncertainty settled.

"She's a good kid, I think."

"That's what Diane always said."

He paused, but I decided to go ahead and take the conversation in my direction. "The police interviewed you, I guess," I said.

"Yeah. Everybody she knew, I suppose."

"They tell you about the murder weapon?"

"Oh yeah," he answered. "I got asked all about muzzleloaders."

"You know," I said, with what I hope he took as eagerness, "I always see on TV how they get forensics people to identify bullets and stuff. You think they can do that with muzzleloader shot?"

"I don't know," he answered. "I'd guess a lead ball would deform pretty easily on impact, but you'd think the same would be true of all lead bullets. There's no rifling in the barrel of a muzzleloader, so I don't know what there is that would leave a mark on the ball."

"Yeah—that's kind of what I figured. I guess I'll ask Deputy Bowling about it when I see him next time."

"You got interviewed, too, huh?"

"Oh, yeah. When you find the body of a murder victim, you go right to the top of the list of suspects." About now, a crowd of school kids came by. "Hey, talk to you later," I said, stepping away.

"Sure," I thought I heard him say. Why the school kids would be interested in his muzzleloader gun club, I had no idea. But it was West Virginia.

I should have expected it, but it still took me by surprise. Not a hundred yards from Harlan Stephens's setup, I found the Lovingood clan, set up pretty much like they had been up at the ramps festival. Instead of selling ramps-based food, now they were set up to give demonstrations of dutch oven cooking using real fire and coals.

There was a little crowd of school kids here, too, and I watched while Mary Lovingood whipped up a batch of folded biscuits on a board, using nothing but her hands and an old bone-handled knife. She was dressed in a vaguely historical-looking dress and apron and cap, and she used an old blue graniteware drinking cup to cut the biscuits into circles and moon-crescents, tossing them into a buttered dutch oven and then slipping the lid on before setting the whole thing right on the edge of the fire. "That's all there is to it," she said, though the kids looked like she'd done a magic trick. "I'll give you all a taste in a few minutes, if you stick around."

None of these kids looked like they'd miss that for the world: Free food! Cooked on a real fire! "Hi Mary," I said. "Is Bill around? Or Sut?"

"Jim!" she said, apparently seeing me for the first time. "Just go on around the trailer."

"Save one of those biscuits for me," I said, heading back. Bill Lovingood and Sut were sitting on folding lawn chairs under a striped awning hooked up to the top of the RV trailer. Sut had his knife out, and was working on one of the folk-art canes that he specialized in. I'd heard that he sold them as far away as the Tamarack, down in the southern part of the state. Although it was barely noon, beer bottles stood open in front of both men, standing on the closed lid of a Styrofoam cooler like the one I'd seen whirling around below the dam on the Mon.

"Gentlemen," I said, by way of greeting.

"Jim," they both said. "Sit a spell," added Sut, gesturing to another folding chair.

"I don't think I've seen you down here before," said Bill Lovingood, as I sat down on the grass; I didn't trust my weight in the rickety chair. Bill Lovingood's tone didn't seem especially friendly, I thought.

"I've been down here to Prickett's Fort," I said truthfully. "But I've never come down for one of these reenactments before."

"No need to relive the old days, I suppose," said Sut, who was shortish and stocky, sporting a white Colonel Sanders beard.

"I never realized how often you guys must get out for this kind of thing. Time was," I added, "when I thought of the Lovingoods as keeping far out of touch with the modern world. But I bet you do all right, selling at festivals and things like this."

"Huh," said Bill.

"We do all right, I guess," said Sut. He glanced at his nephew. "But we don't really need it to get along. We're still pretty self-sufficient, up at our old place."

"I'm glad to hear it," I said, though I wondered why Sut had seen the need to tell me that.

"I don't suppose you have any of that ginseng tea in the cooler," I said. I was thinking about whether or not I should mention that I might be coming out to their place with Emily Smart in a couple of days. My instinct said I shouldn't tell them, but sometimes in conversation I can't keep my own mouth shut.

"We didn't bring any here," said Bill. "Since there's guns here, we always see a few state troopers, and they like to give us a hard time whenever they can."

"Do you guys know if Mike Merrill is here?" I asked, the reference to the law bringing him to mind. I hadn't seen him so far, and as far as I knew he was still in the county jail, though it was at least possible he might have been let out on bail.

"Still in jail, I reckon," said Sut.

"He's got Billy Mayhew looking after things down here," Bill Lovingood added. "Same as up at the ramps festival."

"That sure was a strange thing with Darla Jones getting killed," I said then.

Some sort of look passed between the two men. "You think Mike really did it?" asked Bill Lovingood.

"I'm sure he was there. The nose doesn't lie, you know." Although I couldn't help reflecting that the person with the nose might draw the wrong conclusion, I didn't say that. Mike was already suggesting to the sheriff's office that they—and I—had leapt to the wrong conclusion, even without a good explanation for his having been there at the scene. I was pretty sure that when they did test the puke for DNA, it would turn out to be his. He'd probably say that he saw the body and just lost it. That he'd not seen the murder itself, or the murderer. But that wouldn't explain why he'd tried to shift the blame to me.

All I really knew was that I hadn't been arrested yet, that I hadn't even been called back in for more questions. Probably Deputies Bowling and Evans could see it as clearly as I could: if Mike had ridden in that cruiser and had only hinted to Bowling that I was the guilty party and hadn't come right out and said he'd seen me do the killing, his changing the story now didn't make much sense, except if he was trying to cover his own tracks somehow.

"I can't see who else it could have been," I said. "If it wasn't Mike, it could have been anyone at the festival, and the question would be who he is covering for and why."

"Huh," they both said, at pretty much the same time, prompting another glance between them.

"You got anything you want me to tell the deputies?" I asked. "I'm sure they'll be coming back to talk to me, soon enough."

"Nothing," said Sut Lovingood. "Nothing."

There was no point in saying to them directly that this was exactly the response I'd expect if they themselves had something to hide. I couldn't be certain they did: they might be telling the truth, they might be lying, and I might never know at all.

At this point, Mary came around the RV, a little paper plate in her hand. "I had enough biscuits left for all three of you," she said, putting the plate on top of the cooler. I picked one up and ate it, and so did the other two.

"Now that's the taste of the old days," I said, earning a smile from Mary. "I see why you guys come down here and do this."

I spent the afternoon wandering and thinking when I should have been working more seriously on the investigation. When I finally realized I was missing an opportunity, two of the things I'd come there for still hadn't gotten done: first, I had wanted to figure out if Bill Lovingood knew—or cared—that Diane Smart, the mother of his daughter, had died. Second I needed to go back and talk some more with Harlan Stephens and probably even see if I could get him to introduce me to Merle DuPont. The latter two were still on my own personal list of persons of interest for Diane Smart's murder. Her body had been found right on the proposed line of the PaVaMa easement, and it still seemed at least possible that it had been her surveying work that had brought her into danger. And coworkers came right after family and lovers when it came to murder suspects: you had to know someone pretty well before you'd want to kill them, and that was usually as true for humans as it was for bigfoot. For a bear, on the other hand, all you needed was opportunity and proximity: there was nothing personal in it at all. If Diane Smart had been killed by a bigfoot, I might be wasting my time if I was looking for a motive.

When I finally came out of my reverie, everything was winding down at the fort. The school kids had been bused away a couple hours earlier, and now most of the casual tourists and visitors had gone, too. Most parks usually closed down after dark, and sure enough, a woman in a park ranger's uniform came up to me as I was walking along the split rail fence.

"Now it's really starting to look like it must have looked two hundred years ago, don't you think?" the park ranger said.

We were facing away from the parking lots, but we could still see one of the railroad bridges over by the river. Even so, she was right, at least as far as my own imagination could tell. She went on: "Everyone's been trying to pay the bills so far today. Now's when the real reenactment begins. Everyone's out in the camps, now, and they'll be doing their best to be authentic."

"But there's almost nobody here to see it," I said.

"Well, you can't make the tourists and kids wear correct

costumes, but everyone who's staying will be dressed right," she said, looking at my tracksuit pointedly.

"Oh, yeah," I said, although I doubted that she'd be changing her outfit. "I came down on the rail-trail: I'll be heading back up toward Morgantown here in a few minutes. I'll bet it'll be pretty hard for some of these folks, though," I said, "to give up their phones and internet access until tomorrow."

"Maybe," she said. "I've always heard them say that everything outside the tents has to be authentic eighteenth century, but inside the tents, it's another story, and electronics and electricity are allowed. Maybe some of them will go whole hog anyway. Or cold turkey."

I had to laugh. I had questions to ask and suspects to quiz, but tomorrow was soon enough.

Maybe it was a foolish romanticism on my part, but I didn't really want to break up the fragile illusion of authenticity they were building so carefully for each other—and for a couple of folks with cameras, I noted—by strolling in among them in my tracksuit. So I waved to the ranger, went back up to my bike, and rode northward a few miles until I found a little cliffside with a couple big rocks that would serve as a fine temporary shelter for a bigfoot. And I tried, in my own little way, to imagine myself in another time.

CHAPTER 10

WEDNESDAY

———

Is it wrong of me to admit that I woke up sore and aching from my night under the clouds and stars? I hadn't packed the hammock, even though I knew that I wouldn't sleep as well without it. But still, I had forgotten how very hard the rocky ground could be. Even when I had stayed up in the Homeland last, when I'd visited Martha, I had slept in a kind of bigfoot nest, which had not been as comfortable as Martha's hammock but had still been a place made for sleeping. The spot I had chosen last night, while out of sight of the trail, just hadn't been as comfortable, period.

Fortunately, my bike tire had not yet lost all its air and I didn't need to use the pump this morning. I was hungry, and in need of coffee, so I rode down into Fairmont proper, looking for a breakfast place. Coffee, a couple of fried eggs, a tall stack of pancakes—that would hold me for a while. The reenactment itself wasn't scheduled to start until ten, and even then, from what I could tell, it was going to take at least a couple of hours. It would be late afternoon at the earliest before I'd be getting back to Morgantown.

Emily Smart had sent me a text saying Friday was good for her if I still wanted to help her clear the rest of the stuff out her mom's place. I texted her back and confirmed, and I reminded her that tomorrow we'd planned to go visit the Lovingoods. I texted Seth Jones and told him to meet me at my office at ten o'clock on Friday morning and to remember to bring the pickup. There was the rest of my week all sorted out, I realized. Even so, it hardly seemed a good plan for making any progress on finding Diane's killer. But I couldn't exactly feel bad about doing favors for Emily or deny I felt very protective of her: I've always been a sucker for youngsters with nowhere to turn. But I also couldn't see myself making much progress on her case unless something unexpected happened today at the reenactment, which didn't seem likely at all. I still had more ideas about what might have happened than I wanted. What I needed was something that would let me focus in and eliminate some of the possibilities.

I didn't know if I'd be able to wrangle my way into a conversation with Merle DuPont today or not, but I'd have to try. It still seemed important to ask him about why he'd been at the memorial for Diane Smart. As far as I could figure, he shouldn't have been there. Her boss, sure; her boss ought to have been there. But her boss's boss's boss? Everything odd is worth investigating when you don't have any other leads.

When I finally made my way back to Prickett's Fort for the reenactment, though, I saw that I'd probably never get to talk to him today. The rangers were handing out a little program that described the battle and the setup for it to the visitors and tourists, several dozen of us. The role of George Washington, as I might have guessed, was being played by DuPont himself. When your company sponsored the event, I realized, you could choose your own role, though Washington had been in his early twenties at Jumonville Glen, and DuPont was well over fifty. So much for historical authenticity.

I could see him already, in the distance, an anachronistic white

146

wig on his head like an English barrister. The colonials were all dressed in buckskins, some fringed like refugees from the 1960s or like the university's Moonshiner mascot. Some were a bit more practical. The French were nowhere in sight at the moment, but the program indicated they'd probably be dressed like eighteenth-century French regulars, not too different from what I'd seen Sean Bean's various opponents wearing in the *Sharpe* series on TV. The only action that seemed to be going on when I got to the park was campsites being cleared and tents being taken down. According to the program, they'd be packing everything with them using a couple of horses and mules.

Eventually, the beasts were loaded, and the whole troop moved down to the creek and stumbled across at the ford, really not that far from where the creek emptied into the Mon. Once they were across, we were all allowed to move up to the creek side; the engagement was going to be just across the little waterway where we could see the action. A couple of photographers dressed in buckskins were moving among the reenactors, filming with their phones, it looked like. Soon enough, everybody was pointing, and a scout came running back, presumably to report that the French had been spotted.

Guns were pulled out of saddlebags and brought down from human backs, too. It looked like every single colonist was loading up: pouring black powder in, tamping it down with a bit of wadding, pretending to slip in a leaden musket ball, then tamping it down, too. Some of the reenactors, it was obvious, were more practiced than others, but even the quickest took a surprisingly long time to go through this process. This was one of those moments when something you know intellectually becomes so much more real when you see it in person: if the French had had modern weapons, the battle would have been over even before the colonists were loaded up and ready to fire.

Diane Smart, I realized, had been shot by someone she knew and knew well enough to trust at some level. With a modern gun, you could aim and shoot before someone could really dodge, but unless you had a musket ball all primed and tamped down in a muzzleloader, there was no such thing as an accidental or spontaneous gunshot, much less rapid fire. And Diane Smart had been shot from the front, facing her killer. Seeing these reenactors do their thing was already making me rethink the whole crime: this was no case of a surveyor being shot by some backwoods crank defending his land—or his patch of marijuana—from a sneaking outsider. She had faced down her killer, daring them to shoot her, probably never believing that they would. It eased my mind a bit to realize that Diane Smart would probably not have trusted a bigfoot that way. If she knew us well enough to always recognize us, that is.

Eventually, the guys portraying the French came within shooting range, and there was a flurry of firing, and slow reloading, and firing once again. Huge clouds of gray smoke rose from the two little groups, and eventually the French cried out for a halt, and we could see some kind of brief ceremony of surrender taking place, with "George Washington" accepting a word of parole from the surviving French lieutenant. Then it was all done, and the wounded or dead on both sides stood up and shook hands with one another, pounding each other on the back. A meeting of old friends, probably.

I didn't know what else I should have expected. Of course, the reenactment couldn't go on and on to what followed after this battle—to setting up a new camp, to taking prisoners and guarding them or letting them go, to reporting back to various higher-ups in the English and French armies, and to starting a new Seven Years War. These people all had lives to get back to, work to return to tomorrow, after two days off in the middle of the week.

And strange as the whole exercise seemed to me, they must have been having fun, meeting up with old friends and making new ones.

I stuck around for a while. The spectators who'd watched with me began milling around with the reenactors after they all waded back across the creek. There was a little station where spectators could sign up to get emails about future reenactments and even to join some sort of society where they could participate if they wanted to. Harlan Stephens spoke to me again while slipping a copy of the paperwork into my hands whether I wanted it or not. "If we can get enough people together," he told me, "we can plan even more complex engagements. And a lot of us always get together and go to Gettysburg every year, you know. There's a lot of interest in the Civil War."

"Thanks," I said, uncertainly. "I don't really see myself as a re-enactor."

He looked me up and down. "I could see you as a kind of Daniel Boone–type woodsman," he said. "Simon Kenton, maybe. Or Paul Bunyan."

"Yeah, I don't think so," I answered. I didn't want to know what made him think of those three, when he looked at me. One of them wasn't even a real person. But I didn't think I'd have a better chance to raise one of the subjects that was on my mind. "I think I saw Merle DuPont at Diane Smart's memorial."

"Yeah, I talked to him," Stephens said.

"I was surprised to see a CEO making the effort."

To this Harlan Stephens offered a little laugh. "Oh, the three of us go a long way back," he said. "Went a long way back, I guess."

"Yeah?"

"Merle and I went to high school together," he told me. "Good old Tunnelton High. Diane was a little younger, and she lived over the border in Mon County. But I knew her family."

"And you both worked for DuPont?"

"Sure. Everybody's got to work for somebody."

I didn't point out that DuPont worked only for himself. There was nothing in Harlan Stephens's words or manner, I thought, that suggested anything odd or unusual, but he could have been lying, in one way or another, as far as I knew. Even as he was telling me this, I realized that I wouldn't get any kind of different tale out of DuPont. It was too easy to check: Tunnelton High was probably gone now because of the consolidation of the schools in Preston County, but the records would be somewhere, and probably a phone call could confirm what Stephens was saying. What it might mean was another question.

The bike tire was still holding air when I got on again for the ride back up to Morgantown. What Harlan Stephens had told me about his relationship with Merle DuPont had all my attention. My instinct told me that this was one coincidence too many, and I wondered what Deputies Evans and Bowling would make of it.

But as I rode back up the trail, I started to look at it differently. The truth was, it was a small world here in West Virginia, and all sorts of folks might have all sorts of connections: connections to one another, connections to Diane Smart, connections to me, for that matter. None of those connections made them criminals or murderers. I could spend a lifetime—a bigfoot lifetime— trying to track down everyone who had some link to her, but there had to be a way to pare things down. And something was nagging at the back of my mind about the Lovingoods. I wondered suddenly whether the Lovingood homestead was in Mon County or in Preston County. The Homeland was close enough to the border between the two that their holler could be in either. Bill and Diane would also have been fairly close in age, I thought.

Maybe I could sort those things out for certain tomorrow when I went up there with Emily.

Thinking about Emily and her father reminded me of what I was hiding from the deputies. The very thought helped me focus a bit. If my links to Diane Smart and to Darla Jones had made them take a second look at me, they'd also look a lot closer at Bill Lovingood if they realized that he was Emily's father. Or if I told them he was, for that matter. I could probably hold that little detail in reserve if I needed to set the dogs onto some trail other than my own at some point. It wasn't honest to hold it back, but I could always say that Emily and I had talked about it and that I'd been under the impression that she'd told them herself. I'd hate to put her in that spot, and it wasn't really fair to her, but it was good to have something in reserve, even if focusing the deputies' attention on Bill wasn't a nice thing to do.

I eased my mind by telling myself that things were sure to be somewhat clearer after she and I went out there tomorrow. I'd meant to try to get a street address for the Lovingoods when I'd seen them, but I had forgotten, and by now I was halfway back to Morgantown. I was sure we could find the place anyway. At least I hoped we could.

Was it possible, I asked myself, that the two killings really were connected? There had been a lot of time between them: Diane Smart had been missing for the better part of a month before the ramps festival. There was nothing similar at all about the ways these women had been killed, but they were two of a kind, in some ways: both single mothers of adult children, one kid each. Surely, Bill couldn't also be Seth Jones's father. It seemed clear now that I'd probably need to ask Seth to tell me a bit more about his mom. Or maybe all the similarities were just coincidences, the kind of small-world parallels that I kept reminding the deputies could always happen. The kind that, in the end, didn't mean a thing.

That left me nowhere at all, so I spent a good part of the ride asking myself if Mike Merrill really was the one who'd killed Darla Jones. There were only two possibilities: either he had killed her, or he hadn't. In either case, there had to be an explanation for what he'd done in the aftermath—waking me up in the first place, showing me the scene, driving off to fetch the sheriff's deputies, and then pointing the finger at me. If he was guilty, the details all made sense. He'd made sure I had a chance to put my fingerprints—yes, bigfoot have them, too—all over the scene, and of course everyone had seen her sitting at my picnic table. If he hadn't killed her, I supposed there were two more possibilities: either he knew who had done it, or he didn't. If he didn't know, he'd done everything just about right, except maybe for hinting that I'd done it. And asking for a lawyer just when he had. And barfing at the scene and not admitting it.

If he had seen whoever had done it, he must be very scared of them now. Maybe he was even intimidated enough to assume that Big Jim Foote could take care of himself and that it was safer to point a finger at me than it was to name the real killer. But who in the world had been at the ramps festival that could be so intimidating?

It was also possible, I reminded myself as I pedaled along, that one or both of these poor women had been killed for who they'd slept with, or who they'd wanted to sleep with, or who they hadn't wanted to sleep with. Of course, I hadn't slept with Darla Jones, but she'd talked and laughed with me long into the night, and anyone who'd been at the ramps festival could probably guess what she'd been thinking. There were humans and bigfoot both who found cross-species sex attractive, even addictive. The best explanation I'd ever heard for it had been from a bigfoot who had told me that when she was with a human male, she knew—if only for a short time—that the two of them were thinking and feeling the same things, or close enough, anyway, to make a true connection. There was a yearning, she'd said, that only sex with a human could fulfill, because all the rest of the time, their thoughts and their feelings lay just out of reach. It was the flip side, she'd told me, of why we kept ourselves apart: there was a chasm between us that couldn't normally be bridged. But it felt like it could be during sex. Or so she'd said.

I'd lived enough history, and I'd seen enough stories on TV, to know that a human female who could feel such a thing, who wanted to feel such a thing, might well be killed by the human males around her, a kind of deadly punishment that was driven by motives I'd never clearly understand. The human psychologists seemed to think in terms of anxieties over purity, anger over rejection, and a desire for power over others, but those feelings didn't really match anything I had ever felt. And there it was right there: that unbridgeable chasm. I could see the situation in my mind, read the words the psychologists wrote, and even understand them as words. I still had no clear idea what it would feel like to want to kill someone for any such thing, but it obviously happened, among the humans at least, all over the world, and it had happened here in the US, driven by American race prejudice, and probably by other things, too.

Could sexual jealousy, possibly inflected by racism or speciesism (as Emily had named it), have killed Darla Jones? If so, I'd have to seriously consider Bill Lovingood as her killer; Emily had also claimed he called my people "biggies," after all. Of course, I'd briefly considered him as a suspect first thing, before I'd discovered the ramp-less puke, which had pointed so convincingly to Mike Merrill. I remembered all over again that Darla Jones had made it clear enough that Bill Lovingood had been pursuing her at the ramps festival, even while his wife was sitting there with the rest of the clan. I'd known enough of the Lovingoods over the years to know some of them could carry a mean grudge. But Bill was surely not the only one at the festival who'd seen her chatting me up. Could Bill really have intimidated Mike so thoroughly? I'd have said he was a jerk, but not a threat.

What about Diane Smart? She was the reason I was thinking of Bill Lovingood at all. Emily had told me that her mother had broken things off with Bill after she found out he'd taken Emily out to the Homeland. The way Emily had put it, it seemed like she'd been angry about him introducing their daughter to us bigfoot. But Emily couldn't have been more than four or five years old when it happened, and her understanding of the emotional dynamics of that time might be very far off indeed. The anger, that was something that she probably remembered correctly, and she probably remembered it being directed toward Bill, but the reasons for that anger might have been caused by almost anything. I didn't think Emily had lied to me, though that was always possible, but there might well have been things about her mother that she had no idea about. One of those things, I guessed again, was a secret that had gotten her killed.

I knew it would be a disaster for me if both women's links to bigfoot were the motives that lay behind their deaths. Whatever else happened, I couldn't tell the sheriff's deputies that the motive for any crime was prejudice against the bigfoot. I would have to come up with some other motive, some other explanation, a purely human motive, which would probably be easier if I had a better understanding of human motives in the first place. Regular old human jealousy might be good enough, I hoped, though even that would put me uncomfortably close to the center of Darla Jones's case. But I had to think about these things: I needed to be ready if an explanation was needed. Although I still hoped to figure out what was really going on before the sheriff's deputies did, they might find some piece of evidence I knew nothing about and might put it all together before I did.

Of course, I could still be barking up the wrong tree entirely. Maybe it would be a good idea for me, when I took Emily out to the Lovingood homestead tomorrow, to try to take Mary aside and talk to her when Bill wasn't around. She might not want to tell me anything, but I figured I needed to try. And I'd probably need to remind Emily, before we even went out there, that Bill still hadn't been ruled out as a suspect. Certainly not by me, and maybe not by the sheriff's office, either. She needed to know that so she could take care of herself, just in case it turned out that she needed to.

All of this was a lot to think on, and it was nothing to put me into any kind of good mood, but at least if there was only a single killer, maybe that really meant no bigfoot had done the killing. Maybe, if I was right, I could scratch them off the list of suspects.

For a second or two, I thought things might be looking up, but then, halfway back home up the rail-trail, it started to rain.

The rain had pretty much stopped by the time I got back to my office though my tracksuit was soaked right through by then. One of the sheriff's cars was parked just up the street from my place. Not a stakeout, I guessed, but someone looking to talk to me. Not an arrest, or they would probably have brought two cars.

Deputy Evans stepped out of the car, putting one of the sheriff's oddly stiff hats on his head. He strolled over as I was making my way from the storage shed where I kept the bike to the front door. "Deputy," I said to him. "How's the investigation?"

"Which one?" he asked, and I guessed that they were having some of the same doubts I'd been having. There really were too many coincidences, and there was no question that I was linked into the coincidences all too clearly. I knew that they'd be talking to me more.

"Well, I was thinking of the Diane Smart case," I answered simply. "Come in, sit down."

He did, taking the big old hat off again as he came through the door and then balancing it on his knee when he sat. I left the soaking tracksuit on and sat in my chair behind the desk. "Cheese puff?" I asked, pulling the bag from the drawer.

He looked at me as if I was out of my mind. "Those things are terrible for you," he said.

"Yeah, I suppose." I didn't see that there was any reason for me to get down to business. He was the one who had come to visit me. "They taste good, though."

He must have agreed, since he took a handful for himself. "Look, Foote," he began. "I'll be straight with you. The accusations that Mike Merrill is making don't hang together all that well, but at this point, there's probably as good a case against you as there is against him. We're probably going to have to let him go."

"What happened to the case?" I asked. "You know that barf was his."

"Yeah, yeah. Everybody knows the barf was his. Now he's saying he threw up after he found the body, and that he didn't see anything else at all. He thought it was you that killed her at first, but now he doesn't know. He panicked: he made some mistakes, told some lies, maybe, but now he's telling the truth. You made some mistakes too, as you probably know, and if we wanted, we could claim you were trying to deflect the blame away from yourself."

"Huh," I said. "Is he telling the truth now?"

"He might be. But it doesn't matter if I think he is or not if a jury won't be able to tell."

"No prints on the hatchet, then."

"Nope. Darla Jones's, but nothing else we could use." We sat looking at each other for a minute, but he spoke before I did. "You got anything else you can tell us, any new ideas about either case?"

"You don't think there's any connection, do you?" I asked, fishing.

"Just you, at the moment," he said. Whether I was supposed to take this as a threat of some kind or not was not clear to me at all. But it did seem to suggest that they hadn't yet figured out that Emily Smart's father was Bill Lovingood.

"Well," I answered slowly, considering. "I didn't kill either one of them. You probably won't believe me, but I've never fired a gun in my life, though I probably could if I had to." Just as well, I thought, that I hadn't made it up to the candy shop/gun store yet to test fire one of theirs. To make the point even more firmly, I held my hand up so he could get a good look at my thumb and fingers. "I'm not sure I could hold a gun right and fire it, regardless," I added, "but an old-fashioned muzzleloader sure isn't where I'd start, if I were going to learn to use a gun now."

Now it was his turn to say "Huh." He looked, considering. "But you could have held Darla Jones's hatchet." It wasn't really a question.

"Yeah, I could," I said. "I can do a lot of things, but I'm better with lifting heavy things than I am with squeezing and fine control. That big old bicycle of mine even has old-fashioned coaster brakes, you know."

"Why didn't you tell us this before, about your hands?"

"Tell you what?" I asked, serious. "That my hands have been this way since I was born? Most of the time I don't even think about it myself." I usually hated to call attention to the hands, but it seemed like I needed to convince Evans that I really shouldn't be taken seriously as a suspect. I needed them to look less closely at me, rather than more. It was ironic that now I was literally giving him a close look at my hands.

"I can see that, I suppose," he said, nodding.

"Look," I said to him then, "I am as interested in seeing that whoever killed these two is brought to justice as you guys are, whether it was one killer or two. Is there any kind of question you can't ask, any rock you want me to try to turn over for you? I am a professional investigator, after all."

He looked as if he was considering the offer but then just shook his head.

"You know," I said then, "I just came back up from Fairmont, riding the bike, and it gave me a lot of time to think. Morgantown's a funny place, I decided."

"Yeah?"

"Yeah. Everybody knows everybody else. If I told you to go talk to Hobo Joe and Kenny Hetrick, my guess is you'd know exactly who I mean."

"Yeah, I know 'em both, at least to pick them out on the street."

"I'm not saying you should talk to either of them, I just mean it as an example. If something happened to those two guys, do you have any idea how many people you might identify as being a connection between the two of them? I'm pretty sure they move in different circles, as much as anyone can in a small town. But that's just the thing about Morgantown: it's small. It would be more of a surprise if you didn't find some kind of link between Diane Smart and Darla Jones. Besides the fact that both their names start with D."

"And?"

"Well, I just mean that if you find some connection between the two of them, it may not mean anything at all: not everyone who knew them both needs to be considered a suspect, for instance. Including me, I suppose. I'll tell you the truth, the one truth that's most important to me in all of this: I didn't kill either of them." Of course, I'd say the same if I were lying to him, and I couldn't count on him being able to see the truth somehow in my expressive bigfoot face. "All the same," I went on, "I am starting to wonder if the two cases aren't related somehow."

"You got anything more than a hunch?" Evans asked.

"You mean like the fact that Mike Merrill was the person in charge of the concessions down at the Prickett's Fort reenactment this week, or that Harlan Stephens was there, as was Merle DuPont, and that I also saw Stephens and DuPont talking together at Diane Smart's memorial service?"

He looked startled. They were all the right names to get his attention. "I don't think there's necessarily anything to any of those things," I said. "Morgantown's just a small world, like I was saying. And Stephens told me that he had known DuPont and Diane Smart ever since he was in high school. It's a perfectly reasonable explanation. But there's a flip side to the fact that Morgantown is a small place. Maybe one reason to guess that the cases might be related is that it's hard to believe you've got two killers to catch at the very same time."

"Could be a coincidence."

"Yep. Could be. Doesn't mean it is." I didn't mention that I had just flip-flopped on my own claims about the significance of coincidences, and he didn't call me on it, either.

"Hmm," he said, sitting quietly for a moment, before reaching for another couple of cheese puffs. "I'll pass this along to Deb Armstrong and Deputy Bowling," he finally said. "We'll see what there is to see. But if you have any more ideas, or you see anything else that fits these two women together, you let us know right away, all right?"

"Of course," I said, lying to him already. The identity of Emily

Smart's father, I seemed to have decided, was her secret to tell, not mine.

He dusted the orange cheese powder off his hands, and looked down at his hat, and I could almost see the wheels of his thoughts turning. Not all the cheese powder had come off his hands, and if he picked up his hat, there was a chance it would rub off onto the hat, and that simply wouldn't do. I reached behind myself to pull a tissue from the box on the file desk, and handed it to him silently.

"Thanks," he said, using the tissue in one hand to carefully place the hat on his head, then wiping his hands more carefully. "Keep us posted."

Later, I got online and ordered the lemon chicken from one of the Chinese food delivery restaurants and waited for it to arrive. I couldn't decide if the two whole days I'd spent riding down to Fairmont and back had been a waste of my time or not. Somehow, my thinking about what was going on had changed, but when I tried to put my finger—or my thumb—on just what evidence I'd come across that made me change my ideas, I couldn't quite do it. The feeling that something had changed made me very worried. I'd had the feeling before, and it usually worked out without causing me any problems. But not always.

I spent some time on the web, looking at maps and satellite photos of the area, trying to figure out some route Emily and I could take to get out to the Lovingood homestead tomorrow morning. It should have been easy, but they were nearly as far off the map as the bigfoot Homeland. The dirt tracks that led to their homestead weren't on any of the maps, and they didn't really show up in the satellite images, either, which had been taken when the trees were all leafed out. I thought maybe we'd start by going out toward Arthurdale and coming back to their place from that direction, but even so, I knew it might take me more than one try to find the right way to get there. Traveling by road wasn't always the most direct way, as I knew well enough.

I sent Emily a text to confirm that she'd pick me up at ten. Shortly after that, my lemon chicken arrived; I'd already paid online, but I gave the driver four dollars as a tip. I used a fork, never having gotten the hang of chopsticks. Every time I'd tried with my bigfoot hands, I'd never had any success.

CHAPTER 11

THURSDAY

———

After three tries and a lunch break in which we consulted the maps all over again, we finally found the right unpaved turnoff from the road. It was already midafternoon, and from this turnoff, we still had one more turn to navigate to reach the Lovingoods' long and winding tree-covered drive. Emily had a GPS unit stuck to the dash, and even I laughed to see the little animated map showing the car just floating there against a gray background, not a single road anywhere to be seen on the "map" it showed. I spent most of my time looking out the windows, trying to see in every direction at once, still not any more certain that we were on the right track than the GPS unit was.

"Holy shit!" Emily said all of a sudden, slamming on the brakes and bringing the car to a sudden stop. I looked forward to see one of the younger Lovingood cousins, I think it was Joshua, pointing a rifle our way.

"It's all right," I told her. "Keep the car running." Then I got slowly out of the car and shouted toward Joshua: "Hey man, it's just me, Jim Foote. We're just coming up to have a little talk with your Uncle Bill."

The rifle shifted a little, now only pointing in our general direction, rather than in our specific direction. "Who's with you?"

"Well, you probably don't know her," I said, "but she's one of your cousins. Probably best to let us come on up."

Joshua looked suspicious, but he put the gun down, leaning it against a tree, and waved us forward. There was a brightly colored folding lawn chair by the side of the trail, and it looked like Joshua had been spending his time carving walking sticks, the kind you can buy at just about any tourist shop in the mountains. Mostly they were just sticks; Joshua had left the bark mostly on them and had drilled a hole through the top where a leather thong would go. Around the top, he'd stripped the bark off, and it looked like he was carving a rudimentary face in the exposed wood. These sticks didn't take much talent, but if he had the patience to keep at it, he might eventually become a respected folk artist like his great-uncle Sut. "Take the left-hand branch," he said when the car drew up. "Everybody's probably up to the main house, I'd guess."

The whole hollow, of course, was the Lovingood homestead, but over the generations, at least three or four different houses and cabins had been built, in addition to various other structures. There were always a few kids, and I'd always heard they were raised by the whole village of Lovingoods, eating and sleeping and staying in whichever house they fit into most easily. A bigfoot was always raised by their mama, but there still seemed to be something attractive in the Lovingood way, though I'd always heard the Lovingood kids were just about always in trouble of one kind or another once they went away to school. Some dropped out, and some never came back to the hollow. Some, probably, did both.

I looked over at Emily as she drove us up the narrow track toward the main house. At least for today, she was one Lovingood

163

kid who was coming back, even if I didn't know what sort of reception she'd get.

The drive ended in a kind of informal driveway circle. Three cars were already in it, as was the aging RV that'd I'd seen at the ramps festival and at Prickett's Fort. I told Emily to go ahead and pull around them all, and to find or make a spot at the end of the circle, so the car would be ready to go when she was. "We might as well go on in and see 'em," I told her.

"Would he really have shot us?" she asked, finally.

"I doubt it. You'll probably get a chance to ask him later, but my guess is the gun wasn't even loaded and might not even be functional. If you keep a rifle outside almost every day and don't expect to ever really need it, it's probably easiest to just use a decoy. He probably had a handgun in case there was a real emergency."

"That's not exactly reassuring," she said.

"He's just making sure people who are lost don't ramble this way by accident. It's kind of a game the Lovingoods like to play, I think: the role of the eccentric country hillbilly. But really, they're just good country people. If you were a stranger, and your car broke down here, or if you were in some kind of trouble, you'd probably be treated better here than if your car broke down in Pittsburgh," I said. "They'd give you what help they could, probably even feed you, and send you on your way." I didn't go any further, but I couldn't help but reflect on how this was probably different from the reception she'd get from Ezra if she ended up where he stood guard.

"Hmm," she said, and I didn't think she sounded like she was convinced. "Let's find out," she said. "The car hasn't broken down, but I do feel like I'm in trouble."

"Fair enough," I said. I'd never have phrased it that way, but

I wouldn't say she was wrong. We opened the car doors and stepped out.

Side by side, we walked up the wide steps to the porch on the big house. It was a big two-over-two brick house, twice the size of Horatio's. It had probably been built about the time of the Civil War with bricks baked right here on site. I had noticed a satellite dish tucked up on one wall when we were driving in. That hadn't been there that last time I'd been out here, but I couldn't say I was surprised to see it. Once we were on the porch, I knocked, and a voice called out from inside, "C'mon in!" I thought it was Sut Lovingood's voice.

It was Sut, I saw, once I'd grown a little used to the interior darkness. A TV was on in one corner of what used to be called the parlor, and Sut occupied a recliner, though it wasn't reclined at the moment. Bill Lovingood was there, on a nearby couch, and Mary hovered nearby, along with two cousins or brothers—they were hard to tell apart, and I always figured they liked it that way. Hank and Thomas, I thought. Probably everyone had gathered in here when they heard the car coming up the drive; I couldn't imagine they hung out together like this all the time. "Jim Foote," Sut Lovingood said, making sure everyone knew just who I was, while I was still looking around. "What brings you out, and who's this you've brought us?"

"This is Diane Smart's daughter, Emily," I said, glancing Bill Lovingood's way. "And she's got a right to be here, I think, since she's also Bill's daughter."

"Little baby Emily, all growed up," said Sut, and I could see that everyone's eyes went to her, including his. There was a momentary silence, but Sut Lovingood was nodding. "You've got some of her look," he said to Emily. Sut's words reinforced just how long Emily had been away. I wasn't sure how to understand his comment about her resemblance to her mom, though. Maybe his memory was just that sharp, or maybe they'd all been reminded of her recently.

"Thanks, I think," said Emily. It looked for a moment as if she was going to stop there, but then she pursed her lips and went on. "I—I suppose you all might know that my mother died recently; I was only a little girl the last time I was out here, I know, but I thought—I don't know, I thought I should come up here and reintroduce myself." She looked around, while I mentally kicked myself for not pointing him out to her.

Before I could say anything, though, old Sut himself had spoken. "This is Bill here on the couch," he told Emily. "And of course, you're always welcome here. I'm right glad that Jim here knew us well enough to bring you on out." I wasn't sure, but I suspected he was asking himself why I hadn't mentioned her when I'd seen them at the reenactors' camp. "Course we remember you."

Emily gave what looked to my eyes like a shaky smile. She turned her head, looking around the room probably trying to gauge just how much welcome any of the others had for her and not being very reassured by what she saw. Bill certainly wasn't doing his part, I could tell, and I had to wonder if Mary had ever heard that Bill even had a daughter.

It seemed like Sut was seeing pretty much the same things I was seeing, and he levered himself up out of his chair with one of his own canes. "Come on, everyone," he said, once he was on his feet, "Bill and Emily here have some catching up to do, I think, and we don't need to sit here watching them like some reality TV show. Jim," he said to me, "I'd like a word or two. The rest of you, I'm sure there's someplace you can be."

I'd never gotten in very far from the door, and I was the first one out. I waited on the porch. Sut was the last of the Lovingoods to come out of the door, and he closed it firmly enough, giving Emily and her estranged father as much privacy as he could. I had seen Mary come out with a look on her face—anger? sadness? fury?— and I wondered if I had lost any chance to talk to her privately today.

"Let's, uh, let's sit a bit under the old maple here," he said to me, heading down the stairs and taking my agreement for granted. "You can start by telling me how you knew to bring Emily out here to us."

There were a couple rough Adirondack chairs under the tree, green paint mostly flaked away, and Sut fell into one, though I thought it was low for him. The one I was in was certainly low for me. But he seemed to know what he was doing. "She ask you to find her dad?" he asked further.

"No, it was her mom. She asked me to find her mom."

"And it turned out Diane was dead."

"Yeah."

"You know who killed her?" he asked. Before I could answer, he waved his hand at me. "Don't get anxious, now. We know she was killed; read it in the paper, you know."

"Yeah," I said. "It's a mess. I don't know who killed her, and neither does the sheriff, though they're probably trying their best to fit it to me, despite my best efforts to convince 'em otherwise."

"You?" he said, with what I thought might be genuine surprise.

"I found the body, you know. And you know I was there when Darla Jones was killed up at the ramps festival, too."

"Huh," he said. It was one of those words that I knew could mean almost anything to a human. I used it that way myself, of course. He probably said it just to let me know he had heard me, and we both sat silently for a minute or two, thinking. Eventually, he spoke again. "You know, Jim, I think I'm glad you came out here for this visit. I might have a bit of work for you; I don't quite know yet. But I'm mighty glad you brought little Emily out here: we lose too many of the younger ones these days."

"It happens all over the state, from what I hear. Young folks don't want to stay where there's no jobs anymore."

"True, true."

"Emily always knew Bill was her father, I guess," I said, trying to answer his earlier question. "She and her mom just always pretended he was in Texas."

Sut gave a little bark of a laugh. "Wishful thinking, I suppose," he said.

I didn't think I wanted to follow that up, so I shifted focus slightly. "Emily was under the impression, I think, that her mother was angry with Bill for introducing her to the bigfoot and taking her up into the Homeland."

"Well," he said slowly. "That could be. But unlike my Julie, Diane always said she could never live up here, and Bill told her he'd never move down into Morgantown. Could be that she was just looking for an excuse to cut it off entirely." I'd been there when Sut had first met Julie Rogers, thirty some years before down in Calhoun County.

"I was sorry to hear about Julie," I told him. She had died several years earlier.

"It was the smoking that got her," Sut told me. "Lung cancer."

"That must have been hard."

"We had our share of laughs. When Diane wouldn't move out here for Bill, it made me appreciate what Julie had done even more."

"Yeah," I said. "I told Emily when we were driving out here today that there was no way to be sure that Bill would want to have her in his life on any kind of ongoing basis. I've got no idea what he thinks of this." I'd also reminded her that he was still on the list of possible suspects for her mother's murder, but I didn't think I should say so to Sut.

"Sure, sure. He's got a temper, you know, but they'll work something out, I think, and they don't need either of us in there looking over their shoulders." He was silent a moment. "Who do you think did kill Diane?"

"To tell you the truth, I haven't ruled anyone out yet," I answered. "You hear about the weapon?"

"She was shot, the paper said."

"That's true, as far as it goes," I answered. "But she was shot with a muzzleloader, which is why I was down at the reenactment camp at Prickett's Fort. There can't be too many of them around." I wasn't about to tell him that we still had one or two up in the Homeland, though he might actually already know.

"Well," he said, "far as I know, we only go down there to make a few dollars; none of us are reenactors."

That had been his chance to tell me whether or not they had muzzleloaders here in the hollow and he'd let it go by. "I got the impression the reenactors were city people, mostly," I said. "People who don't already live out in the woods."

"More'n likely," he said. "You know, Jim," he went on, "I was thinking after we saw you the other day that you might have actually met my granddad, back in the days when he ran the still."

I almost laughed. "I was thinking the same thing," I said, "when I tasted Mary's biscuits. Took me right back there."

"That was all done with, before I was old enough to know him. Now, instead of selling moonshine to make ends meet, we sell ginseng tea and ramp cookies." I wasn't sure, but I thought he meant the comparison to suggest that things hadn't changed for the better. "And I do manage to sell a few canes," he added. "All of us do one thing or another—and often enough, two or more things—to make enough to get by."

I couldn't see where he was headed yet, but I figured I should just let him get there in his own time.

"For my granddad, breaking the law by running a little still was just good economic sense. A little moonshine never hurt nobody."

I didn't figure he really needed me to contradict him. He surely knew that alcohol had, indeed, been known to hurt people. But suddenly I wondered whether there was a logic to what he was saying. "You know," I said, "my grandpappy once told me he'd met some of the guys who were behind the Whiskey Rebellion. Running a still is an old, old tradition in these parts."

"That it is, but some of these youngsters are too busy with homebrewing to be running any still nowadays. Though I will say, some of the hops they've started growing up here is mighty good. Last year, they even sold some to a microbrewery down in Clarksburg."

"Every little bit helps, I'm sure."

"That it does, mostly." He put his hands up on the end of his cane and used it to lever himself up out of the low chair. I got up from my own to lend him a hand, but he managed it on his own before I could get to him. "I can still get around, even if it's not as good as I used to. Let's take a little stroll."

So we did. The Lovingood houses ranged from log-built, to brick, to mobile, though each tended to be in a little grassy clearing in the woods. Chickens and a few ducks wandered freely; in the winter, I supposed they'd be in a henhouse or something. Fifty years ago, they'd still kept a few milk cows up here, but now it was too easy for one or another of them to get into town for milk and butter and ground beef to make it worth the effort. I'd seen Mary at the same grocery store in Sabraton that I shopped at once or twice.

A well-worn network of paths connected the various buildings, and Sut led me uphill toward what looked like a burning pile: out here where there was no regular trash pickup, anything that the Lovingoods didn't want to recycle or haul back into town ended up on the burning pile. Eventually, most of the stuff they threw out would burn or rust away up here: this pile must have been a feature of the Lovingood place for just about forever. I gave a little laugh, thinking that one of Sarah Lloyd's archaeologist colleagues would probably love to conduct a dig there. Without saying a word, Sut poked around the edges of the pile with his cane for a minute or two, and eventually I saw that he'd rooted out a little orange plastic bottle, half melted at one side.

"You see that?" he asked.

"Sure," I said. "Looks like a medicine bottle."

"Huh," he said again. "Medicine." I let it slide: he'd come out with whatever was bothering him sooner or later. "No label, you notice. Never had one, I think."

"Illegal?"

"I'm sure of it," he said. "There's someone up here who seems to be taking a damn lot of prescription meds, always in these unmarked bottles." I couldn't help thinking of the pills I'd gotten for Horatio, back in Morgantown. I'd also taken them out of the labeled bottle before I had given them to him.

"Who is it?" I asked, figuring he must have at least a good guess.

"I think it's probably Mary, Bill's wife," he said. "You know anything about how to get her off them?"

"If she's addicted," I said, "it's probably a matter for professionals. You sure it's not just some drugs her doctor gave her?"

"There's never any labels on the bottles," he said. "It's too damn suspicious."

I couldn't argue with that. "Anyone else taking 'em?" I asked.

"I can't be sure," he answered. "It could be, but most of the time I can't even tell with Mary—but I'm pretty sure in her case." I shook my head: talking to Mary might be more difficult than I had anticipated.

"You know where she's getting them?" I asked.

"We don't have all that many contacts down in Morgantown," was his answer. "I was wondering if maybe you'd look into it for me. I could pay, maybe. I'd like you to stop the flow of drugs up here, to say it plainly."

I thought about that: the Lovingoods made money in all sorts of little ways, here and there, from however many canes old Sut could sell to Joshua's rustic walking sticks, and now wild-grown organic hops, apparently. But mostly, they'd always gotten along by not needing too much money, by being as self-sufficient up here as they could be. And prescription drugs, legal or illegal, couldn't be cheap. "We'll keep it all in the family," I said in answer. "I am sure that's what Martha would tell me to do."

"She's done a good job for you all, hasn't she?" he said.

"I think so," I answered. Unless I was mistaken, Sut was mentally comparing the job he'd done to the job Martha had done. It must have been hard for him to ask me to help him do his job. But of course, I was always helping Martha out too, one way or another, so it seemed the least that I could do.

Eventually, he left me to wander on my own. What he wanted most, he'd told me, was to see the supply cut off: someone, maybe even someone here at the Lovingood place, was bringing these drugs in, and someone (or more than one person, even) was hooked on them. He was no fan of the drugs, he said, but the regular commerce, the repeated link to some criminal network in Morgantown, or Fairmont, or Kingwood, I thought, must have bothered him almost as much. It was a challenge, he said, to all of their independence, a danger to their way of life.

I had nodded when he said that, thinking of my own thoughts about the bigfoot guns: I had come to see them as a challenge to our independence, too, not so much for our reliance on human black powder and musket balls, but for the very way they changed our relationship to the past. Sut wanted continuity for his people, not the radical change that would come with moving more fully into the mainstream of human society. The Lovingoods had always been willing to break the laws of the wider human world. It wasn't really the illegality of these drugs that Sut was worried about any more than he was worried about selling ginseng tea out of season; it was the way he could see that this addiction would draw the world to the Lovingoods and the Lovingoods to the world. Sut thought the Lovingoods belonged in their place.

It was a perspective, I thought, that I could understand and respect.

Before he left me, I'd asked Sut if he could maybe ask Mary to come out and find me, but an hour or more passed and I didn't see her. Eventually, though, a dinner bell rang, and I figured that meant Emily and I were both invited.

Eighteen people sat down at that dinner table, including me and Emily. It probably said something that she chose to sit next to me, though Bill was at her other side. Mary was a bit farther down the table, and I watched her, as best I could, to see if there were any signs that Sut's suspicions were correct. Good old human jealousy, I thought of a sudden. Mary, too, could be made to fit the bill for the deaths of Darla Jones and Diane Smart: the two dead women were her husband's former lover and a potential current one, I thought, remembering Darla Jones's complaints at the ramps festival about unwanted attention from Bill. Mary may have married into the Lovingood clan, but from everything I could see, she'd taken to her new life with a kind of beautiful enthusiasm, as the quality of those dutch oven biscuits had made clear; the drugs, if Sut was right about who was taking them, I didn't really understand. Regardless, I couldn't imagine that she hadn't learned, over the years she'd lived out here, to fire a muzzleloader. Though how she might have transported Diane Smart's body to where I'd found it wasn't quite so clear. But if Sut was right, and she really was addicted to opioid painkillers, Deputies Bowling and Evans, at least, would want to consider her.

I wondered, now, if that was the real job Sut had in mind for me. He'd made no accusation at all against his nephew's wife. If anything, he'd presented himself as concerned for Mary's continued health and well-being. But asking me to stop the drug traffic—that might be accomplished in more than one way.

When it rains, it pours, I thought wryly. Now I had two murder investigations and a drug trafficking ring to close down, and no certainty at all that any of the three were related. I knew it was a small world we all moved in, but could it really be that small?

With all of this passing through my thoughts, I probably paid less attention to how Emily and Bill were getting along than I should have. From what little I did see, the two of them seemed to be adjusting well enough, though, as usual, it was hard for me to be sure. He passed the butter when she asked and even offered me some of his cousins' beer.

"I couldn't believe what I was seeing when you two pulled up in that little Nissan," he said then. "Big Jim Foote, riding in that tiny little car? Your back must really be killing you now, I thought, seeing you bouncing up our drive!"

"Yeah," I answered him. "I had the seat all the way back. I'm not much of a fan of riding in any car, but I didn't see any easier way of bringing Emily out here."

"Well," he answered, "I knew her mama didn't want anything to do with me, but like I told Emily, I'm glad to know her now." The smile he gave might have been perfectly sincere, but something about it looked wrong, I thought. Emily didn't react, though, so I told myself it was nothing. I wondered whether he had any inkling of what his uncle Sut had shown me that afternoon.

Not long after the big meal was done, I wedged myself back into the front seat of Emily's little car, and she drove us back into Morgantown. "What did you think?" I asked her. "If you can even say, so soon," I allowed.

"They seem like good people," she said. "But I don't know how they live out there, so isolated."

"They've got cable TV," I said. "And the internet. Nowhere's really isolated these days when you have those things." It was true, I realized as I said it. Sut's worries about being overrun by mainstream culture seemed to be a little less reasonable when I remembered he hadn't seemed bothered by the internet. Before we'd left, he'd even slipped a little piece of paper into my hand with his own email address on it, and I'd given him one of my cards in return. "Keep in touch," he'd said when he handed me the address, and I knew he meant if I had learned—or done—anything about what he'd asked me to do. It was a question, I realized again, of just what it was that Sut was asking me to do, and why.

"But you were right," she said then. "He called you a biggie when you weren't around."

"I'm not surprised."

"He said you couldn't be trusted."

"Me?"

"All of the bigfoot, I guess," she answered. "He said you were always lying, that it was a way of life."

"I guess that's true enough," I answered, trying not to be annoyed. "As long as you count hiding as lying." There was a small silence, and I spoke again. "Everybody's got to decide who it is they can trust: if there's anything I've learned, it's that you make that call on the basis of individuals, not groups, or," I hesitated, "species. There's bigfoot you can trust, and some you can't. Same as humans."

"Not all lies are betrayals, you mean."

"Yeah, maybe you could put it like that," I answered, even though I didn't feel like something was quite right there. But what it was, and what would ease her mind, I didn't know.

We managed not to make any wrong turns getting back out to the main road, and the GPS was easy to program with a destination this time. It was full dark by the time Emily dropped me off at the office. She agreed to come pick me up again at ten the next morning. "I think I told you before: I've got someone with a pickup coming along to help clean out your mom's place," I told her. "I hope that's okay."

"That's great, Mr. Foote," she said. "I'll see you then."

A few moments later, I was back in the office, sitting down to check on my email. The Lovingoods may have had internet out at their place, but my phone hadn't been able to get a signal out there, and I had most of a day's worth of spam to sort through.

Most of it was the usual junk: no Nigerian princes today, but one male enhancement remedy; one offer of life insurance; and two emails from Harlan Stephens's muzzleloader group, which I sincerely hoped I would be able to unsubscribe from soon. The subject line of one message in my junk folder said, "Information about D. Jones," however. I couldn't stop myself from opening it up.

It was unsigned, and the sender's information was the kind of garbled junk that suggests an anonymous rerouter: I doubted I'd be able to trace it at all. The message inside was short: "For information about Darla Jones's death," it read, "meet me at midnight," and it gave an address that I thought was somewhere on or near the northern end of the university campus.

My first thought, of course, was that the email must have been from Mike Merrill. He must have been released by now, and he had every reason to think that I'd be interested in information about Darla Jones's death. But was he going to give me a tip, or was it a trap? Either way, I thought, I might be able to come away with some useful information. I can't say I was worried for my safety in any trap that Mike might set: he was only one human, and in the dark, there was no chance that a human could spot me if I didn't want to be seen. There were trees enough in that neighborhood, I was pretty sure, so I could go unseen until I wanted otherwise.

Was there anyone else who might use such a topic to lure me out in the dark of night? Whoever had killed Darla Jones might want to put me out of the picture if they thought I might be able to make a case against them: that included Mike, of course. But there might be others if Mike wasn't the killer.

I thought that I should probably just forward the message on to Deb Armstrong or to one of the sheriff's deputies. But if the police turned up at this midnight meeting, whoever had sent the message would simply fail to show themselves. That's how this kind of thing worked: it would work to lure me there but no one else. It was far more likely to be a trap than an honest exchange of information, especially since it wasn't clear what they could possibly want from me. But could I afford to let it slip past?

In the end, I decided that I couldn't. I set my alarm for eleven, and I got what sleep I could in the meantime.

CHAPTER 12

LATE THURSDAY, EARLY FRIDAY

———

I managed to wake up with the alarm, though it wasn't easy to make myself roll out of the hammock. The was nothing new on my email when I checked it, so I put on my darkest tracksuit; there was no point in wearing the one with the easy-to-see reflective stripes if I wanted to stay unseen. I called up an internet map site just to make sure I knew where I was going. The address was pretty much where I had thought it was, at the boundary between the university and a nearby residential neighborhood. It would take me about twenty minutes to get over there: less, if I didn't mind being seen.

All too quickly, it was time to go. I locked up the office and made my way up the rail-trail to the arboretum, which was nominally closed after dark, but there wasn't any gate or fence to keep anyone out. I worked my way up the nature trails, out past the basketball arena, and then across campus, building by building, until I was close to University Ave. I almost laughed out loud when I realized where I was headed—a trio of little buildings, each labeled with the university's familiar logo and sign: "Crime Scene

House." All three were used by the Criminal Justice department for practical exercises or exams in what they called forensics on *CSI*. Now I knew it was a trap: a gun, or something, was just waiting for me, and someone was waiting for a chance to turn one of these cute little houses into an actual crime scene.

But I could move silently and could make myself nearly invisible to human sight—bigfoot night vision is apparently much better than a human's—and it wasn't hard to pick out the outlines of the ambush. I could see four guys, big by human standards, but not one of them was on the scale of bigfoot. Two of them carried baseball bats, but if the others had weapons, I didn't see them. If they weren't all former football linemen, they definitely had that look. I didn't know any of them by sight, which meant that I was already at a disadvantage; my whole purpose in showing up was to try to learn something about who I was up against. I hadn't had any real expectation that I'd learn anything about who had killed Darla Jones, and now I knew I wouldn't learn anything if I didn't engage with them somehow. But even that, I thought, was dangerous and no sure thing; they certainly looked like they had come to the meeting with violence in mind.

Well, maybe I could change their minds. From the size of them, I assumed they were probably counting on strength and numbers to keep them safe, rather than guns or other weapons, but I'd need to be careful, regardless. Eventually, I knew, I'd need to make the first move.

"Good evening, boys," I said, stepping out into the open.

If I was any judge, all four of them looked at me and my size and had a second thought or two. At least none of them attacked right off. I was glad to see that no additional weapons had been drawn; they were here to send me a message, not kill me outright. I relaxed a bit.

For a few moments, no one spoke.

"Someone said you guys had some information for me," I finally said. "But there's really only one thing I need to know, and that's who hired you."

They exchanged a glance or two; no one seemed to want to take on the job of spokesperson. "We don't like PIs sticking their noses in our business," one of them finally said, a big blond with a wide neck.

"Oh, so you guys are with the cops?"

Only one of them laughed, one of the guys with the bats, and I did my best to mark him down as one I needed to watch out for. Sure enough, that was the one who spoke next: "No, we're with the hospital, and we're gonna put you in it." He cocked the bat back and stepped forward, starting to swing; I saw the others closing in, too.

It always feels like a failure of some sort when I let things end up in violence, and I always feel guilty for fighting humans, no matter how big they are. I can never shake the feeling that they are only the size of juveniles, youngsters, kids who don't know any better and who don't deserve to be hit full strength. So I did my best to take it easy on them. I managed to catch the swinging bat in one hand, but while that was happening, the other guy with the bat caught me on the leg, and I'm afraid I lashed out a bit in pain by backhanding the first guy and knocking him down, while I kept hold of the bat. The other three could see right away that now I had all the advantage of the greater reach. And they probably couldn't anticipate my speed.

I ended up giving all four of them a couple of taps, trying to make sure not to hurt them too badly. But I was hurting enough already that I wasn't really laying off too much, and I probably broke a few bones. In two minutes, they were all down, and I was breathing heavily. They hadn't run from the conflict, I had to give them that. I spent a few moments making sure they were all still breathing, and they seemed okay as far as I could tell.

It could have gone worse, I thought to myself, but I knew already that they'd gotten in more hits than I had realized; besides those first two attacks with the bats, I had a cut on one cheek (from a punch?), and one leg and one hand were very sore, but neither was broken, I hoped. I had a pretty good knot on the back of my head, too. I knew I'd be limping for a few days, and nursing a serious headache as well.

I guessed I'd be okay. Of course, I was no doctor, and if I wasn't sure how badly I'd been hurt, I knew even less about these football players. Probably, they'd need medical attention, and I had no way of controlling what kind of tale they'd tell. I could see clearly enough now that this was just the kind of trouble I should have known to stay out of. I should have brought the deputies along after all.

Sooner or later, though, these guys would either be speaking to the cops or they wouldn't. If they didn't, I didn't need to do anything at all, except maybe come up with some kind of story for how I'd gotten hurt. If they did talk to the cops, they'd probably tell them that Big Jim Foote had beaten the four of them up, after some kind of unspecified late-night run-in. They'd probably get rid of the baseball bats if they went to the cops themselves, but that would mean leaving the crime scene. Hmmm.

I thought, briefly, of calling for an ambulance. But that would put me on the scene, and lead to questions I really didn't want to answer. For all I knew, the cops had already been called, anyway; the fight hadn't taken long, but it was probably loud enough, and I had no idea if anyone had seen us.

I glanced around and noticed I wasn't too far from a blue campus safety phone, and I breathed a sigh of relief. The thugs might have chosen the Crime Scene Houses as a joke, but it was my good fortune. Another look didn't reveal any obvious surveillance cameras, though I might have missed one. I stumbled over to the phone, pulled a used tissue from my pocket and picked it up to call the campus cops. No point in leaving any prints. Someone would be over pretty quickly, and they'd find four unconscious and hurt bruisers, two baseball bats, and no good explanation for what they'd been up to. If I was lucky, I'd be able to dodge the consequences entirely, even if they did blame me. It was the best I could do.

After I made the call, I knew I had to get out of there. A heavy limp was the best I could manage, though, and I knew I had left blood at the scene. Depending on how the campus cops handled it, they might or might not realize that there was blood there that didn't come from the four boys. Any DNA test, of course, would come back garbled—they might guess it wasn't human, but probably they'd just think the test or the sample had been corrupted somehow. I had to keep them from getting a sample from me, though, so I couldn't be there when the squad car arrived. I did my best to melt back into the shadows, but it's not so easy when you're bleeding and hurt.

The truth was, I probably needed some medical attention myself.

I hated to bother them, but I'd been told more than once not to worry about it, so I hobbled back downtown as best I could, and then over the Walnut Street bridge. It was harder than I expected. I'd pretty much stopped bleeding when I got to Sarah Lloyd's porch, but the pain wasn't going away.

"Jesus, Big," Nathan said when he finally saw who was knocking at his door at one o'clock in the morning. "What the hell happened?"

"I, uh," I began. "I took a bad spill on the bike."

"In the middle of the night?"

"Well," I answered, not really expecting him to believe me—or Sarah, when she'd heard it, for that matter—"it took me a while to make it over here, and I couldn't go to Morgantown General, you know."

"I'll get Sarah up," he said, heading for the stairs. "You should probably go on into the kitchen," he added quietly.

I turned on the light on the way, poking my head into the little downstairs bathroom. The face I saw in the mirror looked damaged, more than hurt. This was a bad one, I thought. I perched on one of the kitchen stools and tried not to leave any blood anywhere, though I probably failed.

When Sarah finally came down, she was dressed, and she had a little medical kit with her. She had a sewing kit, too; Nathan must have told her I might need stitches. Nathan trailed after, a couple of athletic bandage wraps in his hands. "Who did this, Big?" Sarah asked, obviously concerned.

"Some guys," I answered, deciding she deserved the truth. "We didn't get much of a chance to talk."

"They okay?"

"I think so," I said. "I called the campus cops to check on them."

"Christ, you're a mess." There wasn't anything I could say to that because I knew it was true. Sarah had patched me up before, but I'd never been hurt this bad. She started just by cleaning the blood off; then she thought about putting a couple of stiches into my cheek before deciding on a little butterfly bandage instead.

"Where else does it hurt?" she asked.

So I pointed out a bruise on my ribs, the damage to my hand and my leg. She bit her lip as she ran her hands over the skin and fur. "I think the fibula's probably broken, Big, and maybe one or two ribs. But I can't set the bones," she added. "Is there anyone else you can ask?"

"I'll see if I can get up to the Homeland," I told her. "I might be able to get some help up there." I didn't much look forward to the prospect of making that trip.

"Don't waste any time about it. The ribs'll probably be okay, but the fingers I don't know about. And if the fibula in your right leg is broken, you'll probably always have a limp if you don't get it set."

I didn't want to lie to her, but it only took me a moment to realize that I didn't even know when I'd be able to get out to the Homeland again. If nothing else, getting beat up by four human males probably meant I was supposed to be laid up and out of circulation, at least for a few days, and maybe permanently. Someone, I guessed, was thinking that these were critical days, and they didn't want me pursuing the investigation into Darla Jones's death. That fact, slowly, made it through the aches and pains to the thinking part of my brain. The thing that struck me now was that I hadn't really been pursuing any investigation of Darla Jones's death; I had spent the last few days looking for Diane Smart's killer. So maybe this ambush really did mean that the two cases were linked: something the killer actually would know better than anyone else, myself and the police included. But if someone wanted me out of the picture—and out of it right now, it seemed—then *in* the picture was pretty much where I needed to be, at least until I'd figured out what was going on and who had set those guys on me.

"I'll do what I can," I finally told her, and she frowned in response, but didn't argue. "Tonight, though," I asked, hesitantly, "do you have anything for the pain?"

The two of them looked at each other, as if there was something they knew that I didn't. "Nothing stronger than aspirin," she said. "Did you ever get anything for that friend of yours?"

Horatio, she meant. Yeah: maybe I could get some of the pills I'd given him back. They were painkillers, after all, and prescription strength, no less. "Tomorrow," I answered. "I'll talk to him tomorrow." Because I was tired, and all I needed at the moment was sleep, even more than I needed anything for the pain. Sarah and Nathan could see the shape I was in clearly, and they let me crash right where I was.

I woke up just enough to hear the twins heading out to school in the morning. "When did *he* get here?" I heard one of them ask Nathan on the porch, but I didn't hear the answer. I sat upright as slowly as I could; I had aches pretty much everywhere, but my hand and leg were the worst. I checked the sheet that Sarah had put down in front of the fireplace, and I saw that I had managed not to bleed any more. It was only a small victory, but I wasn't above claiming it, at least in my own mind.

It looked to be an ugly day. "You gonna get in any trouble over this?" Sarah asked me when I made it into the kitchen again. The first aid kit she'd used last night still sat on the counter.

"Could be," I had to admit, "though I hope to avoid it."

"Can you?"

"I suppose it depends on what the guys who beat me up tell the cops," I answered. "I was only defending myself, but they were there to assault me, so they might prefer to tell some other story."

"All four of them?"

"Yeah, that's the question," I acknowledged.

"So, the best-case scenario is that you're the innocent victim, broken bones and blood and all, and you left the scene but didn't go to the hospital or a doctor or the police."

"Yeah. I'll probably have to say I was disoriented. Not thinking straight."

"Well, no one would argue with that, I suppose." I think that was an attempt at humor, though she wasn't smiling.

But she had gotten me thinking. From the police perspective, my actions really would need explaining: the kinds of injuries I'd taken weren't minor. Maybe I could go out and see my new doctor, Dr. MacDonald. He wasn't, I was sure, the type to inquire too closely into how I'd come by these injuries, and I already knew he'd prescribe the kinds of drugs I would need. Then again, that might be the very reason he'd refuse to see me; he probably wouldn't dare to get mixed up in anything that the police were likely to be concerned with. And if I went out to see him, I'd probably need him to look at least at my leg, which meant I'd probably have to shave them both. I could just picture the resulting dialogue: "You shave your legs?" he'd ask, incredulous. And I'd have to say, "Yeah, I'm a competitive swimmer." Even I could see that that conversation was not likely to go anywhere good.

"I'll have to act as if the injuries are no big deal. I told Nathan I'd had a spill on my bike: maybe that's what I'll have to say." I told Sarah.

"The police will know it's a lie."

"True," I answered. "They'll know it. But they won't bother to try to prove otherwise, unless they think I committed a crime and they can prove it."

"Sounds like a house of cards, Big," Sarah said to me. "So many ways this could go wrong."

She was right in that, but what could I do? This had to be a break in the case, and there must be some way I could use it to leverage my way to the truth. But here I was, my head aching as much as any other part of my body, and I knew I wasn't thinking clearly. You know you're in trouble when you start to think that putting yourself on prescription painkillers will improve your thinking, even though I really didn't see what else I could do. "I've got a friend," I told Sarah finally, "who might drive me out the Homeland, or near enough." I was thinking of Emily Smart. "I can probably get the leg set out there, and splinted, too, if I can take some of these wraps."

"Of course," she said. "Anything you need. You know we won't tell anyone you've been here."

I knew that the twins might very well tell, but I still had hopes of wrapping this all up before it would matter. If only I could find the thread that would start unraveling everything. Dimly, I could see that there was a mixed metaphor in there somewhere.

"I can't thank you enough," I said. I could see her getting ready to tell me that I wasn't well enough to go. "No, I've got to get moving. I really can't just hide out here." I reached for the aspirin bottle that she'd brought out last night, but I couldn't get my hands to work well enough to get the cap off.

"And you think you're ready to get back to work?" she asked, taking the bottle from me and opening it easily.

"Ready or not, I've got to," I answered. "Thanks again," I said, and washed three of the tiny little pills down with a last gulp of coffee. Then I stood, my lower leg really hurting now, and I stumbled out of the house.

I don't know how often I've seen it on the television, when a cop or a detective or just some regular Joe of a human gets clobbered and beat up and then pushes through it somehow, going ahead with the investigation, with life, moving a little roughly, maybe, or with a visible bandage or a wince or two, but really not all that inconvenienced. Maybe humans are just more resilient, more able to work past the pain, more driven somehow, but I doubt it. Those guys I beat up last night, for example, were probably at least as bad off as I was, as unable to move smoothly or easily, as distracted by the pain, and as eager to make it go away. Pain can't really be shown on TV, and the narrative makes its own demands of action and movement.

It was some other force that was pushing me. Narrative be damned, I thought to myself, as I worked my way down to the level of Decker's Creek, the downhill movement somehow hurting more than the uphill. Part of me looked at every little stand of trees I saw along the creek as a refuge: there, my mind or my body was telling me, there is enough space that I could hole up for a while, recuperate, stay out of sight of human and bigfoot alike, regain my strength until I could come out again, strong and able. But that voice was one that I knew I had to overrule. I'd known people—humans and bigfoot both—who'd broken a small bone in their foot or ankle and had managed to stumble around for a few days before getting it taken care of, the pain growing the worse all the while. On the one hand, I didn't want my pain getting any worse, but on the other, I hoped maybe I could still make it a few days more, maybe wrap up the cases, and then lay up and get healthy. I wasn't really thinking straight, like I said.

It was even more troubling when I realized that my body was whispering something else to me; it was pushing me on to Horatio's house, hinting that the pills he had there would make all the pain go away. I'd only taken two of them before, and they were just codeine, but somehow it was like the pills were speaking right to me, promising me ease. I couldn't help but listen: who doesn't seek ease, or relief from pain? I knew I'd need to be careful, that that whispering was dangerous.

I thought of Sut Lovingood, living right up on the border of the Homeland, worried about how painkillers were encroaching somehow upon his folk, tying them to something criminal that was worse, somehow, than when his grandfather had run a still, because it was a thing from outside, a thing he had no control over. Martha would have put things in very much the same terms, I knew, if some human addiction had reached my people in the Homeland, and I had to wonder whether or not it had. I'd taken the pills myself; I'd given them to Horatio—I hoped they did him only good. Could bigfoot become addicted to them? I began to be certain that they could. I knew what Martha would say: it was my job to keep that from happening. No one else's.

I was in a state to match the blackest of Horatio's moods by the time I made it up the steps to his porch. I took me several knocks to rouse him; the sun was well up, and he ought to have been awake for an hour or more. I thought of just breaking through the door, but my hand and my back rebelled at the thought of the pain it would add to what I was already dealing with. He did finally let me in.

"Jamie," he said to me, the welcoming in his voice cutting through at least some of the irritation I felt at his use of my old name. But then he looked a bit closer. "You look like hell, Jim," he said. "Come in, sit down if you want."

"Thanks Horatio," I said, slowly—very slowly—lowering myself onto an old oak rocker he had in the front room.

"Human trouble?"

"Always," I said, with a wry, half-formed laugh. He shook his head. "Yeah, but every time I turn around," I added, "it starts to look like it's bigfoot trouble, too. Or that it could be."

"That kind," he said, and somehow his words, or my pain, turned a kind of key in my mind, unlocking something I'd always known but never really felt so clearly. I'd known him for seventy years or so, ever since I first came down to Morgantown. Even then, he'd been a grumpy, hard-to-please old cuss. But for the first time, I understood what it meant that he had been doing my job back then, in the 1940s, and maybe even for years before that. Why I'd never really understood it, I didn't know—maybe he had just handled everything, myself included, so smoothly that you couldn't really see the work he was doing, his grumpiness a kind of cover for an underlying competence. Today, for the first time, I admired him. "That kind," I said, smiling through the pain. "Do you think, Horatio, I've done a good job?"

"Huh," he said, taking another long look. "You really are in the middle of something, aren't you? And beat up pretty good, by the looks of it. How many were there?"

"Four."

"They live?"

"Far as I know," I answered. "I think they should be all right."

"Witnesses," he said. I didn't know if he was criticizing me for letting them live or not.

"The police ask a different set of questions when they find four dead bodies," I told him.

"True enough, true enough. I'll answer your question, little Jim," he said then. "I don't see the Homeland on TV, and the only bigfoot I see on it are human jokes and fantasies. You're doing your job just fine."

I nodded, leaning forward on the rocker. Before I could say anything, he spoke. "Now, what do you need from me to keep it that way?"

"I—," I said, hesitating. "Right now, I need to take a couple of those painkillers I brought you." At first I thought he was going to refuse.

"They do bring a powerful relief," he said. "Almost enough to make me forget my hurts. Take what you need," he said. He looked away for a moment, then looked back at me. I wondered if he was telling me that even if there was pain I needed to get past, the pain was a reminder of something I didn't dare forget. "They are in the glass there. But leave me what you can."

"I'll just take two," I said, levering myself to my feet and stepping toward the sideboard. It seemed to me that there were fewer in the little stemmed glass than I thought there ought to be. "I won't forget."

I didn't take the pills right away. There was another thing I needed to take care of before I did. The walk back up to my little office building took some time: every step, it seemed, hurt more than the last. Finally I made it and unlocked the door to the office. I sat for a few minutes at the chair behind the desk: just sitting, just taking the weight off my leg.

When the pain finally grew a little less sharp, I stood up again, and the pain came back. But I went out the back door and unlocked the little garage door. I took the bike, and walked over to the corner of the building, and I smashed the front end as best I could into the corner of the building. If I were doing it right, I'd find some way to get some fresh blood onto it, here and there, but I didn't feel like opening up any of the gashes that Sarah Lloyd had been so good about closing up. I lugged the thing around to my front door and dropped it there.

Then I climbed into the hammock and swallowed Horatio's two little pills. They knocked me out even more quickly than the others had.

Eventually I heard a knocking at the office door. And Emily Smart's voice. "Big?" she said, a question in her voice. "Mr. Foote? Are you all right?"

I couldn't refuse to answer, so I lumbered out of the hammock and limped to the door. The light outside told me it was late in the afternoon. "Come in, Emily," I said, only realizing after I spoke that she wasn't alone. Seth Jones was standing beside her, a little porkpie hat on his head.

"You guys know each other?" I said, confused. Luckily, I always kept two chairs across the desk from mine.

"I was here, waiting for you this morning," Emily answered, "when Seth drove up. He was looking for you, too, and we figured out that you meant him to help out with my mom's apartment."

"Oh, yeah," I said, and I could tell that my brain was not yet back up to full speed. I had forgotten all about my promise to help Emily this morning and about my hopes of getting a little more background information about Darla Jones from Seth. Was there anything else I was forgetting? The pain wouldn't let me forget what had happened last night. And it didn't seem to be leaving room for me to remember much else.

"Are you okay?" she asked again.

I debated telling them the truth for a moment, then decided to go with the lie. "I had an accident on the bike," I said lamely. "I didn't make it back here for a while today."

I couldn't tell if they believed it or not, and they weren't saying. But they looked at my various bandages and wounds, and I could tell they were concerned.

"Do you need any—uh—aspirin or anything?" Emily asked. I saw her eyes glance towards Seth, and I figured she knew I couldn't see a doctor. And that Seth had no idea why I couldn't.

"No," I said. "Thanks." I paused, trying to think.

"You need us to drive you to the urgent care place or the emergency room?" Seth asked.

"I, uh, it's not that bad," I managed to say. "You guys get the apartment cleared out?" I asked, changing the topic.

"I doubt that I'll get Mom's security deposit back," Emily Smart said, "but, yeah, we got everything out. Most of it we just dumped."

There wasn't much I could say to this, so I tried to think of some other topic to raise. I glanced at the clock. "You guys want to get some dinner?" I asked.

They looked at each other, and something passed between them that I couldn't recognize. Before either of them could say anything, there was another knock at the door and it opened sooner than I could even speak. It was Deputy Bowling, and I'm sure my face must have shown something, although I didn't know what. I really wasn't ready to deal with him yet. He didn't seem to notice. "Emily Smart and Seth Jones," he said, instead. "You guys know each other?"

He must have been quickly recalculating the possibility that the two deaths were related somehow. "I introduced them," I said, whether it was literally true or not. "Emily needed help cleaning out her mother's apartment, and I knew Seth had a truck." I looked at Emily and tried to suggest with my look that she and Seth might be best off leaving. Whether she understood or not, something must have clicked.

"Thanks for your help, Mr. Foote," she said. "Sorry about your bike accident." And she stood up, and Seth did too, and they walked out of the office. Bowling let them go.

"Bike accident?" he asked when they were gone, and I didn't know whether I should be irritated that Emily had brought it up or not.

"You must have practically stepped on the bike, outside," I said, still uncertain about whether to lie to him or not, or how much of a lie to tell.

"Looks like someone hit it with a baseball bat," he said, and I suddenly felt like I could like him if circumstances were different. But I managed to keep from laughing. The pain helped, of course.

"Tree branch, baseball bat: not that much difference really, I guess."

"I'd tell you to be careful where you're going," he said, "but I can see it's already too late."

This time I did laugh. "Yeah," I said.

"So, there was an emergency call out last night: four guys, two of 'em still in the hospital, even now. You know anything about it?"

"College students?" I asked.

"Three of 'em," he said.

"Sounds like a normal Thursday night in Morgantown, to me."

"One of them might have described you," he said.

"Huh," I answered. No reason for me to do all the work in this conversation. It wasn't one I really wanted to have, after all.

"Look, Foote," Bowling said, seeming to have come to pretty much the same conclusion, "I really don't think you had anything to do with Diane Smart's death, or Darla Jones's, either. But I'd appreciate it if you could share anything you know about either case, if you've got anything."

"Huh," I answered again. "I've got nothing you can use," I finally added. "Nothing but some suspicions. You'll be the first to know, if I get anything more."

"Yeah, well," he answered. "These four guys, I just thought I'd tell you, they say they got some good hits in on whoever beat them up, enough to put him in the hospital. But nobody's shown up in the emergency room yet. So, uh, keep your eyes open, okay?"

I couldn't tell if he meant it as a friendly warning or as a promise that he was keeping his eye on me. "Give my best to Deb Armstrong," I told him as he stood and got ready to leave.

CHAPTER 13

STILL FRIDAY, INTO SATURDAY

———

All the time I'd been talking with Deputy Bowling, the little pill bottle I'd borrowed from Sarah and Nathan Lloyd had been sitting right there, on the corner of my desk. When the deputy left; I opened it and took the lone pill that remained. It probably wouldn't knock me out like the two pills I had gotten from Horatio had, but the pain insisted. I made it back to the hammock and wished that I had actually taken more of the pills back. It was my prescription, after all. The feeling in the leg wasn't good at all, and I really did need to find some way out to the Homeland so I could have Martha look at it. Maybe I could get Emily Smart to drive me out there; I should have asked her before she left, but once Bowling arrived, I couldn't really expect her and Seth to stick around.

Emily and Seth had seemed to hit it off well enough, and I wasn't sorry that I had forgotten to meet them in the morning, especially since I'd been in no condition to help with their work anyway. I thought about the two of them while I tried to fall asleep. I knew I really didn't have any business trying to play matchmaker for two humans: I hardly understood them one at a time. One part of me had hope for the two of them that I couldn't suppress, but I didn't think it was a good sign that the secret of my bigfoot identity was already a secret they couldn't share. It was something I'd have to think about when I got out of all of this.

I also needed to think some more about Bowling's last words. I beat up four guys at midnight, and he asks me to pass along any evidence I might find. The best I could figure, it looked to him like maybe I was making progress on the case, or on one of the cases anyway, and apparently he hadn't gotten enough out of any of those four guys to make any connections he could follow. Except to me.

I couldn't fault his logic. I couldn't see why anyone would have sent four guys after me, unless I was getting too close to something they wanted to protect. Maybe some guy wanted Emily for himself and he thought I was some kind of competition. If so, I might need to warn Seth to watch his back. But four guys seemed like overkill for anything like that. It made more sense to suspect that whoever had sent them was someone who'd already killed twice. Although why the killer hadn't hired guns, rather than thugs, didn't seem clear at all.

Nothing made sense, I thought as I finally drifted off to sleep.

I woke because my lower leg was on fire. Or it felt like it was. I had broken bones before, and I knew that the pain would eventually lessen, but right now, it wasn't going anywhere. Something would have to be done. I rolled out of the hammock and stumbled around the office for a while, straightening things up, washing a couple dishes in the tiny sink, standing on one foot too much of the time. It was all just avoidance: I needed to do something.

One choice was to drop everything, make my way out to the Homeland, and let Martha and the other healers out there do what they could. I'd be safe out there. Probably. I still hadn't ruled out entirely that Diane Smart had been killed with one of the Homeland guns, though no bigfoot would be foolish enough to set only four humans on me. If I could just get to the Homeland, I could focus on getting well—take a few weeks' vacation.

Doing that would mean leaving things down here in Morgantown to simmer in my absence, however. Although I thought Deputy Bowling might actually be on my side, he wouldn't be able to ignore my disappearance, and it wasn't as if I could tell him where I was going. If I wasn't here, he and the rest of the police might make out a case against me that I couldn't easily fight. And then, if I ever did turn up down here again, I'd be arrested straight off. That would not be good at all.

I had to admit, I was tempted anyway. I thought, let it work out that I could never come down to Morgantown again; I could retire out to the Homeland for good. Another decade or two and the Jim Foote identity would have grown too old to inhabit anymore anyway: why not make this an early retirement? I'd done a lot of good for my people down here over the years. I deserved it. Someone else could take up the work. Maybe Mel was ready. Not that it mattered. I hadn't really been ready when I had taken the work onto my shoulders, and I'd managed, one way or another. But I couldn't do that to her yet.

At least Horatio had stayed here in town when I'd started working down here; he'd always been willing to lend a hand if I found myself in trouble. Just yesterday he'd let me take some of his pills. Now I wondered how much of his grumpiness was simply directed at me because I was doing the job that he couldn't really do any longer. It put him in a different light.

What I truly needed at the moment, I thought again, were some more of those painkillers so I could wrap up this case, or these cases, and then get my leg seen to—a vacation that didn't involve incriminating myself. I headed out the door, stumbling back down to the Decker's Creek Trail on the way back over to Sabraton.

As I was walking I realized that something wasn't right, and I knew it. About the time I went under the Pleasant Street Bridge, I finally realized that I'd gotten up, and had even gotten out the door, without making a cup of coffee, even instant coffee. Now it had caught up with me and I needed my coffee fix. I could head up the hillside now and be in the Cottonwood Café in a minute or two; I could get a cup there. What was wrong with me? I never got up without coffee. "It's just the pain," I said to myself. "Once that's taken care of, everything will be all right."

But it wasn't the pain speaking, I realized, standing there under the bridge. It was the painkillers. Sure, I was probably addicted to the caffeine in coffee, if addiction was the right word, but could I become addicted, just that easily, to painkillers? Not that it really mattered if I could, or if I was; I couldn't let it continue, regardless. I climbed up the hill, trying to find some way to cherish the pain in my leg.

It was still too early in the year for the downtown farmer's market, so the coffee shop wasn't filled with Saturday morning customers the way it would be in July. I ordered my coffee and a bagel and looked around. Kenny Hetrick was the only other patron I knew, and he waved me over to his table.

"How are you doing, Big?" he said, before even getting a good look at me. "Ouch," he added, once I had carefully sat myself down, "not so well, I guess."

"I'm calling it a bicycle accident," I said, figuring that told him everything he needed to know.

"Got it. You need anything?"

"Right now, I just need some time to sit and to wake up. To

think, maybe. What're you working on?" Kenny always had his laptop open, when he was here, was always typing, though I suspected a lot of it was social media rather than academic writing.

"I'm working on a paper for the big Medieval Congress in Kalamazoo," he told me, and I nodded along, encouraging him to tell me all about it. I sipped my coffee. He went on: "I'm thinking about writing a paper about medieval wild-men: big, hair-covered guys, living outside of civilization, out in the woods. The payoff will be where I look at the Middle English poem *Sir Orfeo* as making use of the wild-man motif."

I couldn't help giving him a sideways glance. "Wild-men, huh?" I said.

"Come away, o human child," he recited. "To the forest, and the wild, with a fairy, hand in hand, for the world's more full of wild-men than you can understand."

Something about the quotation seemed wrong, I thought, but this was all part of the game that Kenny and I played. He was letting me wake up and not making me work too hard at it.

Before I could think of a suitable response, the door opened and Hobo Joe came in. I wouldn't have said Kenny and Joe moved in the same circles at all, but Kenny waved and said "Joe," the same way he'd called me Big. Before I knew it, Joe was unloading his backpack onto one of the empty chairs at our little table, plopping his hat down on the top of it when it was down. "Big, Kenny," he said by way of greetings. "Be back in a minute."

He came back from the counter with a flat white, of all things, sitting down at the fourth chair. "Nice day," he said. Then, "Big, you look like a train wreck."

"Close enough," I answered. "Bicycle, pothole, tree."

"Uh-huh," he said, glancing at Kenny. "And you, Professor, what's up with you?"

"Just enjoying the feeling of not having to stress out about the end of the semester anymore," he said.

"Having summers off must have been nice," said Hobo Joe, though as far as I knew, all his time was his own.

"Seasonally unemployed, actually," came the reply. Watching their by-play was fine by me. I still wasn't quite working at full speed, mind or body. But Hobo Joe didn't seem to notice.

"You get my note?" he asked, turning my way.

I had to think for a moment, then remembered the note he'd left on my door, pointing me towards Dr. MacDonald. "Yeah, I got it."

"You must be psychic," he said.

I had no idea what he meant, and it must have showed on my face.

"Looking for a doctor before running into a tree on your bike," he said, with a gesture at me, as if he could point out my various aches and pains.

"I, uh," I began and stopped. I had been about to say that the drugs hadn't been for me, but that probably wouldn't have been very smart. Now it was Kenny who was playing the role of observer, but what he was making of our conversation, I had no idea. "Just lucky, I guess," I finally mumbled.

"Huh. If you call that luck," he said.

"You went to see a doctor, Jim?" Kenny asked then. I scowled in answer, realizing that he knew enough about me to know that it wasn't something I'd normally do. "Part of an investigation, really," I told him, looking at them both. I knew better than to let this go on. "Can't talk about it, at least not right now. Anyway, I've got places to be. You guys have a good morning," I said, rising from my chair. "See you next time."

It was probably a good thing, in the end, that I had dropped in for breakfast; it took my mind off Horatio and his pills and it reminded me that I needed to get my bike fixed. I went back to the office and picked up the wreck I'd made of the bicycle last night. It was only a matter of minutes to take it over to the shop and ask them to put it right. "Looks like a pretty bad spill," said the guy who took it off my hands, and at least I felt like my story wasn't too obviously false, even if I doubted that Bowling had believed it.

Carrying the busted bike hadn't made my leg or my ribs feel any better, and before I knew it, I found myself heading back over to Sabraton. I was thinking about Horatio again; he would just have to let me borrow another handful of pills. He wouldn't like it, but he'd let me do it, or so I told myself. When I got to his little place, though, there was no answer to my knocking.

Sooner or later, if he didn't answer, I'd have to go in. I didn't figure there was any point in waiting. For all I knew, he was out: the pills made him feel better, too, and he'd probably been happy to have the chance to get out of the house again, maybe go to the store. The door was unlocked, anyway, so I wasn't really worried about it at all.

When I got to the sideboard where he'd put the little glass of pills, though, I didn't see it. I looked in his china cabinet, and the glass—or one just like it—was back in its place, empty. "Huh," I said to myself in frustration, trying to think where he might be hiding them. Nothing in the little medicine cabinet in the downstairs half bath. Probably should try upstairs, I decided.

I saw him as soon as I got to the top of the stairs, lying on his old oak bed, dead. There was no doubt in my mind—there's a kind of stillness that sleep or unconsciousness never reaches. I knew he was old, and I knew he was dying, but he'd always seemed unkillable to me, a fixture in my world, grumpy as could be, steady and always there. There are some things you just can't imagine, or at least I can't; I have to live through them before they even seem possible.

He looked peaceful enough in the bed, and my first instinct was to think that time had finally caught him. But my mind was saying otherwise, telling me that he'd taken all the rest of his pills together, eased his lingering pains all at once and for good. It was a conviction that I couldn't shake, and I wondered now if this wasn't, in fact, the help that Horatio had been asking me for. Another one of those things I couldn't even think until it had happened.

I sat down in the rocking chair in the corner of the little room, angry and suddenly ashamed. I'd come here, I realized, with my own pain outweighing, in my own mind, any pain he might have had—but his death was telling me now that he had known a pain I'd never felt. He must have, to want to end it so much. His last lesson to me, maybe. All I knew, for the moment, was that it hurt, with a new pain no pill could cure.

That wasn't true at all, I realized. There actually were pills for this kind of pain: the same pills I'd come here looking for, probably. I still didn't know whether, or if, bigfoot get addicted in quite the same way that humans do, but I knew well enough that I'd been acting an awful lot like an addict when I'd come here, ready to steal the very pills I'd brought him as a kindness. My anger, shameful as it was, was anger at Horatio for taking pills I'd come to see as mine.

But where could I get any others? I could make my way all the way out to Dr. MacDonald's office again, though it was quite a haul and the bike was out of commission. He'd probably write me a new script. I still had enough cash in my pocket, fortunately. Then I'd have to come back into town and find another pharmacy. I probably shouldn't go to the same one since I'd had to give my name when I filled the old prescription. Well, there was more than one grocery store in town where I could get it filled. This could all be done, but it would take me the whole rest of the day. Too long, given the way I felt.

I remembered Sut Lovingood's suspicion that someone up at his place was either hooked on pain pills or was selling them. Pursuing that was a far better plan: the Lovingoods were friends of the Homeland from way back and they'd have to help me out. I needed to get Horatio's body up to the Homeland anyway, before any humans discovered that he'd died, and I could easily divert my trip from the Homeland over to the Lovingoods' hollow. It wasn't quite on the way, but it wasn't that long a detour, either.

It seemed like a pretty good plan, I thought, killing two birds with one stone. Fortunately, I'd found a position in the old rocking chair where my ribs didn't hurt, and my leg wasn't too bad. For the moment, I didn't want to move at all, and I could finally think.

I understood a few minutes later that I had gone from recognizing my own symptoms of addiction to wrangling how I could get another batch of pills into my hands. Surely, surely, I told myself, I'd rather have the pain. The pills wouldn't get my fibula set: they'd make it so I didn't care if I got it done or not. The pills were the enemy of thought, even if I didn't have them, even more than the pain itself was. And the enemy of feeling, too. They changed what I was, which was part of their terrible appeal.

So I sat there some more, and I did my best to think. I had responsibilities, and I needed to remind myself clearly of what they were. First, I needed to get Horatio's body up to the Homeland, either by carrying it myself, or by some other means. Perhaps I could get Mel to carry it for me if I didn't think my leg would take it, or maybe Kenny Hetrick or Emily Smart could help me. I probably should help out Sut Lovingood, too, if I could: this was a danger that I didn't want anyone to share, and if there was any chance of prescription drugs leaking onto the Homeland, I had to stop that, too. From what I could see, bigfoot certainly were at risk of addiction, and I didn't know if the secret of the Homeland could survive even a single bigfoot addict. Even if it was me. Too much could go wrong.

Also, I needed to clear up the mystery of Diane Smart's death, and maybe Darla Jones's, if they were related. At least Horatio's death was no mystery, I told myself, one small relief, among all these other worries. My mind kept wandering back to the Lovingood place, as I couldn't help thinking of it as a source of pills, a source of help. Sut hadn't even been sure who was taking the pills, or who was supplying them, so why was I so focused on them now? I tried to remember just what he'd said, just what he'd asked me to do, but all that came clearly in my memory was something Bill Lovingood had said, joking with me about riding in Emily's car. "Your back must really be killing you now," he had said.

Given the pain in my ribs and my leg, eased as much as it could be now as I sat in Horatio's old chair, why was I thinking about that comment? It was the word "now," I finally decided, just that one little word. But it meant that Bill somehow thought that I'd had back trouble before. Of course I hadn't; my back never hurt. I'd seen enough on TV to know that back trouble was incredibly common among humans, but something about bigfoot body structure meant that our most common aches and pains were elsewhere, shoulders and hips, usually. Sarah Lloyd could probably explain it physiologically. Bill Lovingood, not so much. He probably assumed bigfoot complained about back pain as much as humans did: he might tell himself—and others—that bigfoot were just animals, but I'd bet that he wasn't so different from most. He probably didn't really have the imagination to think that bigfoot were really any different from him.

Even that line of thinking didn't seem to cover why he'd said "now," and I couldn't get it out of my mind that in fact I had indeed told someone recently that I had a lot of back pain: Dr. MacDonald, the ultimate source of the very pills Horatio had used to take his life. Could there be a connection between Dr. MacDonald and Bill Lovingood?

Of course there could. Morgantown was a small place, and there was a connection of some sort between almost every two people who lived here. I'd said as much to Deputy Evans. But was there any way Dr. MacDonald could have told Bill I was having back trouble?

It would never have happened if Dr. MacDonald had been a reliable and discreet physician. But I hadn't gone to him for his reliability or his discretion. Or, rather, I went for the one, but not the other. I went to get a bogus prescription, and I hoped he'd have no one to gossip to about it. Could he have told Bill? Perhaps my imagination was too active, but I didn't have any trouble at all imagining their conversation. "Big Jim Foote," the doctor would have said. "He one of yours?" And Bill Lovingood would say, "No, but I know him. What did he want?"

And it struck me how things would play out if Bill, for example, had had a string of folks he had some kind of control over, folks who'd go to Dr. MacDonald to get their own bogus prescriptions, and then pass them along to Bill, who'd market them, somehow, maybe selling them under the table at events like the ramps festival or the Prickett's Fort reenactment. Maybe other places, too. Maybe even up in the Homeland, though what coin a bigfoot would pay in wasn't clear to me. Yet. I knew that Diane Smart had gotten drugs—legitimate ones, I had presumed—from

Dr. MacDonald, and I knew that Darla Jones had been complaining about Bill and about some pressure he was putting her under, though I'd thought it was something else at the time. It was thin, but the pieces all fit. It might even be true.

The other pieces could be made to fit too, I saw. Mike Merrill, if he knew what Bill was up to, might indeed have been intimidated—not by me, but by Bill—into lying about what or who he'd seen on the night Darla Jones had been killed. And Bill, if he'd sicced four thugs on me, might very well have wanted them to hurt me pretty bad but not kill me. Bill might be a fool in many ways, but I doubted he'd want the whole of the bigfoot Homeland turning on him. What he really wanted, probably, was for me to be out of the picture, hiding out up in the Homeland while my bones could heal. In fact, it looked a lot like he might get that very result, though I'd have to try to put the police onto his trail before I went.

That had to be my next move. Taking Horatio's body up to the Homeland wasn't a responsibility I could dodge, and really, I didn't want to dodge it, but I could set the dogs on the trail first. I had to do that, and I had enough that they might go for it. It might even be enough to make a case they could take to court. If there had been any compelling physical evidence on either death, they would have made an arrest already, so the case the cops would need probably wasn't going to be based on physical evidence anyway. An account that fit the pieces together was what they had to be looking for. They must have most of the pieces, and all I needed to do was fill in a couple of blanks for them, show them the outline.

I had a sudden thought, and pulled out my phone. I sent a text to Emily Smart, asking her if she'd kept her mother's pill bottles when she and Seth Jones had cleared out the apartment. "No," the answer came back in a minute or two. "Was that important?"

I wrote back a brief note telling her not to worry about it. It probably wouldn't really matter. I followed it up with another text asking her what she'd done with the trash. If the police could get a search warrant on Dr. MacDonald's records, they could probably find out what he had prescribed for her. It would be nice if I could show them the physical link on an actual pill bottle, but I thought they had enough to go on.

"We hauled everything out to the dump ourselves, even the medicine," Emily wrote in the next text, "even though we probably shouldn't have. It was all just too much." I pictured myself wading through the mountains of stuff they had up there at the dump, and then quickly replaced that mental image with one of Deputies Bowling and Evans going through the garbage, which was much more pleasing. Though they'd probably delegate that work to someone lower down than them. Still, I could dream.

Of course, if they got MacDonald's records, they'd no doubt see that I'd visited him, too, with timing that might actually look suspicious to them, although my business with him and Horatio was entirely unrelated. Well, I could tell them that I'd honestly been in pain, I supposed. It was a lie, but not the only one I'd be telling them. "Seth says the pill bottles were in a white plastic trash bag," came the next text, and I was interested to see that she and Seth were together this afternoon. "Say hi to him for me," I wrote back. Then, "I'd like to talk to you both this evening, after I talk to the cops. There may have been a break in the case."

We set up a plan to meet, though I told her I had no idea when I'd be able to get away. They were hooked, of course: they'd wait all night to hear who'd killed their mothers. I dreaded with all my heart having to tell Emily Smart that her father had probably done it, but I didn't see any lie I could tell that would save her— or me—from that.

My next text was to Deb Armstrong. I told her that I had some information on the Diane Smart case, and asked her to meet me, with one or both of the deputies, if she could manage it, at my office in half an hour. I looked around and saw Horatio's keys on the table next to the bed. Now all I had to do was get up out of the chair, which I managed, with a return to pain that I could anticipate but not really prepare for.

There was nothing for it but to charge ahead. I grabbed the keys, hobbled down the stairs almost on one leg, locked up the little house and made my slow way down the trail and back up the hill to my office.

CHAPTER 14

STILL

SATURDAY

———

All three of the detectives were waiting outside my office door when I got there, all in their various uniforms, and I was glad I'd estimated a full half hour for a trip that would have normally taken me only ten or fifteen minutes. There wasn't much foot traffic around here on a Saturday afternoon, but anybody who walked by the end of the block would probably see them waiting, and if I wasn't lucky, I'd have a reporter for the paper coming by before too long, just snooping. I unlocked the door and went in. "Hold on a minute, you guys," I said to them. "I've got another folding chair here in the back somewhere."

I disappeared into the back, debating about whether or not I should do anything about my various aches and pains. Not that I had anything stronger than aspirin. I finally decided I didn't have the time. I moved a spare tracksuit from where it was tumbled on a chair and shuffled back out front. I handed the chair to Deputy Evans, who had been left standing by the others. He'd be the one sorting through the trash, if any of them were.

"Jesus, Big," said Deb Armstrong once she'd gotten a good look at me. "They let you out of the hospital?"

"Haven't been," I admitted, settling slowly into my own chair. "I've been working on the Diane Smart case," I added, trying to turn their attention away from me and my condition.

"What do you guys know about Dr. Philip MacDonald?" I asked, shifting their attention even further. It was the best opening I'd been able to come up with as I had made my way back to the office.

"What the hell does he have to do with Diane Smart?" asked Bowling. I noted that he hadn't answered the question. None of them had.

"Well, for one," I answered, "he was the prescribing physician for all the meds in Diane Smart's medicine cabinet."

"That right?" asked Bowling, turning to Evans. The other deputy was already scanning through some documents on his tablet.

"Yeah, we got that," came the answer a minute later.

"And?" Bowling said back to me.

"He on your radar at all these days?" I asked.

"Might be," said Bowling, clearly unwilling to give anything away.

"There's talk," Deb Armstrong said, "that he writes a few too many prescriptions, too often."

"Don't you guys have some sort of statewide database for that stuff?" I asked. "So you can keep track of who's getting all those drugs?"

"We're supposed to," said Bowling. "But you know, as we get told all the time, prescribing legal drugs isn't a crime, unless we can prove the doctor in question is acting in bad faith."

I thought for a moment about describing my visit to Dr. MacDonald, but I wasn't clear enough on what happened at a normal doctor's visit to say whether or not his verbal examination would count as evidence of bad faith. I decided on a different line of approach.

"You guys ever get a report on that pile of puke out at the ramps festival?"

"Are you saying these killings are connected?" asked Bowling, who I decided really was the sharper of the two deputies. Deb Armstrong, I figured, probably wasn't especially familiar with the Darla Jones case, unless the deputies had also considered they might be related.

"It was his puke, right? Mike Merrill's? I figured there must be DNA evidence?"

"Yeah, it was his," answered Evans, quickly manipulating his tablet, calling up the report in question, I hoped.

"Any evidence of painkillers in the barf?" I asked.

"There was," said Bowling, not even needing to check, which gave me an idea of how Evan's schtick with the tablet was more or less an act. "We asked Merrill about it, and he said he had a legitimate prescription. Lucky guess, or have you got something better?"

"It was a guess," I answered, "though I thought it was pretty likely. Did you get the name of his physician?"

The two deputies shared a look, and I wondered whether one had urged getting it and the other resisted. "No point in it, once we decided we couldn't hold him," Deputy Evans finally answered. "You think it was this Dr. MacDonald?"

"I wouldn't be surprised. I think you might do well to see if you can get a warrant to search his records. Can you do that? Can you get a warrant for patient information?"

"If there's sufficient cause," said Deb Armstrong. All three shifted in their seats. They seemed to be getting impatient, as if I wasn't giving them anything they could really use yet. Now that

I had them sitting here in front of me, I was less certain about whether there was anything I had that they could move on.

I decided I might as well just dump the whole thing on them. "I know that Diane Smart got at least some drugs from him, and I'd lay odds that Darla Jones did too. And Mike Merrill seems likely. Some or all of those three, I think, may have been passing pills along to a dealer, probably a guy named Bill Lovingood. For one thing, Bill Lovingood just happens to be Emily Smart's father."

"What?" said Deb Armstrong and Bowling together, before Bowling went on. "Bill Lovingood is her father?"

I mentally cursed myself for not handling that better. I would have been better off dropping that little information bomb at a less compromising moment. "She hadn't seen him since she was five, she told me. Until I took her out there to meet him a couple days ago," I added, knowing they wouldn't be happy to know that I had known, but also thinking that I'd better tell them the truth. "I figured you guys must already know about Bill Lovingood being her father."

"She said he lived in Texas! That she didn't have an address or number for him."

"Yeah," I said, with what I hoped would come across as sympathy. "I guess she and her mom always said that, if anyone ever asked. Emily said that she knew his name, and that he lived around here, but that he might as well have lived in Texas, for all she ever saw or heard from him."

"But you're saying," Bowling said, "that Diane Smart and Bill Lovingood were doing business somehow, with prescription drugs."

"Or she was refusing to do business with him. All I can see," I said, "is that everything in these cases makes sense if there's somebody out there who had leverage on Diane Smart, on Darla Jones, on Mike Merrill, and probably over some other people too, and that Bill Lovingood knows them all, was in the right places at the right times, and I'd bet he knows MacDonald, too. It could possibly be the other way, though: Diane Smart and Darla Jones might have been refusing to work with Bill Lovingood, they might have had leverage on him that he couldn't allow. Since they're both gone, we might not ever know for sure, but that's the story I'd tell their kids, if I had the choice." All three of them looked thoughtful. "Anyway, if Bill Lovingood had enough leverage on Mike Merrill, Merrill would do everything he could to make someone else out as guilty for the killing of Darla Jones. Even me. I'm fairly sure Bill Lovingood knows how to load and fire a muzzleloader; all of the Lovingoods probably do. And I'll bet you'll find that their business in selling food at festivals and reenactments is a fine cover for selling pills."

"The whole clan might be in on it," Evans said. I hoped that meant I had them half convinced. I hoped even more deeply, though, that Bill had acted alone, that Mary and the rest of the Lovingoods were as innocent as children, give or take Mary's own possible addiction. Even if I'd solved the case, the truth of it all would be painful to everyone in the Lovingood clan. Including Emily.

"I suppose," I said, hoping to steer the conversation a bit, "that Bill Lovingood's hold over Diane Smart must have been something going back to the time they were together, around when Emily was born. Maybe you can trace some old connection to Darla Jones, too, though I don't know what—she may have grown up around here, too, and she was about the same age as Bill and Diane—maybe they all knew each other, back in the day. And if Mike Merrill was taking the pills himself, that might also be part of why he wasn't willing to point the finger at Bill."

"Huh," said Bowling. "There might actually be something to all this," he said, and I couldn't tell if his comment was grudging or admiring. Possibly both, I guessed. "What finally tipped you off, if you don't mind saying?"

I hesitated. I had been worried he would ask that. The last thing I could tell them was the truth. I didn't want to admit I'd been to Dr. MacDonald myself, looking for drugs, and that it was Bill Lovingood's comment about my back hurting that had eventually made everything click. "It was something Sut Lovingood said," I finally tried, "when I was out at their place with Emily Smart. He was worried about Mary Lovingood. She's married to Bill, but I could see there was something strange about how they interacted. It all kind of unraveled from there." It was vague, but maybe it would do the job. Best just to press on. "I'd really appreciate it, you know, if you could keep my name out of things as much as possible. I've known the whole Lovingood clan for years, and I'd hate to have them know I'd turned Bill in." Sut, I thought, might understand, maybe Mary too, but the rest I couldn't predict, and they could make all sorts of trouble for me. I knew some of their secrets, but they knew the one about me that I couldn't ever let out.

"How do you suggest we do that?" Deputy Evans asked.

I shifted in my chair, setting all my injuries to hurting again, though I tried my best not to show it. "I guess maybe you could follow up on Diane Smart's prescriptions, tying them up to Dr. MacDonald, and then try to find evidence of links to Darla Jones and Mike Merrill in MacDonald's patient records. If they are there, and I suspect they are, use that evidence to pry open the Darla Jones murder, and hopefully it will all come out that way. It's still possible after all, that Mike Merrill really saw whoever used that hatchet and just has been too afraid to name the real killer. But I've got to hand it to Bill Lovingood: there's not much here to pry open." I kept silent about knowing that Diane Smart's pill bottles were now lodged in the landfill.

Deb Armstrong had a look on her face. "We've been saying the same thing about the Diane Smart case. It sure would be nice," she added, "if you'd picked up some physical evidence for us." And I could see her eyes tracking over my various injuries. But she didn't ask me a direct question, and, for better or worse, I didn't say anything. If they thought my story about a bicycle crash wasn't reliable, let them prove it. I certainly didn't want anything about my physical condition to go into evidence: they might even insist I see a doctor. Another doctor. And I was glad I'd already taken the bike into the shop. I didn't need them impounding it and using it to show I hadn't really had any crash at all.

"I guess," Bowling said then, "maybe we could ask around, too, find out if there's any word around town about Bill Lovingood dealing in prescription pills. It's nothing I've heard, or we'd have been on this angle before, but maybe we can find someone who knows something. This is all pretty weak," he said.

"I know," I answered. "But it's the best I can do, and I think it might even be true."

"Well," he said, "that's all well and good, but we probably need more than the truth. We've got to make a case we can take to trial." Even so, he seemed to understand that there was nothing else I was able or willing to give them. He stood up, and the others stood up too. "Thank you, Mr. Foote," he said. "We'll see what we can find out."

Deb Armstrong lingered a few moments after the other two had left. "You okay, Big?" she asked.

"I'll be all right," I said. It was the only thing I could say.

"I know Deputy Bowling was hoping you'd tell us you'd been

beaten up by four guys, night before last. One of those guys mentioned your name, said you'd been there, wanted to press charges on you for assault."

"Me?" I said, my best impression of a look of human innocence doing who knows what to my face. "I had a crash on my bike."

"Yeah, we know. If you're hiding something, Big, you've got to know we'll probably figure it out. You might as well tell us."

"Look, Deb," I said cautiously. "I suppose if I had been beaten up by some guys at the Crime Scene Houses, it would only have been because I'd gotten a tip, lured out there to take a beating, maybe. And maybe those guys might be able to name the person who set them onto me, if I'd actually been there, but maybe they were paid anonymously, too. Check their pockets, check their email, check their texts: I'm sure you already have. Maybe Bill Lovingood is in there, somewhere. But of course I wasn't there."

"Crime Scene Houses?" she said.

"I'm sure that's what Bowling said, when I talked to him yesterday," I answered, though I had no way of remembering if he had or not. It didn't matter: they all must know already it had been me, but I needed to tell them again that I wouldn't acknowledge it.

"I hope you know what you're doing," she said. I hoped I did too. She left shortly afterward.

I texted Emily: she and Seth were already at The Station, and if I got over there quickly enough, there would still be time for me to get some dinner. I rooted around in my back room, looking for the little bottle of aspirin that I knew was there somewhere, but of course I couldn't find it. I gave up after a few minutes, and took my aches and pains back out on the street.

From the hostess's podium, I could already see the two young people at a table in view of the bar, and I limped over to them without waiting to be seated. "Hi, Big," Seth said as I approached, and the hostess, who'd been trailing behind me, must have peeled off, seeing I was being welcomed.

"I still can't believe you fell off your bike," Emily said. "You look terrible."

"At this point, I've told a lot of people it was a bike crash," I told her. "I'd appreciate it if that would be all that you know."

Her eyebrows angled in toward one another, in one of those expressions that bigfoot just don't have. Puzzlement, I guessed. "Either of you guys got any aspirin?" I asked them.

Seth shook his head no, but Emily rooted around in her purse for a moment. "Ibuprofen?" she said. "Is that okay?"

"Yeah, that'll do," I answered. "Anything to take the edge off." She handed a couple of the pills to me, and I popped them in my mouth and swallowed them dry.

"A beer maybe?" Seth offered.

"No thanks. Not even one of yours," I said, reminding him he'd asked me once before. He nodded. I reminded myself to be careful: Emily might know my secret, but Seth didn't, and I didn't want to say anything that would give it away, though the pain wasn't making it easy to keep my thoughts in order. I'd have to do my best, regardless. I sat back in my chair, thinking where to begin. "You guys think your mothers might have known each other?" I wondered again how much of all this trouble could have been avoided if I had thought to ask the question much earlier.

They looked at each other for a moment, then Emily spoke. "We wondered about that. But as far as we could guess, they didn't." So much for Morgantown being a small world, I thought, where everybody knows one another; even if I'd asked the question earlier, it wouldn't have gotten me anywhere.

"Well, I'm pretty sure they knew at least one person in common," I said. Then I bulldozed on ahead, trouble or not. "They both knew your father," I said to Emily. "Bill Lovingood."

She looked unhappy, I guessed, but it was Seth who spoke. "One of the Lovingoods who was selling food at the ramps festival?"

"Yeah, that's him," I said.

"I didn't know he was your dad!" he said, turning to Emily.

"I barely know him," she said quietly. "My mom never talked about him much." Of course, I knew this already, but it was interesting to see her talk about it.

The waitress came by at this point and I ordered a burger and fries. "Just water," I added, knowing that even this little delay was all too welcome to me on account of what would have to come next. "Look," I finally said to the two of them when the waitress had gone. "There's no easy way, no fun way to say this, but I think Bill may have killed both your mothers."

Emily gasped, but fortunately neither of them spoke aloud. "The problem is," I added before they even could, "the problem is that there's precious little hard evidence. If there was, the police would have arrested him long ago."

"So Mike Merrill really didn't kill my mom?" asked Seth Jones. He seemed confused, understandably enough.

"I think he might be hiding the identity of the real killer, too afraid or too intimidated to tell the truth. I can't blame him, really: he's got to be in fear for his own life. But I hope he'll be willing to talk soon."

"I—I thought he was a friend of yours!" Emily finally managed, also confused, if I was any judge.

"I've known him all his life," I told her, "but I've never known him well." I hesitated, then charged ahead. "The thing is," I said to Seth, "Bill knows a secret about me, a really important one, and so I've always considered him to be trustworthy enough, just because he's never told it. But I should have looked closer at him sooner."

Emily looked like she was trying to figure something out in

her own head. I waited, trying to give her space. Seth seemed to be waiting as well, which was nice to see, I thought. "Are you afraid he'll tell your secret, if the police arrest him?" It wasn't at all what I expected her to ask, but once again, I should never be surprised when the human thought process surprises me.

"I suppose it could happen," I answered slowly. "Though I don't think the cops will believe him, if he tells it. And I'd guess he knows that, so maybe he won't say anything."

"Hmmm," said Emily. Seth sat there quietly, plainly wondering if he was going to be let in on the secret. I was pretty sure Emily knew it was not her secret to tell, and I didn't see any reason to tell him yet. If ever. Though if the two of them became a couple, that might have to change: I wouldn't want the secret to lie between them. This was a complication I hadn't really thought through, but I knew I'd been through worse.

Seth finally broke the silence. "Why do you think he did it?" he said. "Why do you suspect him, I mean."

"To tell you the truth, I think he's been supplying prescription painkillers to who knows how many people out in rural Mon County and probably Preston County, too. Maybe even Marion County. I think he must have had a network of people who were getting prescriptions from a shady doctor around here, and that he and the doctor set it all up, blackmailing patients, maybe, into a bigger scheme. It's possible that your moms were supplying him with drugs that he sold on to others. Or it might be even more likely that he was trying to blackmail them, trying to get them to do it. Who knows how many others were supplying him?"

"My mom would never have been selling prescriptions!" Seth said, and I thought that Emily had been about to say the same thing.

"That's what I finally figured, too," I said. "Your mom, too, Emily. Probably what happened is that Bill pressured people into this scheme: he had something on people, some kind of leverage. One reason he might have killed, though, would have been if someone he thought he had a hold on slipped out of his grasp. Or if someone threatened to turn him in. And your mom, Seth," I said, "she told me straight out that he'd made her an offer that she could refuse. I didn't know what she meant at the time, but I think this was it." Neither of my two listeners spoke. "If so, she knew a dangerous secret about him. And I think your mom knew it, too," I told Emily Smart.

"So they were killed to keep his secret."

"Maybe so," I said. "We might never know for sure, unless he confesses, but that's the story that seems to make the most sense to me. I just came from telling the police about all of this, so I am sure you'll be hearing from them, but I'm also hoping to hear that they've made an arrest before too long."

The two young people looked stunned, and I felt bad when, just a moment or two later, my dinner was delivered. It hurt to chew, it hurt to lift the tiny weight of my sandwich, but I was hungry, and I had to eat. It had seemed, as I was saying it, that the least I could do was to tell these two that their moms had died resisting, died *for* resisting, Bill's scheme. I didn't know if it was true or not, and maybe the police would find a different story, tell them something worse about their moms. I hoped it wouldn't come out that way. But it was out of my bigfoot hands, at this point.

"You going to be all right?" I asked Emily when Seth had gone to the restroom.

"I just met him," she answered. "My father, I mean."

"Yeah. I wish it hadn't worked out like this."

"Are you sure about this?"

"All I know," I answered slowly, "is that it's the only thing I can figure that ties everything together. Including how I got my ribs broke and stuff," I added. "I feel terrible," I said.

"Aren't the ibuprofen helping?" she asked.

"No, I mean I feel terrible that you lost your mother and now maybe your father, all in the last couple of weeks." It was true, I did feel terrible about it, to the point of feeling responsible, somehow. "I can't make up for either of them," I said finally, "but I guess I want to say, you can call on me, any time, for anything, you know."

"You have any kids?" she asked.

"Yeah, one." I said, not wanting to go into that story at all.

"You close?"

"Not at all, I'm afraid." It didn't seem right to keep this from her. "He's—he's a handful," I finished lamely.

For some reason, this made her smile, and I hoped for the best. That she could smile at a moment like this had to be a good sign.

"I am just having such a hard time," she said, "trying to wrap my head around all this. I would never have said she had anything to do with illegal drugs, you know?"

"I know," I answered. "I never saw it, either. Bill never offered to sell me any drugs; in fact, I can't think of a single person I know who takes illegal pills." Well, I thought to myself, Horatio doesn't really count—that was still different, somehow, in my own mind. "But it's all over the state: it must be right in front of all of our eyes, a whole shadow economy that most of us never see."

"I suppose you're right," she said, heaving a sigh. "I suppose we don't want to see it."

"Unless we're in it," I said, thinking uncomfortably of myself. I hoped she wouldn't see the lie, wouldn't recognize it in me.

"You guys go on, get out of here," I finally told the two young folks after Seth had returned. "I'm going up into the hills for a couple days to see an old healer I know who can maybe help me with my leg. But I want you to know," I said seriously, "I'll give you whatever help I can, while all of this works out." I didn't dare say that I knew what they were feeling, especially because I really had no idea what the human response to that kind of loss might feel like. "I'll always feel like this awful business is something the three of us have gone through together: it's a bond I feel, and I'll always be happy to do you a favor, if you need one."

I had just enough money to pay the dinner bill for the three of us. Whether they'd ever let me pick up some part of that larger tab, only time would tell.

Before I left The Station, I texted Mel, who needed to know about Horatio. "Drop whatever you're doing, if you can," my fingers picking out the letters on my little phone, which wasn't easy even when I was feeling my best. "Meet me in thirty minutes at Horatio's house."

It was dark out by now, and no one paid any attention to me, limping or not. I made it over to Sabraton before Mel got to Horatio's house, but not by much. "He's dead," I told her by the door. "But you could probably see that coming."

"Well, it's not often I get a text like that," she answered. "I figured it was something serious. But what in blazes happened to you?"

"I've kind of been on a case," I told her. "Two human murders, not just the one I told you about before. I'm just lucky there didn't turn out to be a third killing: they only sent four after me." I didn't tell her who I thought had been behind it; that would all come out soon enough. "I'm going to take him up to the Homeland," was what I did say to her. "The place is yours, if you want it." I knew that the house was owned by the same little holding company that owned my building, itself held by a kind of bigfoot trust I'd set up myself, a long, long time ago.

She looked around. "I'd like to see him," she said.

We went up the stairs to the little bedroom. Horatio was just as I'd left him, of course. He wasn't a small bigfoot, and Mel

223

could see me sizing him up. "You sure you don't want me to help take him up there?" she asked.

"I owe it to him," I said. "I found him some painkillers, and brought them to him, a few days ago. He took enough to end the pain, I guess."

"You broke the law?"

"No one will find out," I said, hoping it was true. Mel really had no idea how often I broke the law anyway. "Look, you don't have to decide if you're going to stay here tonight, Mel. Let me know when I come back down. But could you maybe keep an eye on the place for a few days, at least? I don't know if his neighbors will look for him, or even notice he's gone."

"All right," she said. "I'll tell them he told me he was going to move in with some younger relatives." It was what we always said, down here among the humans. "You be careful," she added.

I nodded in answer. I managed to lift Horatio's body up onto my shoulder, though my sore ribs didn't make it easy. The leg hurt a lot, too. "I got him now," I told Mel, and then I took as much time as I needed to get him down the stairs.

It was dark enough when I got out onto the porch that I couldn't really see the expression on Mel's face, but I was pretty sure it wasn't a happy one. "I'll manage," I told her again. "My leg hurts," I admitted, "but I'll get Martha to look at it when I get there. And I'm due for a rest, I think." Not that I could be too far out of sight: Bowling and Evans might have more questions for me even if they could make out a good case against Bill. But I couldn't wait around for them. And neither could Horatio.

And so I set off, before she could really try to stop me.

CHAPTER 15

STILL SATURDAY, INTO SUNDAY

In the dark, I didn't really need to worry too much about carrying Horatio's body along the rail-trial. I didn't think there'd be any runners out at this time of the night, and down here in town, the trail only crossed streets a couple of times. It was pretty well out of sight otherwise. But I certainly didn't find myself making good time.

I almost regretted the whole attempt when a beam of moonlight angling between the trees showed a little black bear not a dozen yards ahead of me. I stopped. I wasn't sure which of us was more surprised. Winter really was over once you started seeing the bears again, but I was pretty sure I wasn't in any danger. I saw its snout twitching, probably trying to make sense of my live body and Horatio's dead one. Then it shuffled off the trail. It didn't want to mess with me any more than I wanted to mess with it. Horatio didn't get a vote.

Then I was moving again. Every step up the trail, it seemed, brought new pain, and I knew I wasn't thinking straight, even as

I went. I didn't need to think, really: the path was something I knew by heart without thinking, and it was easy enough, a mild grade right up along Decker's Creek, through the springtime woods—until I got to the point where I had to leave the trail.

I stood there, doing nothing for a moment. This was why I hadn't wanted Mel to come along: this is where I had left myself no choice but to accept the pain. I closed my eyes and when I opened them, I moved. I had to do it, and I did. The hillside trail, if you could call it that, gave me no kind of respite or ease. I won't say I hallucinated my way up the mountain, but it wouldn't be all that far off if I did.

All of the way, I couldn't get out of my head the feeling that I was in a kind of reenactment myself. Bill Lovingood, if he really had killed Diane Smart, had carried her around in these hills, leaving her up where I'd found her, where I was sure he had hoped she'd never be found. I was also taking Horatio's body up so that no humans would ever find it. True, Bill had probably not been injured when he was carrying Diane's body, but still, it couldn't have been easy for him: a time of all-too-real intimacy between the living and the dead. For my own part, I kept thinking how I'd failed Horatio somehow. Although I knew better than anyone how dangerous it could be to imagine I ever knew what a human thought, my hallucinating mind couldn't help wonder if Bill had also felt like he'd failed Diane: what else could drive someone to carry a body up and hide it in the woods? Surely he was punishing himself, even while trying to cover his ass.

I truly thought I was hallucinating, when I heard a voice say, "Not another step, Jim!" I kept moving, not wanting to lose whatever momentum I had. "I'll shoot!" I heard, and something in the voice made me stop, made me look.

It only took me a moment to realize that it was Bill, especially once I saw that he had a long gun pointed at me. In the early morning light, I wasn't sure if it was the same gun he'd used to kill Diane, but I guessed it was. "I knew you'd be coming up this way, sooner or later, when I finally heard from those boys. But who's this you're carrying?"

"Horatio. He died last night. I had to bring him," I said. "His last trip up to the Homeland."

"Just like you, then," he said, and I knew it was a threat. The pain might have hindered my clear thinking, but something about the danger had cleared my mind up remarkably.

"You can't shoot me, Bill," I said, hoping it was true. "Too many people know," I added, realizing as I spoke that it actually was true: until now, I had had a plausible tale, a likely story, but he wouldn't be pointing a gun at me now if he hadn't done the killings. And he'd just admitted to sending the thugs. "I already laid the whole thing out for the deputies." I didn't need to tell him that it was his own words that had given him away. "You should never have set those boys on me, you know. You must have known they couldn't shut me up."

He said nothing, but I thought that maybe he was looking uncertain. Maybe he'd let me talk some more. Now I was even more certain why he'd told those boys just to beat me up, not to kill me: he knew that if he killed me, and it ever came out, Martha would find some way to pay him back. He might be afraid of being arrested by the cops, but he must be just as afraid of Martha and the rest of us. Maybe more. "If you shoot me now, you know there will be a feud with the Homeland that you'll never survive. Maybe you can get a lawyer to get you out of whatever trouble you've made for yourself in the human courts, but you know Martha will find a way to catch you and finish you. No telling what she'd decide about trusting the rest of the Lovingoods either." I didn't know if the implied threat to his family would move him at all, and I had even less certainty about whether Martha would back me up on it.

"No biggie's gonna tell me what to do!" he shouted.

"Fair enough, fair enough," I said, trying my best to sound reasonable. "I'll tell you what," I said. "I'll put a good word in with Martha for you: she'll let you be, let you go, as long as she can be sure you never gave any of those pills to anyone from the Homeland. You might go to jail for a few years, maybe, with a good plea bargain, but if you keep the secret, if you kept those drugs off the Homeland, we'll make sure there's a place for you up here when you're out. If you gave any of us drugs, though, I'll give you straight to Martha."

"I never did!" he swore, and I knew then that I'd make it through to him. This was the final choosing point for him: if all his bridges had already been burned, maybe he would shoot me, maybe even kill me. But if he'd kept the drugs among the humans, and he continued to keep quiet about the bigfoot, I knew Martha would back me, and he knew it too. He might be a fool, but not a complete one: this was one judge and jury he could get on his side, and he grabbed the chance while he could. "I never did that," he insisted. As much as anything, I figured that was probably because he'd never thought of it or had never figured out a way he could make it pay. But if it could buy him even a piece of a future now, he wasn't too proud to take it. Even from a bigfoot.

"That's it then: you can run from the cops, or you can turn yourself in. Either way, when it's all cooled off, we'll find a place for you out here. Even with the rest of your family, if they'll have you."

"They will," he said confidently. I didn't tell him that I thought Sut might see things otherwise.

"Well," was what I said, "you'd better get moving. I've got to take Horatio up the rest of the way."

I could see he wasn't happy, but that was hardly a surprise. He'd gotten himself into a mess he couldn't really get out of, and it was going to hound him one way or another, sooner or later. "I guess I'll take my chances with the cops," he said.

I nodded, gritted my teeth, and struggled on up the mountain-side.

"That you, Jim?" I finally heard, and I knew I'd made it to where the almost-trail found the edge of the Homeland.

"Ezra," I grunted, catching his scent in the dark.

"Huh," he said. "I guess old Horatio finally died."

"Yeah." There wasn't any more to say, or any more that I could find to say. I moved on into the Homeland.

A moment later, Ezra was at my shoulder. "Here, lean on me," he said. "And take your time. We'll get him there."

Between the two of us, we did. Martha couldn't have been happy to see us, and not only because it was the middle of the night; we all feel diminished when one of us dies. And there aren't all that many of us in the first place. I don't remember what she said, to me or to Ezra. We took Horatio's body out to one of the rocky ledges where I knew she'd be in charge of building up a fire later in the day. It was too dark then for her to look over my injuries, but she must have known I was in pain.

She told me to sleep, putting me right into her own hammock, and I did. When I woke, she had a little smokeless fire going near her place, and a couple of squirrels cooking. "I figured you'd need something to eat," she said, "after carrying Horatio's body."

I ate both of the squirrels while she looked on. "You're hurt from more than just stumbling up the mountain with a burden," she said. "What happened?"

"Four humans with clubs," I said, figuring she might or might not know what a baseball bat was. "Bill Lovingood set 'em on me."

"Bill Lovingood?"

"He killed that woman whose body you took me to see. And one other, probably."

"Huh," she said, and I knew I'd need to tell her the whole tale later. "Better take a look at you," she said then, "see if there's anything to be done."

I didn't say anything, and she examined me while I was still in the hammock. "The ribs are probably broken, and the leg definitely is. The cuts look all right."

"I had my human friend look at the cuts," I told her. "But she couldn't do anything about broken bones."

"Nothing I can do with these, either," she said. "Except to tell you not to do anything to make 'em worse, I guess. And to say that you probably shouldn't have carried old Horatio up here. Mel would have done it."

"I know, I know. But I owed it to him." She nodded, saying nothing, and she let me go back to sleep.

I slept until right before the burning. The Homeland is pretty remote, and when you stand up on the ledge where we do the burnings, there's not a human place in sight other than the Lovingood homestead—not a house, an airport, a cell tower, or anything else. And we do our burnings at night, so there's no smoke to be seen, either. If the Lovingoods saw the flames, they'd be curious about who had died up here, and tomorrow they'd probably send someone up, just to ask politely who it'd been.

There's no formal ceremony when we burn our dead. No bigfoot has ever wanted to have their body buried under the ground—and I've known a few humans who've felt that way, as well, some of them miners—and probably nobody wants their body mauled by a bear, either, even after they are dead. There were some bigfoot who said we'd first given fire to humans, thousands of years ago, and some who said maybe it had gone the other way around, but no one knew for sure. Fire was an old, old bigfoot tool and an old, old opponent. Just about everyone in the Homeland came by to add a stick or a branch to the burning. Some, I guessed, hardly knew old Horatio since he'd spent so very little time up here in the Homeland, but not one of us here didn't know someone who knew him. So they all came, just about. Only a couple old guys, just as grumpy and angry as he was, I always thought, didn't make the effort. There's always someone.

I'd been to human funerals before. I'd even briefly stopped in at Diane Smart's memorial. Humans talk their way through death at these things, I've always thought. They talk to each other, giving eulogies and sermons. Humans and bigfoot alike are alone in their deaths, but humans respond by invoking community, somehow. Bigfoot say goodbye in silence, in privacy. It was past the time when we could speak our minds to Horatio, for good or ill, and our silence was a reminder of that, more than anything. Maybe it mattered that we were all silent together, invoking our own kind of community. As long as I'd been thinking about it, still I couldn't decide if bigfoot and humans were more essentially similar, or irrevocably different. But when the fire began to die down, he was truly gone.

I stayed with Martha, of course. Somehow, she found someone to bring out another hammock, or lend one, and I slept in it almost the whole next day, letting her take her own back from me. It would have been nice, I thought more than once, to take a couple of pills and just let them wash the pain away for a time: although sleep helped, it didn't come easy. Whenever I woke, I half expected to see someone from the Lovingood clan, come up to the Homeland to ask about the burning, to say their piece, and maybe their goodbyes, in their human way.

Well, they had their hands full over in their hollow, no doubt. If Bill had been arrested, the whole Lovingood family would have been turned upside down, but it would explain why no one had come. We had always expected Bill to follow in the footsteps of Sut, whenever Sut himself died, and they needed a leader there as much as we bigfoot needed someone like Martha. Even Martha couldn't guess who that leader might be.

When I woke up the next morning, the pain was a bit more manageable, I thought, though once I got up and started moving around, it seemed to come back quickly enough. But Martha was sure: the bones were starting to knit up a bit, and it was just a waiting game now. "You'll probably have a limp, though," she told me, and I figured she was probably right.

I felt like there was something important I needed to talk to her about, but for whatever reason, I couldn't think what it was. The pain, probably. But I did remember something else. "I told Mel she could have Horatio's house," I told her.

"Yeah, I talked to her yesterday, while you were sleeping," she answered.

"That all right?"

"Sure. Just do whatever paperwork you have to do with the trust when you get back down there," she said.

"Of course I will," I answered. "I might take a little money out to get some work done on the place, too. I don't think Horatio has changed a thing in over fifty years."

"Well, you know best about those things," she answered.

"There is something else," I said, finally remembering.

"Yeah?"

"Yeah. You remember I asked you about the guns?"

"The ones up here in the Homeland, you mean?"

"Yeah. I think they've got to go. We need to get rid of them. At the very least, they have to come down into town."

"We've always kept them up here," she said then. "I don't think Ezra will give his up."

"Always," I said. "Always is the issue. We may have had those guns for more than a lifetime, but we haven't had them always. And that's exactly the issue. They are too human, I think." I hoped I'd be able to convince Martha. I hardly knew how to explain it to myself, but I had to try. I glanced guiltily at the hammock, still hanging from a couple of trees near Martha's space. "Human culture," I said finally, "is all about things, objects, possessions. Our world," I said then, "is something else. We have stories and lore that we pass down, but things, somehow, are like anchors that weigh us down, tie us down. Because they are things that tie up to stories. The gun that Ezra has: it's not just a gun, it's a gun that Davy Crockett gave to Ezra's grandpappy. When things and stories get mixed up like that, you get something more human than bigfoot, I think. What things like those guns do is they tie us down to the human world."

She laughed, and it wasn't long before I knew she was laughing at me. "I remember you telling me about how you tried to clear out your little storage area one time, how you said you could hardly bear to get rid of anything at all."

"Yeah, yeah," I admitted. "I know it sounds crazy, but whoever first decided that some bigfoot had to live among the humans, they got it right. Mel, me, Horatio: any bigfoot living down in town will be tied up in the human world: there's no way to avoid it, period. Call it the sacrifice we make. But it's for the good of the Homeland. If you want the Homeland to be safe, I think, we've got to make sure it doesn't get to be just like Morgantown. Today it's a couple of guns; tomorrow maybe it'll be cell phones. Or prescription painkillers."

She looked at me, and I could see that she was thinking. The truth was, this was my job as much or even more than it was hers. I was supposed to deal with the interface between the humans and the bigfoot. Those guns, I'd come to realize, were very much a part of that interface, even if they'd been around so long as to seem familiar and traditional. Which was exactly the problem, as I was trying to explain.

Martha must have been thinking along the same lines. "Keep the corruption at the interface, you mean," she said slowly. "Down in Morgantown, where it belongs."

"I wouldn't have phrased it like that," I said. "But yeah, that's the idea."

"If I put it like that, I think I can get you those guns. But what will you do with them down there?"

It was a good question. They were genuine old guns, I knew, and they must have some kind of significant monetary value. Martha wandered off, sometime after the sun was at its highest, and she told me she was going to see about bringing in the guns. I supposed I could sell them: a dealer or an auction could get a good price for them, and the money could go right into the trust. We had enough, as a rule, but we could never have too much laid up for a long, harsh winter; that I knew.

But probably, however I sold them, I would have to come up with some kind of story to explain how I'd gotten them, how these incredibly rare antique guns were just now coming to the market, completely unknown and unheard of. Provenance, that was the word. The truth, obviously, was out of the question. The more the guns were worth, I knew, the more likely that people would suspect they were fake.

Well, this was the kind of thing I could worry about later. Lying to humans was my job, after all. Keep the corruption at the interface, Martha had said. She always did have a bad habit of telling the truth, which was the real reason she was living up here in the Homeland, and why I lived down in Morgantown.

I slept through the night again, enjoying the night air. When I talked with Martha the next morning, she told me that Ezra hadn't been very willing to give up the gun that he had from his pappy, but he had given it to her eventually. Martha was persuasive, I knew. It wouldn't hurt if I could figure out something or other to help him out, maybe, in the future, she implied. I'd give it some thought. I felt a twinge of guilt for having considered, even briefly, that he might have shot Diane Smart. I really would have to find some way to do him a favor.

I was getting increasingly restless, in part because I knew that things must be happening down in Morgantown that I needed to try to keep an eye on. Probably Deputy Bowling was ready to beat me with a baseball bat himself, for the way I'd disappeared after trying to sell him a theory about the murders. Luckily, I thought, I had been telling them the truth as far as I could figure from my run-in with Bill, and surely they'd been busy tracking down the evidence and the confirmation they'd need. Maybe they'd already arrested him; maybe they'd gotten Dr. MacDonald, too. And the guys who'd beaten me up, if I was lucky.

They'd start wondering more and more, however, the longer I stayed away. They'd have some kind of question for me, or want to check on something: I didn't have any illusions that my disappearance hadn't been noticed. They'd want some kind of story, too. Not a provenance, but an alibi, I supposed. I'd have to come up with another plausible lie.

I would manage.

I was still in the Homeland on Monday afternoon, getting ready, in fact, to make my way slowly back down into town, when Sut Lovingood came up, shouting out for Martha from far enough away to let us know he was in the neighborhood.

Martha called out to him, and I stood up, carefully. My clothes were a mess, but at least I had them on, I thought.

"Good," said Sut, still huffing a bit from the climb. I saw he was using a walking stick. It was one of his own, I thought. He'd used one when we had our chat at the burning pile, too. "I was hoping you'd still be up here, Jim."

I looked at her, but Martha seemed to be letting me answer. "Sut," I said quietly. "I hope I haven't brought too much trouble down on you."

"Oh, none we haven't brought on ourselves. And I did ask you to do what you could, as I recall." He had taken a seat on a nearby boulder, leaning the stick beside it.

"I guess the sheriff's deputies came and talked to Bill?" I asked.

"Talked to him, arrested him, took him away." He paused, maybe thinking of what to say next, or how to say it. "He killed both those girls after Mary got hooked on pills. That was how he said it all got started, getting them for her when her first prescription ran out. And then he just let it get away from him. He admitted to it all, before it was all over." Another pause. "I'm still not sure he's telling all the truth, but no one seems to doubt that he killed those women. I hope to God I never see him again."

"Well," I said, not sure what to say. Bill was his nephew, but I also knew that Sut had raised him like a son. I would worry later about the fact that I'd promised Bill that he'd always have a place at the Homeland.

"You look like those guys beat you up pretty good," he said to me then.

"Yeah, well, at least they didn't kill me," I answered.

"Bill said he'd sent them after you, too, or at least that's what one of the deputies said." I just nodded. Bill had admitted the same to me, as far as I was concerned.

"How's Mary?" Martha asked.

"She's taking it like a trooper," Sut said, with what I guessed was a small laugh. "I think she'll divorce him before it's all done," he added. "I told her I wanted her to stay on, that the family would get her through this. I told her I'd rather have her for a niece than have Bill for a nephew."

Something told me that Sut was telling us something important, something I needed to know to understand how human families worked, but for the life of me I couldn't quite see it. I knew all the words he was saying, but it didn't seem to make any sense. For some reason, though, I thought about Emily Smart.

Martha spoke before I could figure out what to say. "I hope you always know, Sut, we're your neighbors. Let us know if there's something we can do."

"I do know it, ma'am," he said. The word sounded strange in his mouth, until I remembered that Martha and I, of course, were both years older than Sut. But you all had a loss up here," he went on. "We saw the fire, down at our place. Who was it?"

"It was Horatio," I said. "I brought him back up from Morgantown, where he's always lived."

"I met him once or twice, I think. Sorry I wasn't here to throw a branch on," he said.

"It's a kind thought, Sut," said Martha.

All three of us were silent for a moment.

"I should have known about Bill a lot sooner," Sut finally said. "We never made as much money selling those damned ramp banquets as Bill always told me we did."

Sut may not have been able to read the look on Martha's face, but I could see she had no idea what he was talking about. "It wasn't the only thing he was selling, then. He was giving you drug money?"

"Yeah. He was. We don't need a lot up here, you know, like you all, I guess. But we need some: there's always money to be spent, always a need for it. Bill always had a little, and the one thing I will miss about the bastard is that he always had some to give. Though I wouldn't have taken a dime if I'd known where it was coming from."

"Jim here is in charge of all our money," Martha said. "But I don't know that we've ever got much to spare."

"Oh, I wouldn't ask it of you," Sut said. "We'll find a way; we always do. We can raise the price on the ramp banquet, maybe, set up at more fairs, maybe. The Buckwheat Festival over in Kingwood, maybe some other places."

I glanced at Martha, but she had said it right there already. I was in charge of all the money. I pushed myself up from the boulder I'd been leaning against and picked up the two long guns, still wrapped up in their deerskins. "I'll tell you what," I said to him. "We've got these two heirlooms we've decided to get rid of. One of them, passed down from Ezra's grandpappy, was given to us by Davy Crockett. If you can find a buyer or a dealer who'll give you a fair price, you and the Lovingoods can have half."

He unwrapped one of them, and I could see he knew what he was looking at. "What'll I say, when they ask me where they come from?"

"You just tell 'em the truth," I said to him seriously. "They're family heirlooms that have been treasured up here for almost two hundred years, that you've got to sell them now because you need the money."

"Huh," he said, and I thought he was thinking. "There's real money in these. Probably I'd only sell just one, put the other one away, hold it for a rainy day."

"Sounds fine," I said. "You got some ideas about how to sell it?"

"I've probably got some connections in the folk-art world, maybe, or at least people who might know some people."

"I'd have been starting from scratch, if I tried to sell 'em," I said. "More than likely, we'll do better out of this deal already." It didn't really matter if we did: it was worth more to me and to Martha to keep the Lovingoods where they were, a reliable buffer on that side of the Homeland, standing between us and the rest of the world; nothing was more important than the Homeland.

"Well," said Sut, standing up slowly from where he'd been sitting. "Time for me to get on home again, I guess. Thanks again, Jim," he told me. "I can't give you any money right now, but I made this for you." He handed me the walking stick he'd been using himself when he'd arrived. "I started on it right after you and Emily visited us, my way of saying thank you for bringing her back to us. I hope I got the grip right. And you can cut off an inch or two at the end, if I made it too long."

It was, of course, a small work of art. I stood up myself, and leaned on it, the hand-grip surprisingly comfortable. "It's just right," I told him. "Thank you. As it happens," I said, looking in Martha's direction, "I can use a cane right now; my leg is broken, I guess."

"And you may need it afterward, too, fool that you are," said Martha. "He carried Horatio all the way up here on a broken leg," she said to Sut. "Mel could have done it, or any of us."

"I'd have been happy to bring one of the cars down," said Sut Lovingood, and they both looked at me like I was indeed a fool.

Martha walked me around a bit, humoring me, I figured, while I got used to walking with the cane. "I really was worried, for a while," I told her, "that Ezra or some youngster had used one of those guns to kill off a human, you know. That kind of killing has always bothered me. Killing a human should be just as unthinkable to us as killing one another. But I didn't know how to stop it." Not that murder was completely unknown among us, I thought to myself.

"Well, one way to stop, or at least slow it down, it is to take the guns out of their hands. I'll tell you, I'm almost as unhappy, as I grow older, about the way we've always killed bears. We share the woods with them, too, after all."

"But the bears are a nuisance," I said, just like every bigfoot I had ever known.

"You might as well say that the humans are a nuisance," she answered, glancing at the cane. She meant, of course, that one human might have broken my leg with a baseball bat, but another had given me the gift of a cane, unasked for and unexpected. "And when was the last time a bear gave you any kind of trouble?"

I told her about the young one I'd seen when I was bringing Horatio back out to the Homeland, how it had sniffed the air once or twice, trying to figure out how much of a danger we were, and then it had moved aside, for all the world as if it had decided to let us pass.

"A real nuisance, huh?" she asked.

She was right, of course. Well, it was a problem for Martha to think about. The bigfoot down in Morgantown knew the humans too well to kill them. Mostly, I thought. But killing bears? That was pure tradition.

"It's definitely best to get the guns away, one way or another. You have no idea how worried I was that the sheriff's deputies would trace some of the black powder I've bought back to me. Buying it always seemed such a small thing, but one curious policeman could have discovered the Homeland. Or at least put me in a mighty tight spot."

"Yeah," said Martha then. "But it didn't happen, and everything seems pretty tied up by now. Well done," she said. "Well done, Jeannie."

ACKNOWLEDGMENTS

___

Big Jim Foote arrived in my imagination—almost fully formed—during a pleasant walk with my wife along one of Morgantown's rail-trail paths a couple of years ago. Which one of us said the fateful words, "Bigfoot, PI," neither of us clearly remembers, but I started work on this book soon after, and I owe the genesis of the book—and so many other things—to her.

Various friends have read drafts, or served as inspiration in other ways throughout, and I particularly wish to thank Erin Jordan, Dana Oswald, and Patrick Conner for early and continuing support. Though she may hesitate to claim the role, Ann Claycomb was invaluable to me as a writing mentor, and I owe her a particular debt of thanks.

This novel was mostly written in coffeeshops: in Morgantown, West Virginia; in Bexley, Ohio; and—for one wonderful week—in Tallinn, Estonia. The baristas who made my morning coffee in those shops are also owed a debt of gratitude. At West Virginia University Press, I want to thank particularly Derek Krissoff, Sarah Munroe, and Charlotte Vester.

Finally, I want to offer a more diffuse, but no less sincere, thanks to the City of Morgantown and its residents. The Morgantown that Big Jim inhabits, needless to say, lies in an alternate world, similar to our own, but very different from it. Necessarily, many of the places and institutions of the two worlds sometimes parallel one another closely, but all of the characters and specific incidents of the book are products of my own imagination, and none of the characters and events are intended to reflect or represent actual people or things they have done.